Cover Photo Credit: Patrick Maffeo

This is a work of fiction. Names, characters, businesses, places, events and incidents are either the products of the author's imagination or used in a fictitious manner. Any resemblance to actual persons, living or dead, or actual events is purely coincidental.

For Bill

Chapter One: Cheat

I have no idea how this happened. How I, the girl that couldn't get a date in high school, the girl who couldn't get a guy to stick with her for as long as she wanted to stick with him, the girl who couldn't divest herself of her maidenhood fast enough, could be in a dilemma like this.

It seems unreal. All roads have led to Bob. The problem is, I am not sure *which* Bob is *the* Bob. Turns out, I had to make my way through a series of red herrings to get to the prize.

I've been thinking a lot about the movie, *The Sliding Doors*. The idea is this: Gwyneth Paltrow's character is living with a shoddy excuse for a boyfriend. She leaves him in bed in their apartment for her commute to work. She runs to catch the train after she is let go from her job. Here is where the story line splits into two directions.

In the first scenario, she misses the train and has to wait for the next one. This is very fortunate for her scumbag boyfriend, who is still in bed at their apartment, where he did not remain alone for long. His paramour joined him there mere moments after Gwyneth left for work. Because she misses the train, she doesn't find out about his shenanigans for months. She gets home from work just moments after the fleusy finishes fucking her boyfriend and leaves. Life goes on as usual. He gets away with it.

In the second scenario, she catches her train. She arrives back home in plenty of time to catch her conniving, bastard, cheat of a boyfriend full on in the act with the fleusy. To her credit, she doesn't sneak back out. She doesn't take him back afterward. Life does not go on as usual. Life, as she knew it, screeched to a halt. She was done with the 'wanker'; she left him and never went back. He gets away with nothing. She gets away with her dignity. Ironically, in the end, this costs her, but that's the part I haven't yet figured out.

What I love about this movie is that I had been in this situation, sometimes literally, sometimes figuratively, several times in my life: Several. Times. The first time, when I caught the conniving, bastard, cheating boyfriend, Kevin, doing it with his fleusy, the fleusy turned out to be my sister Lisa. Right? The bastard told me only a few months prior that he wanted to marry me. How sweet to find out that while he was planning to marry me, and I was not having sex with him because we were, you know, taking things slow, he was sleeping with my sister.

How the hell could that happen? Well, Lisa and I had always been close. We closely resembled each other. If Lisa had a nickel for every time someone had yelled, "Hi, Bebe!" to her across the Medford High School courtyard, she wouldn't have had to raid my wallet for cash. Well, not as often, at least. We were close in age, born thirteen months apart. Irish Twins. We were close in proximity. Our small house in our suburban Boston neighborhood boasted two, count 'em, bedrooms. Of course, one of which was occupied by our parents. This left the remaining smaller bedroom for us to share. We had bunk beds. "Bebe, you get to have the top bunk!" my mother said, mustering some fake enthusiasm to try to fake me out. As if there was any question, since Lisa was a sleepwalker. We were even close in employment circumstance. I helped her get her first job where I got my first job, working as a waitress. In hindsight, that was a mistake. The hindsight began about a minute after I found out that she was fucking my boyfriend.

What was interesting is the way this news was conveyed to me. It was in the form of a special delivery. It was in the form of an ultrasound picture of my niece. Okay, not at that exact time, but close enough. In a way, the joke was on me. Lisa had asked me to take her to get on birth control several months earlier. I said, "Sure." I was happy to take my sister to the Free Clinic to get on The Pill, like my friend had taken me to do six months earlier. I called and made the appointment.

Then I called and canceled it. Right after I found out. Did I mention that she was fucking my boyfriend? Now, I wasn't putting all of the blame on her. Kevin had his share to shoulder. He said he wanted to marry me. He wanted to marry me, and he wanted to fuck my sister. So he had a party of three for a short time, with only one of us not aware of this fact: Me. So when I caught them together, I thought, 'What would Gwyneth do?' Okay, not really, but I took the high road. Collecting my self-respect, I dumped him and in a way, I dumped her-my sister, not

Gwyneth- as well. I didn't take her to get her birth control. Let

him take her! Since he was already taking her! I was done with

the both of them.

Until I wasn't. That part about her showing me the

ultrasound picture of my niece was true. She was born in the

winter, which gave the phrase, "the winter of my discontent"

tremendous new depth of meaning. They got married the

following month and I was even the (wait for it) Maid of Honor.

So. My temper tantrum resulted in an addition to the family,

rather than the abstinence that I had been hoping for. Gambling

never did pay off in our family.

So. Cheat. Cheater. Cheaters.

I wondered how much of my present situation I had to thank myself for. The words, 'You are your own worst enemy' echoed in my head. I'd heard them plenty of times. Also, "Bebe, for a smart girl, you have no common sense." Since I first became interested in having a boyfriend eight years ago, around the age of fourteen, I had not had many of them. What happened was I became sort of, well, over-eager. I was an "I want what I want when I want it" kind of girl. Long on want and short on patience, not to mention boundaries. I had this delusion that when you loved someone (of course! of course!) they would love you back. This was an age of magical thinking in my twenties that most girls outgrow before they hit grade school.

My feelings for David, who I thought of as my first real love, lasted for years and years, as I hoped and prayed that he would realize that we were, in fact, destined to be married. Instead, he steadfastly ignored me as he dated one of our friends. I remained loyal to my dream of him and continued doing things like baking him cookies, and waiting around near his classes so he'd have to pass by me and I'd get to see him (come to think of it, he spent a lot of time passing me by). He dated my friend, with whom I became much less friendly-to the point of nasty-for about a year. I nicknamed her "Horror", and this whole time became a horror show in my memory.

When they broke up, I finally did get my chance with him. All of our time together was surreptitious. In fact, he never acknowledged our relationship to anyone. He almost never spent any time with me when others were present. We had several carnal interludes: in cars, in parks, in other people's houses. Somehow he orchestrated it so that none of it was visible to the world at large. My best friend, Lydia, didn't even realize that David and I had an intimate relationship of any sort.

I accepted this. I continued seeing him even though he continually denied that he was seeing me. Maybe part of the problem for me was that I didn't recognize the dysfunction in all of this. I thought if anonymity was the price I had to pay to have him, then it was small and I would pay it. I assumed it was all temporary. Like I said, 'magical thinking' at its finest.

Maybe I didn't recognize dysfunction staring me in the face because dysfunction was my comfort zone. Growing up, we moved almost every year that I was in elementary school. I've heard that, for some people, this makes them great at forming new friendships and interacting with strangers. For me, it had the opposite effect. Making new friends was something I was not good at. It was exhausting to think about the work and risk it took to reach out to someone to become friends, only to move in a year and leave it behind. After a few years of this, I became very bad at social interaction in general. It was better to remain quiet, observant, and invisible.

I learned to become invisible in day to day life, so when it showed up in my first relationship, with David, it didn't feel as wrong to me as it should have. I felt somewhat uncomfortable about it, but I thought it would eventually work itself out. I didn't have any boundaries set up, no standards, so everything was acceptable. Like Meatloaf said, "I would do anything for love," and I guess I sort of thought that most people were like this.

Now that we were unofficially going out, I felt compelled to be receptive to any physical advances he made. After all, I still believed that we would eventually be getting married, so that made everything okay. I did think about my mother's admonishment from time to time, how "No man is going to buy the cow if he can get the milk for free!" But it was okay if I was going to be *married* to him. I decided that it was also okay if I were *planning* to be married to him.

I began to realize that if we were going to be a couple, only the two of us were going to know about it. I made peace with it. Things progressed fairly quickly for us after that. We would sneak away from prying eyes and make out in his car for hours. I told him that I had never had sex before. I was an eighteen year old virgin, but was ready to cast that mantle off with and for him. I was unsure about his past experience since he never directly answered my questions regarding whether or not he had ever had sex, but I didn't get hung up on that. So what if he had? It couldn't hurt if one of us knew what they were doing.

One night, we went further than we ever had. It was late fall but the weather was warm, and we shed clothes accordingly after we got into his car. We started making out, and kissed for a while before he slid his hands up under my tank top, and under my bra, lingering for a bit before sliding one hand down the back of my jeans, then in my underwear.

I was terrified! He brought his free hand around in front and started fumbling with the snap at my waist. I helped him and then he got it open, and pulled the zipper down, giving himself enough room to slide his hand in between my legs. I wriggled around enough to give him full access. I wasn't sure where he was going to go, but I was fully committed to going there with him. He slipped first one, then two fingers into my private girl parts, exploring, boldly going where no man had gone before. I had an irrational thought: "fingerfucking" described an actual act! Who knew?

I heard him say something, his mouth near my ear. He sounded surprised, but the words were muffled by hair so I couldn't quite make them out. I pulled back. "What?" I said. "You really *are* a virgin," he repeated. I did have a moment to pause to think. He could tell that from two fingers? Then my temper won out and brought me back fully to my senses.

"I *told* you that I was a virgin! I told you *many times*! You thought I was lying?" "Well, yeah," he said.

Being a virgin was a source of endless embarrassment to me; as was not getting my period until I was sixteen years old. I would never in a million years have admitted to being a virgin if it were not true. "What did you think, then?" I asked him. "I thought you'd done it before!" he said. "Why?" I asked, realizing that I had no idea what he really thought of me. "Well, you *acted* like you had done it before!" he said, defensively.

All this time that I had been so nervous, not knowing what I was doing, never having engaged in anything more daring than a kiss and a quick feel that I immediately rejected in a panic, and he thought I'd been having sex with other guys. "I acted like that because I love you!"

Then I had a sobering thought. Maybe my mother had been right. "I never even wanted to have sex with anyone until I met you!" I told him. That was also true. The thought of a guy putting his thing in me was so totally disgusting that, from the age of twelve until a couple of years later when I met David, I was certain that I would *never* want to do that.

In fact, when I first met him a lot of feelings emerged that I hadn't fully understood. Over the months that I spent with him, it started to coalesce into something more definite, and on this night, when he slipped a hand into previously unexplored territory, I finally got it. I had been having this vague, uncomfortable feeling that I didn't recognize, but I could name it now. I understood it for what it was. Desire. Desire for him. This was what it felt like to want someone, to want to be physically intimate with someone. I also knew now that it was mutual. He could deny it in public all day long, but then and there, I knew it. I had him as much as he had me.

So we spent hours on the phone. We spent hours making out. Our making out eventually led to our making it.

When we finally did go all the way, it was in a haze fueled by the several glasses of wine we had drunk over the several hours prior. We were in bed at his apartment that he shared with two other guys, but they were not home, because he was never with me in front of witnesses. I believed that I was making love to my soul mate and that this was the consummation, the confirmation, of our relationship and that marriage was our next logical step. He believed that he was getting laid by someone very willing and able. This was our first and last occasion of sex.

Like so many women have discovered over the centuries from the beginning of time, sleeping with a man to cement a relationship could completely backfire and instead end the relationship. Like, okay, I got her to sleep with me. Done. On to the next. Apparently this was his thought process because that's what he did. If he avoided being seen with me in public before, now he completely shunned me. He no longer took my phone calls. He no longer showed up in his usual places. He was no longer there. I was completely devastated by this. I should have expected it, right? But instead, I was floored. I was just unable to process it. How could this happen? I thought I had done everything right.

Now I wonder how I could have thought that I was doing it all right. I did everything wrong! I had set the bar so low that I was tripping over it and didn't even realize it. I had chased him and chased him until he ran away. I am sad to say that even after all of this, I continued to harbor a secret hope that things would still work out for us in the future. I realized that I had to move on, but I had no idea how to do this and further, I had no desire to do this.

My mother's voice came to me over and over. "Why buy the cow if you can get the milk for free?" The first time she'd said this to me, I had no clue what she was even talking about. What cows? We didn't have any cows! Slowly, I got it. I dismissed this as old-fashioned thinking. "No one thinks that way anymore," I told her. She shook her head, in that infuriating way mothers have of letting you know that, even though you think that they know nothing and you know everything, what's really true is that you know nothing and they know everything. The universal lesson that is so often learned much later in life.

Dark days followed. I spiraled downward into that big, black hole where depressed people go. One component of this darkness was sleep. I escaped into sleep like I used to escape into books, wholly and completely. Another component was negativity. I thought that everything sucked. "Life sucks and then you die" became my motto, which I espoused every chance I got to anyone who would listen. Another component was (stupid) risk-taking behavior, which would persist for years.

I had shared that wine with David at his apartment that night, and after that I started drinking more, and drinking more often, progressing from wine to peach schnapps to coffee brandy to vodka to extra strength (100 proof) vodka. I didn't care much what happened to me at that point. I also knew some people that were into taking tranquilizers. They hung around the courtyard at school. One day someone said to me, "Geez, you're way too hyper! Here, take one of these," and handed me a small, scrunched up piece of tin foil that she said contained a few valium. I pocketed the package, not intending to do anything with it but not wanting to get caught at school with it either. I knew that I felt like shit and I wanted it to stop, but I had no hope that it would get any better.

It was early November when I started thinking how nice it might be to just sleep through Thanksgiving. What did I have to be thankful for, anyway? I risked everything for David and it was for nothing. I had less than when I started. I *was* less than when I started. He didn't care about me at all anymore and, in truth, maybe he never had. So, the upcoming holiday held no appeal for me at all. The thought of sitting around the kitchen table, listening to a chorus of, "So you don't have a boyfriend yet? Why don't you have a boyfriend?" from the relatives was too much for me. Yes, it was sounding better and better to just sleep through the holiday.

Then I remembered the little foil package.

Chapter 2: The Fall

To celebrate Thanksgiving Eve, I finished off a half pint of

hundred proof vodka mixed with orange juice, my go-to drink by

then. I had used the dregs to wash down the valium, and went to

bed and fell right to sleep. Soon, I became aware of feeling really

cold. I felt odd in other ways too, a vague uneasiness. Maybe it

was the effects of the alcohol wearing off, because suddenly I stopped thinking about how much I just wished to sleep through the holidays, and started thinking more rational, reality based thoughts, like, "Oh my God! How many of those pills did I take? What if it *was* bad to have washed them down with half pint of 100 proof vodka!?" My natural, God-given gift of anxiety kicked in and took over. "Shit. Maybe I had really fucked up here."

It was getting harder to move; my legs and arms and head felt so heavy. My brain, my thoughts even, felt heavy. By now, it was pretty late. The house was dark and quiet. Everyone had turned in early, exhausted from the meal preparations that had been going for the Thanksgiving dinner. I picked up the phone and dialed my best friend Lyddie. It was after midnight. Her mother answered the phone. "Bebe, is that you? Is everything okay? Hold on. I'll get Lydia."

"Bebe, what's going on?" she said immediately, since of course it had to be something big for me to be calling her in the middle of the night. "Um, I just called to say goodbye," I heard myself say. I hadn't thought ahead to what I was going to tell her when I called. I was like a concerned citizen, impassively listening and observing. "*WHAT?*" she yelled. "Where are you *going?*" And then I told her about the vodka, and about the Valium, and about how I just wanted to sleep through the holidays, but now I was just so *cold.*

"I guess I took too much and now I guess I'm going to die," I said, surprising myself again, hearing these words come out of my mouth, but then I realized that it was true. If I just went to bed, that could happen. People took too many pills, slipped into a coma, and died all the time, even if it was an accident.

"How many did you take?" she said. "I really don't know, actually," I admitted. I tried again, not wanting to disappoint her further by not having an answer. "I took all of them. And some Motrin, too, I think."

"Oh my God, Bebe! I'll be right there," she said, and hung up. If I was the queen of indecision, Lyddie was my polar opposite. She was the queen of decisive action. Have a problem? Fix it. Now.

Uh oh. She was coming here at one in the morning? Shit. I didn't want to wake them all up. Looking down, I realized that I had never gotten ready for bed; I was still wearing my jeans and flannel shirt over a T shirt. "That's lucky," I thought stupidly, "at least I don't have to change," which was a good thing, since by now I was having trouble even standing up. I got my coat, put my sneakers on, and headed outside to wait for her on the front stairs, like it was any other day and she was just picking me up to go on one of our 'road trips', riding around Medford, blasting the radio and eating Doritos. I sat there shivering, trying to stay conscious.

Very soon, she pulled up. She got out of the car, and to my surprise, her mother got out of the passenger side. They both ran up the stairs, asked me if I was okay. I babbled something back, which I thought was, "Yeah, sure, I'm fine," but I she told me afterward that I said something like: "Yeashruefinehiandniceyouseesyoussguys". They exchanged worried looks. One got on each side of me and they half carried me to the car, depositing me into the back seat. "Oh! It's so nice and warm in here!" I remember thinking just before sprawling across the seat.

"Where are your parents?" Lyddie's mother asked.

"Bed," I managed to say. I was sort of in and out after that; I could hear their voices but wasn't able to make out the actual words. I fell asleep. Or a-stupor.

When we arrived at the hospital, they helped me get out of the car and half dragged me to the ER door. My legs were buckling under me, so this was no small feat. Once they handed me over to the hospital staff, the party was definitely over. I was oh-so-roughly "helped" up onto a gurney and a curtain was pulled to partition me off from the rest of the room. The bright lights were painful and intrusive after the comforting darkness of the night and the car ride. "What's your name?" "What's your address?" "What did you take?" "Why did you want to kill yourself?" "What's your phone number?" The questions came fast from every direction.

I protested, "I didn't try to kill myself! I just wanted to sleep!"

"How much Valium did you take?" How the fuck should I know? I had taken the contents of the foil package, washed it down with some vodka, then took a handful of Motrin because my head was pounding. "Bebe, we're going to call your parents now. We have to pump your stomach."

Now I was awake. Call my parents? No fucking way. "I don't want you to call them!" I protested, but they weren't listening. They were on the phone, and after they had the consent to pump, the phone was handed to me.

"Your mother wants to talk to you," the nurse said. I said, "Hello?" And then I started crying.

My mother was asking, "Why did you do this? What were you thinking?" I was crying too hard now to talk, as I watched them getting ready to pump my stomach, I was getting panicky. What did that mean, exactly? Would they have an actual pump, like to pump air into a tire? But wouldn't that force that shit further down into me? How could a pump make stuff come *out*? Plus, wouldn't it have all disintegrated by now?

Someone said something about how after they started the procedure, I would be throwing up and have diarrhea for a few hours. What? What? That's pretty much the last thing I remembered until the actual "throwing and going" onslaught began. I still have no idea what the actual pumping referred to. I have a vague sense of being given something foul tasting and foul smelling, possibly through a tube inserted through my nose to my stomach which was then removed to allow for the vomiting to begin, but that may not be accurate. I do know that it seemed to go on for days, but my sense of time was terrifically distorted by that point.

I picked a hell of a time to begin taking decisive action. Impulsivity, thy name is Bebe. Desperate times, I thought, more than once, led me here. Eventually I became aware of the changing of the guard. My parents arrived and Lyddie and her mother went home. I was aware, but I didn't much care. I had never been so sick in my life. Whatever it was that they had given me was certainly doing its job wringing every last bit of moisture, mucous, and detritus from my body from any and all available exit points.

It was kind of like laboring to deliver a baby. The waves of nausea and cramping eventually started to come so close together that I was hardly aware of any rest time in between bouts. I had abandoned my clothes hours ago. Fluids of one sort or another were just completely exploding from me; there was no time to even stop to pull down my pants or lean over the bowl. One of the nurses handed me a johnny. "Here, put this on," she said and somehow I did. She placed a stack of about three more close by, knowing that I would be needing them shortly.

I remember thinking that I could have done a better job as a nurse than anyone I encountered at the hospital. These people were very efficient and proficient, but none of them had one iota of caring. They were in there getting things done, but it ended there. I stopped even trying to go back to the gurney to lay down between emptyings. I just "assumed the position," laying in a fetal position on the bathroom floor, eyes closed. All of this was accomplished with one hand tethered by tubing from the needle in my arm to the IV pole. The irony? Now I really *did* wish that I was dead.

I remember that a hospital social worker tried to talk to me. "So what happened? Did something happen last night? Was it a boy?" she asked these questions in rapid succession.

"No," I repeated, "I just wanted to sleep." That was my story and I was sticking to it.

"Usually they do it because they broke up with a boy," I heard her say to my mother earlier. Ha! What a joke! I'd never even *had* a boyfriend, not a real one. Only the fake one who disappeared the minute we had sex. This made what she was saying all the more ludicrous, and made me feel all the more pathetic. I didn't do it because my boyfriend broke up with me; I did it because the boy that I was hoping would someday acknowledge that he was my boyfriend but for now I was just pretending was my boyfriend broke up with me. How humiliating.

I needed to sleep.

Chapter 3: The Ultimate Betrayal

Looking back now, I think of it as my first nervous breakdown. A perfectionist, I was anxious to put this fiasco behind me and move on. Life sort of just went on after that, as if nothing had happened. I decided that I was finished with David, finished with wasting any more of my time on someone who couldn't show that he cared about me. What if I had been wrong about everything? Maybe David never was my soul mate. If *he* wasn't, then someone else out there *was*. Time to pick myself up, dust myself off, and start looking around.

I went back to school and to work. I hadn't missed any actual class time since this all began and ended during the Thanksgiving break. I was in college then, practicing my invisibility in a university setting. I chose this particular university because that was where David told me he was going. Before. Before we had sex. Before he dumped me.

I probably am the only person who attended college for four years and made no new friends. Not one. I was too busy focusing, trying to bump into David on campus, or trying to get finished with my classes so I could get to work. Those college years were a vast wasteland of loneliness. I was completely on the outside looking in for the entire four years.

Work, however, was different. Probably this made what David and Lisa did even worse, since work was the only place that I felt like I was part of things. Like I belonged. Like I mattered. My mother started pushing me to get a job when I turned sixteen. I resisted for months. I was a master procrastinator.

When I was almost seventeen, I decided that I should work because I needed money and my parents had none to spare (more on that later). I called Lyddie and said, "Hey, time to get a job," and she agreed. Lyddie was good like that. We thought about where we should work. It seemed like waitresses had it pretty good. They didn't have to wait for their paycheck; they left work every day with pockets full of money.

I wanted *that*.

We applied and were both hired and started the following week.

Right from the start, I loved this job. For one thing, I was great at it. I had always been a quick learner. I was working on my own almost right away, asking questions when there was someone to ask, figuring it out on my own when there wasn't. Soon they trained me on the fountain, and then the grill. I learned how to operate the dishwasher as I went along out of necessity: when there were no clean dishes to plate the food, someone had to do something. Often that someone was me.

After the 'notable event', I'd only given the barest amount of information to my co-workers about what happened. Although it was true that no excuses were necessary at school, this was not true at my job. I was pretty much working six to seven days every week by then, and I did miss work for the weekend after Thanksgiving. I decided to keep it simple; I told them that I was in the hospital with pneumonia. It so happened that I had a bad cough then; how were they to know that it was from allergies? "I'm fine now though!" I reassured them all. "Not contagious or anything." I didn't even need to produce a doctor's note to excuse the absence from work. I'd never missed a day since I first started working for my boss, Jim, so he had no reason to question my explanation now.

So being a sort of a star at work gave me my well of self-esteem, which had been empty and dry forever, a little trickle of nourishment. I didn't have to sweat it about talking to new people there because there was no time to think about it. I was meeting and talking to new people every day (surprise! Customers are people too). Plus, in order to work together as a team, you had to talk to each other. Although I was uncomfortable at first, it soon became second nature. People listened and responded to what I said because the bottom line was that I was so good at my job that I made their jobs easier, and everyone wanted a piece of that if they could get it.

I finally had a place in my life where I felt appreciated and wanted and important. When Lisa was looking for a job, I didn't think twice about asking Jim to hire her. Why not? It made sense in a lot of ways. I could show her how to do the job, thereby reducing the stress of starting a new job for her. I hoped that once she got on her feet that we'd be able to cover for each other if something came up and one of us needed a day off at the last minute. I also thought it would score me some points with my boss if I brought in an employee who was good. I smugly thought that if she were half as good as I was, that would be plenty better than a lot of the people we had already working there.

Shortly after Lisa came on board, I was invited to a Christmas party. I decided to do a brave thing. I'd never brought a guy to any party before. Instead I spent most of my time stalking David while he pretended not to know me. What better way to start a new chapter than to 'woman up' and invite someone?

I decided to ask Kevin.

Kevin was the manager of the shop where I worked. He had been making it very plain that he was interested in me, so it wasn't an overly risky proposition. I was reasonably sure he'd want to go with me, so when he agreed, with much enthusiasm, I was relieved at first but then relief quickly morphed into terror. What the hell was I thinking? This was one of those plans that looked so good on paper, but who knew what the hell it would look like in real life?

I was still raw, but I was trying to put a good face on it for everyone. "Smile, Bebe!" one of my regular customers, Al, would always say to me when I brought his coffee in the morning. "I *do* smile, when there's something to smile *about*," I protested. "Even if there isn't, smile anyway!" he would say. "It will make you *feel* happy."

That was his story and I have to give him credit; he was sticking to it. I made an effort to smile whenever he was sitting at the counter. Why not? He always left me a dollar tip in appreciation for the huge effort required to bring him his cup of black coffee, and he came in every single day. In no way did I want to jeopardize my income. Also, although I didn't want to admit it, he was right. At first it felt stiff and false, but after a while, I actually *did* sort of feel marginally better with a smile on- with 'a while' being about equal to the amount of time that he was sitting at the counter watching me.

One day, after he had finished his coffee and left, I found an envelope with my name on it under the dollar tip when I went to clear his coffee cup away. He had written a poem for me.

God's Love.

There are so many things in the world today

That need a guiding hand,

We need a firm foundation

Upon which all mankind can stand.

God's love is that foundation,

And can give to all mankind,

A sheltered place in heaven

If we keep him close in mind.

His love is all encompassing,

For everyone to share,

The world would be a better place

If everyone would care.

~Al

He even typed it, and then he cut the page around it into a four by four inch square, with his signature in the bottom left hand corner.

I couldn't believe it. I had stopped going to church by then. I had only been going in the first place because I hoped to catch glimpses of David. Pretty much anything to do with religion now just put me off, so I was surprised to find that I loved this little poem. In the back of my mind, I wondered if maybe he hadn't accepted my story about what caused my absence from work as easily as everyone else had. Was this his way of letting me know that he was on to me?

He stopped coming into the shop shortly after he left the poem on the counter for me with my tip that day. I only saw him a couple more times, then started missing him. One day I remarked to Kevin about how I hadn't seen Al in a few weeks. "Oh, didn't you know? He died." Kevin said. "It's okay. He was old. He died in his sleep," he tried to soften it, seeing the look on my face. "Come on, the guy was, like, 90 or something! He had a bad case of old!" I tried to smile, but quickly finished up what I was doing so that I could run to the bathroom. The tears came, but I pulled myself together fast. He wrote to me about "God's Love", then he went to meet God himself? Too ironic. Even *Al* had left me.

Sometimes you heard people talking about angels on earth. I always dismissed this as total crap. Now, though, I wondered....could it be true? Maybe Al was sent to let me know that there were plenty of people in my life that did love me, and did *not* care if everyone knew? To show me that this is how you treat someone that you care about? I splashed some cold water on my face, then went back out to work,

I decided to take this as a sign. I would stop thinking about the people that didn't think about me. I had been second guessing my decision to bring Kevin to the party, trying out different ways of calling it off in my head, but I stopped that now. I would go. With him. He liked me. He had been talking about the party all week, and how happy he was that I'd asked him. I was starting to worry that I might be one of those people who didn't want to belong to any club that would have her as a member. Deep breath. I was going to plunge ahead, and act "as if".

Chapter 4: Kevin

So we went to the party together. It was fine. There was no electric connection like I'd had with David. The kind that would light me up like a flare if he just glanced at me. The kind that made me feel very interesting sensations below the waist. The kind that kept me up for hours thinking about what I would do to his body if only I had thirty seconds of access. The "OH MY

GOD! OH MY GOD!" sensation when I unexpectedly caught a glimpse of him in my peripheral vision.

No, with Kevin the energy was more like: Hey, did you notice that I'm standing right next to you? Like, a half an inch away? Yawn. Really? Oh, that's nice. Thanks for the heads up. Hmmm, I might go to the mall later. Oh, and I think I have some laundry to do.

Like that. It was sort of a letdown, but in a way it was a relief.

The constant zing of my connection to David, who was in the erotic region of my conscious and subconscious mind every minute of every day was thrilling, but also exhausting and in the long run, what did I have to show for it really? A fractured hymen. A broken heart. A disillusioned mind.

Not much.

So, deciding to embrace 'darn good enough' instead of 'holy shit! I want to rip his clothes off and do anything I want to every inch of his hot body for hours.' It was not a difficult decision to make. After all, David disappeared. Nothing left there. I was left. Kevin was there. He was available and willing and, after we'd been out a few times, he even told me he wanted to marry me some day. Woohoo, right? Right question, wrong guy was my first thought. Then I thought, look what the path of true love and presumed soul mate-ship had got me?

Besides. I'd always heard that the passion train leaves the station quickly after it arrives at the marital bed. It cools down and goes dormant, kind of like the varicella virus goes dormant in your nerve endings after the chicken pox. So maybe it would be better to not have any virus at all, just a benign cloud of good will enveloping us rather than hot lusting love. I decided to go for it and let him know that I was interested in getting married too, but not yet. I also let him know that I wanted to wait until we got married to have sex. After all, I had already had great sex and look how that turned out. It seemed to me that it might be a good idea to put a lot of time and space between hotness and lukewarmness. He was okay with it. Done deal, I thought.

Life meandered on. Still in college, I was spending as little time as possible on campus in classes so I could spend as much time as possible at work making the money to pay for that college tuition. We didn't go out much but since I saw Kevin a lot at work, I didn't feel like I was missing out. We went parking at the lakes from time to time, just enough to know that I could tolerate his body, his tastes, his scents…there was no deal breaker here. The first time he put his arm around me, it felt awkward, like he was trying too hard. I gave him credit for his efforts, though. I decided to help him out. I moved in as close as I could get. I thought, now or never. I had to see if we had any chemistry at all. He leaned toward me and finally, finally, we kissed. Although I was never confident when I was alone with the opposite sex, I was no longer panicked when a boy kissed me. I was feeling kind of neutral about it all. So, okay, he wasn't amazing like David, but he wasn't bad either. He was just different. I could get used to this. Nice, comfy love. Sign me up.

Until I found out that Lisa was fucking him, I never even thought to question him about what he did when he wasn't with me. Never. Once. Thought. What can I say? I was young and not wise in the ways of the world, clearly. He was so nice. I did like him…but I didn't *like* him. Why couldn't I feel that same pull that I had felt for David with Kevin instead? Why couldn't lust and love go hand and hand for anyone you wanted? Why wasn't lust…a transferable commodity? Kevin was nice looking. He was easy to talk to. He was funny as hell. He was a decent kisser. What was the problem? Maybe because I hadn't gone all the way with him yet. Maybe some attractions had to be ignited with a direct penile connection, rather than with daydreams, imagination, and wishing.

Well, too bad. There was no way that I was going to do that with Kevin until we got married. At first I did think that it was a little odd that he had acquiesced so easily to my terms of abstinence, but I thought it was one of the things guys have to do for love sometimes. That he dealt with it by looking at porn and discharging his frustrations into a sock, as all good, frustrated men had been doing for centuries, during all of those years that men were buying cows because the milk was not for free, pal. No wheels were being reinvented here; this was a well-worn path to the altar that we were following. Tried and true.

Except that it wasn't. I guess good old Kev thought that he could have his (cheese)cake and eat it too…oh my God, not going there! So he would marry the chaste, born again virgin and screw the slutty sister to kill time until the wedding night. It's not like Lisa would have thought twice about it. Lisa had a long history of thinking that what was hers was hers and what was mine was hers. Her life had been defined by a sense of entitlement to what was mine. If I had something, she wanted it and would just take it. Permission might have been granted after the fact but almost never before. Lisa's motto was this: Possession of Bebe's goods was nine tenths of the law. And I never made an issue of it. She was my sister, and no matter what, I loved her. I thought that underneath all of the lying, stealing, and treachery, she loved me back, so it was all okay.

This was uncharted territory for us because the punch line was that she was pregnant. Basically, she took my fiancé and, the argument could be made that she took my first born. "You don't have a ring!" she casually said to me one day after Kevin and I had been together for several months. Duh. Foreshadowing.

"Not yet," I said. "I'm not in a big hurry for that," I told her. When Kevin and I talked about an engagement ring, we decided to wait because he didn't have much money, and I didn't have much clue as to what I wanted.

"If we wait, I can get you something really nice," he'd said, and that sounded great to me. If I was going to be wearing it for the rest of my life, it should be something pretty goddamned beautiful, right?

Now, I blame myself. Maybe if I had gotten a ring, Lisa would have recognized that there was a line here that couldn't be crossed. Well, that shouldn't be crossed. No, wait. This was Lisa. It wouldn't have made one bit of difference. When she saw something she wanted, she took it. If it was mine, so much the better. There was no operational moral compass here.

Chapter 5: A Wedding-Not Mine, and a Baby, and a Bad Girl is Born

I was pretty much unable figure out how the man with whom I'd been the good girl, who was doing everything right for a change, had thrown me over for the sister who had been the bad girl, who just did everything. Damned if you do and damned if you don't. What a loser I was for trusting them.

So, they had the baby. They got married. They got an apartment. In that order.

While I was not really jealous of the marriage part or the baby part, I was totally jealous of the has-her-own-apartment part. They lived on the first floor of a two family house on a quiet street on the other side of town. I spent as much time there as possible when Kevin was not there. I loved the idea of having my own kitchen, my own bedroom, my own TV. I felt like I couldn't afford to move out while I was still in college. I was barely able to pay my tuition, even with the help of several thousands of dollars in loans and scholarships. I put independence on the back burner and vicariously experienced it through Lisa.

Time for me to move on. This time, I wasn't looking for a soul mate. I wasn't looking for a husband. I was looking for a lover.

My mission now was to find a willing participant and to just have sex already. It didn't seem like too much to ask. I didn't really know anyone at school, except David. I was still trying to forget that I ever knew him. I looked around at work. The idea of going out with a coworker wasn't so appealing after the fiasco with Kevin. I was very anxious not to repeat *that* particular mistake again.

I decided that maybe I'd have better luck if I paid attention to the customers. There was a pack of wild guys that frequented the parking lot behind the shop at odd times, drinking, yelling, and in general calling a lot of attention to themselves for no good reason. I privately thought of them as The Animals, and mostly stayed the hell out of their way. I remembered the saying that sometimes what you are looking for turned out to be right there in your own back yard. Or the back parking lot.

One of them was a tall, arrogant guy, Buddy, who always gave me a hard time when he came in to not buy something. He was different from anyone I'd ever met. He was very tall, six feet two inches, and he was slim. He seemed to always be wearing blue scrub pants for no real reason except that they were free. Later he told me that his sister got them for free from the hospital where she worked and he stole them from her. Paired with the scrubs was usually a concert t-shirt of some sort, and usually flip flops, even in the middle of winter, for Chrissakes. Buddy had long, curly black hair and amazing blue eyes. They were so vivid that I wondered if they were somehow chemically enhanced. He dropped out of college after two years to go to work. He was now working full time days, and partying full time most nights and weekends.

His one nod to healthy living was that he played a sport. Hockey. Every Sunday morning, he and the rest of The Animals would pile into someone's car and drive a few towns over to the rink. This meant that they also began drinking early on Sundays; as soon as the game was over, the partying began. Or continued.

Despite all of his character flaws, the more I saw him, the more I liked him. I liked his smart mouth. I liked it that I could always come up with a witty comeback to match whatever he dished out. Buddy liked it too; no one else ever stood up to him. I got about an inch away from him when he was giving me a hard time about something, like leaving the store after I'd denied his fourth request for ice in one hour. When we were that close, I had to practically look straight up to see his face. I liked being that close to him. I liked the way he smelled. I liked the sparring. I liked his heat. I liked the sexual innuendo that ran rampant through every single word that came out of his mouth. To me.

So, one night when he said, "If you're not doing anything after work, come out with me," I didn't hesitate. To contort a line from the movie *Moonstruck*, I *ran* to the wolf in him. It was usually after 11:00PM by the time I got out of work to go meet him. He often was well on the wrong side of sober by that time of night, but he made up for it in bravado, and I felt the tug.

I sucked up my courage and marched over to Buddy. He smiled. I smiled right back. He said, "I saved you a beer," and he went around to the trunk of his car. He flipped open the lid on the most enormous cooler I had ever seen, pulled out a bottle, popped off the top, and handed it to me. Bud Light. The kind I liked. I thanked him and leaned up against the side of his car, taking a long swallow of the beer.

He really was good looking, in an off-beat sort of way. I could do worse. Hell, I *had* done worse. Twice. He was fun, funny, and didn't care one bit about anyone but himself. Maybe I could get him to care about me. I decided to try a different approach from what I had used in the past. I decided to be direct.

Later that night, Buddy sat on the hood of a car and then someone else started it up and began driving around the parking lot. Can you say, "recipe for disaster"? The object of this game was for Buddy to not fall off when the driver stopped short, hung a U-turn, or did whatever he could think of to buck Buddy from the bronco.

At first, he managed to hang on, but as the attempts to knock him off failed, the fervor of the driver to beat him increased. He started going faster and faster, and began stopping harder and shorter, until he succeeded in knocking him off. He hit the ground with a thud, landing on his back. He was still for a minute, and while everyone held their breath, I went running over to see if he was okay. He sat right up as I approached him, laughing.

"Are you okay?" I asked him.

"Sure! No big deal!" and he called over to Jim, the driver

of car. 'Hey, Jim! "Let's go again!" Then he stopped, rubbing the back of his head with his hand for a second. "It's a good thing that I have such a hard head! I guess I must have banged it when I fell off." He held out his hand, which was covered with blood.

"Holy shit, Buddy, you're bleeding!" I said. Never a fan of blood, I tried to rise above it so that I could see how bad it was.

After some searching that involved some careful rearranging of his long black curls, what I saw made my stomach flip. There was a wide gash in the back of his head that was full of grit and oozing blood. "Oh my God, you have to go to the hospital. You need stitches." He started laughing.

"What? It doesn't even hurt!" he said.

"I guess the alcohol you've had so far has anesthetized you, because it's one hell of a mess back there," I repeated, "Come on, you have to go to the Emergency Room."

By this time, his friends had all assembled to check out the damage and render their own opinions about what to do. They reached a consensus: go to the Emergency Room. His partner in this fiasco, the causative agent, volunteered to drive him

I reached over to hug Buddy and said, "Don't worry, you'll probably be okay," and then added, "well, as okay as you were before the hit."

He laughed again and said, "If they stitch it, at least they'll give me some good drugs first!" He kissed me quick right on the mouth, said, "See ya," and left.

The next time I saw him was about three days later. His beautiful hair was mostly gone; leaving a nearly bald head. "They had to shave the back of my head for the stitches, so I told them to just shave the damn whole thing," he explained. In addition to fourteen stitches, Buddy also was the lucky recipient of a 1950's style buzz cut. He wasn't completely hairless. He still had his mustache, effectively breaking up the monotony of his face which was *not* now framed by hair. It took some getting used to, but somehow, it worked. He still looked good to me.

I guess we got very close so quickly because of the intensity of that drama surrounding our first time together. We were a couple right away after that. We had a quick conversation regarding significant others:

Me: "You seeing anyone?"

Him: "No."

Him: "You?"

Me: "No."

Glad we got *that* settled. That was easy enough. Later I thought, maybe it would have been better if I'd asked a few more questions. Like, maybe I should have defined what I meant by girlfriend. At the time though, I didn't know what I didn't know.

I was the girl who thought that everyone in court told the truth, because they had sworn on The Holy Bible that they would. Back then, I believed everything that anyone told me. Especially him. I had rebounded some from what had happened with my sister and my supposed fiancé, and had smartened up a little, but not enough.

Time to get on with it. I wasn't getting married, and I wasn't getting younger. If he wanted to put his hands all over me, then I would change my position to facilitate easy access to any part he was groping for. I wanted to *help* him help me. He stayed within reasonable bounds for about thirty seconds; then he went for it. At the last second, he asked me if I was on The Pill.

Shit. No. No. I wasn't.

This bad girl act didn't come naturally to me. I was still just a good girl in--or out of--bad girl's clothing. I had taken on this persona a long time ago, with David, when he thought I had been sleeping around, even though I had only ever been with him. From now on, I would be making a concerted effort not to be naïve and stupid about guys and sex. You know, except for this one last time. To his credit, he stopped short of ejaculation and said no way were we doing it until I had gotten on birth control.

"What about condoms?" I asked, tentatively. "No way. They suck. You know? Plus they can break," which turned out to be foreshadowing. I wish I'd paid better attention to what he'd been saying. Because, as it turned out, he knew what he was talking about.

Anyway, I went back to the clinic to get some birth control. I endured the gynecological exam and the scraping, prodding, and palpating so that I could fuck my boyfriend without becoming a parent. After the exam, we got down to business. How do I have sex but not get pregnant? She started to review the different methods.

"Well, there's the IUD, but if you ever plan on maybe having kids, this method is risky," she said. It really wasn't necessary for her to say this, actually, because once she showed me a picture of an IUD and said that it would be, um, inserted and *left inside* me, I stopped listening.

"No thanks. What else is there?" She showed me a diaphragm, and explained how that one also would need to be inserted, every time, and in advance. Seriously? Well, I never knew when I might see Buddy. He came and went, rarely letting me know ahead of time if or when he would show up. He didn't want to be "pinned down" that way. I saw him when I saw him. He had volunteered no telephone number, saying, "I'm never home." He still lived with his parents, like me, so who was I to judge? I knew what it was like trying to get any private phone time at my house, so I didn't question him too much. As much as

I should have.

He gave me his work number, but said he was rarely at his desk; his job required a lot of field work, but I could leave him a message and he'd "try" to get back to me. If he even got the message, he said. Well, *I* got the message: Don't call me. Looking back, I should have heard warning bells and saw red flags, but at that time, I took it all at face value. The diaphragm, therefore, would require a level of advance planning that would be difficult, if not impossible, for me to execute. Strike one.

Besides, just about all of our physical contact took place in his car, which was not conducive to optimal diaphragmactic installation. The other consideration was that I had been spectacularly unsuccessful in the past when I'd tried to insert a tampon, which was so much narrower and therefore theoretically easier to get into place than the diaphragm, which looked huge to me, like a small bowl, for God's sake! I mean, how could there still be any room up there for his dick once the diaphragm was in place? It seemed impossible. Strike two.

"No, thanks," I said politely. "I don't think that would work for me. What about birth control pills?" I asked finally, not sure why she hadn't led with that, my preferred option.

"Well, The Pill has some serious side effects," she said, "The Pill" with audible capital letters. I was now paying attention. Her tone was so very serious. I heard words like "blood clots", "heart attacks", and "strokes". Hmm, as far side effects go, these were impressive. The upside was that The Pill was something like 99% effective "when taken correctly".

"What do you mean?" I asked.

"You have to remember to take it every day, and at the same time every day, otherwise, the effectiveness decreases substantially. Also, it doesn't protect against sexually transmitted diseases." Well then. I heard everything that I needed to hear. I had no worries about taking The Pill at the same time every day. I mean, that was a no-brainer for an overachiever like me. Plus, look what was at stake. Not getting pregnant. That was a pretty powerful motivator. I couldn't put my parents through *that* again. Sold! "I'll take it." I was armed now, and dangerous.

Our nights out were fairly unimpressive. Sometimes, if I got finished work early enough on a weeknight, we'd drive to a spot where you could see the drive-in movie screen without paying and catch the end of whatever was playing while we ate take-out food. The cheapskate version of "dinner and a movie".

On rare occasions when we had an entire day off together, we'd go to the beach, usually Revere Beach. We liked to go in the winter so we could pretty much have the beach to ourselves. He'd park the car, and then we'd walk down to Kelly's Famous Roast Beef, open all year. He'd get a large roast beef with fries, and I'd get a small roast beef with onion rings and we'd share it all. They packed up the food into open topped boxes, and if it was warm enough, we'd take the food across the street and go sit on the concrete wall facing each other. We did our best to beat off the seagulls while we ate. In the winter, we would just park close to the food source, then run back to the car to eat it. He'd blast the heater for me because my feet were always cold, and never complained that he was wasting gas.

We started going to a little Italian restaurant called DiSanto's. If he got out of work early, he'd call me to meet him there. He'd get some garlicky Italian fish dish and I'd get chicken parm and share. After dinner, we'd head over to the bar side where we could have a few drinks and play on an ancient Ms. Pacman. I was starting to feel like we were really were a couple, and not like I was just mooning after someone who couldn't care less about me. Hello? David. Kevin.

Once I had finally got the birth control issue covered, I was looking forward to telling him the good news. This actually took quite some time. He had always been unpredictable in his habits; he was usually around on weekend nights, but not always.

Sometimes he would show up during the week, but never the same day twice. Hello, enigma.

Finally, he showed up. He came to see me at work. His hair was growing back. He looked more like himself. I loved how tall he was. He had gotten his ear pierced and wore a small gold hoop, and I loved that too. I expected him to be happy with my news and I wasn't disappointed. "Let's get a room," he said. Okay, so that sounded great on paper, but also, it sounded sort of slutty. I mean, get a room, as in, "Let's get a room." Well, what the hell. It would be nice to have sex in a bed, for once, and since it was our first time, it seemed worth it to cough up the cash to do so.

It must have been a special occasion, since he actually picked me up and took me to DiSanto's for supper. I was a little nervous and was more talkative than usual. I wasn't very hungry and was anxious to get to the hotel. He must have felt the same way, because soon enough we were unlocking the door to the room. He had a bag with him, from which he extracted a bottle of champagne. I was impressed. We unwrapped the plastic from the disposable cups provided by the hotel, and he opened the champagne. It was exactly what I needed. After one glass, I was feeling much less nervous. Much more ready.

Well, as first times go, it wasn't the best, but I suspect it wasn't the worst. I wondered if maybe he overstated the amount of experience he'd had with other women, because there was a whole lot of fumbling going on, and not just by me. I was happy to be in a fully consummated relationship finally, and that was what mattered. I was happy we'd had sex. I was sure it would get better. I know we were both nervous but I thought that would take care of itself over time. I was proud of myself for choosing him and following through and making it happen. I wasn't the victim. I had recovered from my two earlier unfortunate relationships and now, the third time was the charm. My eyes were wide open. I was the one in control.

Ha.

Chapter 6: Third Time the Charm

Sometimes Buddy worked as a courier for his company and they would pay to fly him to and from wherever the package needed to be delivered. He could choose to stay at that location for as long as he wanted between flights. When they asked him to fly to Florida, he surprised me by asking me to go with him. He offered to split the cost of my plane tickets since his would be free, and said that his sister lived there and we could stay in her guest room. The main attraction of the trip was getting to spend all of those days in a row with him, and getting to spend all of those nights in a row in bed with him. An added bonus was that it wasn't far from Disney so we could spend a day there before we came home. It would be a first for the both of us. I was happy.

The trip had been going well for us. We had fun going to the beach, driving around in the rental car exploring, blasting Bon Jovi on the radio, and of course, going to Disney. We stayed up late, slept late, ate whatever we wanted, watched mindless TV.

One night, we explored the apartment complex where his sister lived with her boyfriend. There was a large, built-in pool in the courtyard that the apartments surrounded, and in the corner was an outdoor hot tub. I'd never been in a hot tub. He said, "Come on, let's get in!" but I was hesitant.

"Are we allowed to? I mean, maybe it's someone's private tub? Not for public consumption?" I joked.

"Who cares? Everyone's at work. Come on!" he said again. So I did. We had our bathing suits on under our clothes, so we quickly shed our shorts and T shirts and slipped into water.

It felt amazing. The water was perfect, and Buddy was right; it was the middle of the day and there was no one around. He hit the button to start up the water jets and positioned himself with the jet pulsating against his back. Then he motioned for me to come over to where he was sitting up against the wall. I swished my way over to him. He put one hand on each of my hips, lifted me up effortlessly, weightless in the water, and positioned me on his lap, astride him, facing him. We made out for a while, and maybe it was the potential badness of it, thinking that we might be using someone's private property without permission, that made me feel daring, so when I felt his fingers manipulating the fabric of my bathing suit between my legs and pushing it aside, I helped by hooking my fingers into the waistband of his trunks and pulling them down. Wow, my hand felt how happy he was to be doing this, checking again over my shoulder quickly for passersby, seeing there were none, body parts out of site under the water, and feeling him attempt to gain entry.

It was not as easy as I expected, not as easy as they made it look in the movies, that's for damn sure. I thought that the presence of water would make entry easier, but in fact it makes it *harder*. Now that we had started this, however, I was committed to seeing it through. We both persevered and finally, success! He was in. It is also not easy to discreetly receive pelvic thrusts underwater, but soon enough, amidst my giggling, he came. Cross another first for us both off the list. Hot tub sex? Check!

I told him that I loved him about a month before the trip and (okay, after a week had passed) he told me that he loved me too. I was elated. I gave away the milk for free (sorry, ma) but he loved me anyway. We didn't wear much jewelry, but we each had one piece that was very meaningful to us. We decided to exchange the jewelry to cement our commitment to each other. I gave him my gold chain that that my grandmother had given me, and he gave me his gold ring that his grandfather had given him. Now that we sealed our relationship with gold jewelry, nothing could tear us asunder. Right? Am I right?

We were getting along better than ever. We never argued. We had a lot of fun together. We loved Disney, Epcot, and Universal. Sometimes we ate by ourselves, and sometimes his sister and her boyfriend joined us. The days went by quickly. On our last day there, Buddy and his sister thought it would be fun to go do something all four of us together. They decided to go to a water park.

This would not have been my first choice for an activity. I mean, this would not have been my hundred and first choice. I tried to dissuade Buddy from the park idea, but he wouldn't budge; he had been dying to go since his sister told him about it a few months back, and since this was his first, and for all he knew, maybe his last trip to Florida, he wasn't passing it up.

I silently stewed. I was distracted the entire way there, which turned out to take a couple of hours. Also, Buddy and his sister and her boyfriend weren't real planners; they'd just get up and go. For example, Buddy didn't want me to buy my plane ticket home until we got to the airport to actually *fly* home. This made me anxious for days, and every time I thought about it, which was nearly hourly, I thought of all of the reasons why this was a bad idea. Since he was splitting the cost of the tickets with me, I felt like I had to defer to what he wanted. Stupid. Me? I was a *world class* planner. No, worrier. No, planner.

On the way, we stopped for a breakfast of coffee and doughnuts. As we ate, I was wondering about what we would do for lunch. Did the park have good food? Did they even have any place to *buy* food? If they didn't, then what would we eat? Sometimes it seemed like Buddy and his sister could go for hours without eating or even thinking about eating. As long as they had something to drink, they were good. I, like any good Italian girl, was already thinking about what I would have for lunch, and maybe even supper, before breakfast was over. Unfortunately, I was the only functional Italian in the bunch.

Then there was the fact that I could barely swim. This was despite two summers of swimming lessons at the pond near my house beginning when I was twelve. I could manage a dog paddle and could probably tread water to save my life as long as help arrived within, say, three to five minutes.

I also had no body confidence when wearing a bathing suit. Or, you know, ever. Buddy and his sister were tall and thin.

She wore her bathing suit carelessly; she just put it on and seemed to never give it a second thought. The guys couldn't care less how they looked - they knew that they looked great-and just threw on their faded swim shorts without a second thought. I usually avoided any occasion that would require me to bare as much of myself in public as a bathing suit would. Going to a water park made it impossible to avoid and I was extremely self-conscious about it.

Yet another worry was that we were, after all, in Florida, and I was a girl who got sunburned while wearing 80 SPF sun-block in just the amount of time it took me to walk from the bus stop to my house in my much-further-from-the-sun New England home state. Said sun block bottle clearly stated to reapply after swimming. Everyone knew that water a) washes off sun-block and b) increases the intensity of the sun's rays. What effect would spending three hours mostly in the water in the middle of the day have on me?

Also, I wore contact lenses. These wouldn't fly at the water-park; all I needed was little chlorinated water to splash on the lenses to shrivel them up and stick them indefinitely to my eyeballs. I once had a pair of defective lenses, and when it was time to remove them at the end of the day, they had somehow adhered so tightly that just the act of extracting them abraded the entire surface of my corneas. It felt immediately like my eyes were on fire, a feeling that lasted for days. I was not anxious to repeat that ever again.

I considered not wearing them at all. To fully appreciate the panic that this engendered, try this: after you get out of your car, walk about twenty feet from it, then turn around and look back. See it? Nice and clear, right? Now, walk about another three hundred and eighty feet away from it. See it now? Kind of fuzzy? Gotta squint a little? Maybe you aren't even still sure that it *is* your car? Well, that's how it looks to *me* when I'm standing twenty feet away from it without contacts or glasses! Not pretty.

Consider how distressed I was trailing around the park after the others. When they got more than about arm's length away from me, I couldn't be sure who it was that I was following. I didn't even know his sister or her boyfriend all that well, having just met them on this trip a few days earlier. What did they care if I got separated from them? They weren't my babysitters, after all.

Then there was Buddy. How well did I really even know *him*? Not very, I realized. It was unsettling that he still wanted to go to the water park even after I let him know how much I did *not* want to go. I decided that I should swap out the contacts that day for my glasses. Even doing that made me nervous when I considered what might happen to them when I was actually going down on one of the slides. What would prevent the glasses from flying off my face?

I felt a sense of foreboding.

Actually, it was more like a glacier of foreboding. I was a

wreck.

I finally decided that I might as well buck up, shut up, and make the best of it, especially since I didn't see any alternative.

When we got there, we were informed that there were lockers fitted with combination locks to the right of the entrance where we could put our stuff, like keys, wallet, extra clothing and towels, prior to going on any of the rides. So said the gatekeeper. I was relieved at first to hear this. There was be a relatively safe place to put my glasses. The downside, of course, was I would be without my glasses the entire time that we were there. The term "flying blind" came to mind.

The first ride that everyone wanted to try out looked tame. I was game. It was kind of like the slides that you see at the carnival. A nice, gradual sloping downward of the slide into water that was about four feet deep. The fact that it was not over my head gave me courage. We walked up the hundred or so steps to the top, and then they gave us an inflated raft-type thing for us to ride down the slide on. I watched the others that went ahead of me, and they looked like they had a blast, and no one was hurt at the end. And then it was our turn. Buddy and I gave each other a "Ready? Set? Go!" before hurling ourselves downward to the pool at the bottom. I made it! Intact! Maybe I couldn't swim, and maybe I couldn't see a damned thing, but I made it!

On to the next one, which unfortunately was terrifying. It looked like it was about a thousand foot drop straight down into a ten foot deep pool. "No way," I said. "Come on! You can do it!" Buddy coaxed. "No. Fucking. Way," I said. "Oh, come on! I'll be right with you the whole time!" he tried again. Always a pleaser, I didn't want to let him down. It never crossed my mind that maybe *he* was the one letting *me* down. On this slide, it was not possible to go down side by side like we did on the other one. We would have to go one at a time, so for however long it took me to get there after he went, I'd be all alone, unseeing. Maybe that was actually a bonus. I would not be able to watch his descent after he left the platform.

"Okay," I relented, "you go first. You'll wait for me at the bottom?" He nodded. "Great! Let's go," and he started climbing up the stairway that looked high enough to get to heaven, the upper platform disappearing into a myopic mist. I was right behind him. Neither of us were great athletes. He had his weekly game of hockey with the guys and I ran around like a crazy person at my job but that was it, so we were pretty winded when we got to the top. After taking a couple of moments to get his breath back, he was ready. I was still not breathing normally, but that was more likely due to the hyperventilation of anxiety that was gripping me fully now.

"I'm sorry; I can't do it!" I said, looking down, feeling nauseated.

"You can," said the man at the top that was letting us speak our last words before we plunged to our deaths. "All you gotta remember is to keep your mouth shut, cross your legs, and cross your arms over your chest," he said, "and keep them crossed all the way down." Kind of like a corpse, I thought, which was probably fitting since I'd probably be dead before I hit the bottom, if not from the fall from such a great height, then from the heart attack that I was sure to have on the way down.

At some point during the giving of the instructions by the man, I failed to hear the weight of the words "…and keep them crossed all the way down." That was a shame, because it turned out to be the most important thing that he said. It turns out that when you free fall from a great height and land in water, the water is looking for any pathway into you, any unsuspecting corridor, any unprotected orifice.

At the jumping point, I was so focused on trying to slow down my breathing before I passed out that I forgot everything else. I was never a girl who was good at walking and chewing gum at the same time. Plummeting a hundred feet in to a small pool of water is an experience that, once you've had it, you will never forget as long as you live.

On the plus side, if you've been struggling on the toilet in the morning for any length of time, you might appreciate that side effect of a trip down the sky-high water slide with legs not completely fused together.

Enough said.

That was enough for me; I was sputtering water from nose and mouth -and the lower half of my body- for about a half an hour after I landed. Also, my bathing suit was barely still covering any of my important girl parts. Thanking God that it was a one-piece, I struggled to pull it back over parts that were now partially revealed to any and all onlookers. Finally, my man was (of course, of course) *not* waiting for me at the bottom of the slide as he had promised. I somehow managed to find my way out of the pool area and back to dry ground, where I waited, dripping, shaking, half in shock, until he showed up.

"Wasn't that amazing?" he yelled, coming out of

nowhere, laughing. "That was so great, right?" he asked, not waiting for me to reply. "Let's go up again!" he called over his shoulder as he headed for the stairs.

"No, you go. I'm done. Where are the others?" I asked him as calmly as I could manage. I was trying hard to keep my voice steady. I was aware of the tears that had formed and were now seeping from the corners of my eyes, but he apparently had not noticed, or wrote it off to the water.

"Oh, they went over to the other side of the park where the extreme slides are," he said.

Wow; there were worse ones than this one? I couldn't get my mind around that.

"You go," I said. "After that, let's look for something to eat, okay?" I hoped that getting something into my stomach might absorb and offset some of the gallons of water I had swallowed on my trip down the slide, and settle it a little. Now I really *was* nauseated.

"Oh, sorry," he said. "I took a look around while I was waiting for you and they don't sell food here. We'll stop some place on the way back," he said.

I stopped trying to please him after that.

When he returned after his next trip down the Enema Slide, as I'd come to think of it in kinder moments (or the Douchebag Slide in unkinder ones), I said, "I'll just wait for you guys over there," pointing to a shaded area with grass and picnic tables, which was kind of a cruel joke, since there was no food here. I just sat on the bench, waiting to leave.

It took them a long time to exhaust themselves.

Chapter 7: Another Cheat

Florida had been a lot of fun, except for the water park fiasco. After a week of getting up at noon, staying up late every night, and basically never knowing what time it was, though, I was so ready to leave. Life on vacation seemed to move in slow motion, as if underwater. My own normal speed was about a thousand times faster, both in thought and in deed. My patience for life in the slow lane was all used up. I was ready for structure. And coffee. Lots of strong black coffee.

I was feeling pretty good about my relationship with Buddy when we got home. For about ten minutes. A few days went by and I didn't see him or hear from him. Even though he hadn't been around all week, I wasn't worried. He often would disappear for a few days but he always resurfaced. When the weekend came though, and he didn't, I *did* start to worry. Since we'd been seeing each other, this was the first time that he failed to show up for so many days in a row. I tried to casually ask his friends where he was, but it was embarrassing. I was supposedly his girlfriend, and *I* was asking *them* where he was? It was completely humiliating, but I had no other ideas.

They didn't tell me a thing. Maybe they knew where he was and maybe they didn't, but either way, they weren't talking. I tried not to think about it too much. "He'll show up soon," my friend Lyddie tried to reassure me. "Do you know where he's been?" I asked her. She was going out with one of his friends now, maybe he had told her something that she hadn't mentioned to me yet.

"No! Come on, Beebes. You know I would have told you if I knew," she said.

"Okay; I know. I'm sorry, I'm just starting to freak out a little here," I said.

"He'll call you," she said again, and I was almost convinced.

But he didn't call me. Weeks went by, and he didn't come around. It was like he dropped off the face of the Earth. No one knew anything about his whereabouts, and if they did, they must have been sworn to secrecy because not one person gave even one small hint. I did know that he wasn't with me. I had to accept the awful truth.

I had been dumped.

I tried to call him a few times, but he never answered. I went over, and over, and over things in my mind. I just couldn't think of anything I had done to drive him away. What's worse than being abandoned by your boyfriend? Being abandoned by your boyfriend that you slept with. Again.

I felt like a total loser. One good thing, or maybe I should say one less bad thing, was that I hadn't told my parents much about the relationship. They knew next to nothing about him and so I didn't have to suffer through further humiliation fielding parental questions, especially any from my mother, who would have been in "I told you so!" heaven. I avoided my sister's prying questions. She knew I was seeing him because everyone that I worked with knew. There was certainly no way to conceal that. He and I were often together in plain sight of everyone. Well, we were until he vanished.

I had always felt sort of uneasy when I thought of Lisa around Buddy. Most likely, it stemmed from her stealing Kevin. There was also that one time I saw what I thought was Buddy's car drive by and someone who could have been Lisa was in the passenger's seat. It was impossible to know for sure, but I wondered about what I'd seen from time to time. What *had* I seen? I had no idea. They knew each other, of course, but they had never had any reason to say any more to each other than "Hi" and "'Bye", and even that would have only occurred rarely. So what the hell would she be doing in his car with him, alone?

I decided to wait to see if it came up in conversation. After all, I reasoned, if it was innocent, wouldn't she mention it to me? Something like, "Hey! I ran into Buddy today! He gave me a ride home from school. Wasn't that nice?" I waited. Nothing. Maybe it had never happened. Of course, I *should* be suspicious! She was always stealing things from me. Obviously, I would never again put it past her to fool around with my boyfriend.

I ran it by Lyddie. "Are you friggin' kidding me?" she exploded when I told her. "No, I can't think of any reason that she should have been alone with your boyfriend in his car without either one of them telling you about it. None. You have to say something," she said firmly. I decided that we couldn't both be paranoid. I would ask.

I decided that I should ask him, not her. Lisa was not only always stealing from me, but she also had a long history of lying to me. I used to not mind very much about stuff like that. If she needed money, I was happy to give her what I had. If she wanted to wear my clothes, it really was fine with me. But if she wanted to screw my boyfriend, well, that was *not* okay. I *did* mind.

"So," I had finally said to Buddy, in what I hoped was a casual voice, "I thought I saw you drive the other day with Lisa in the car. Did that happen?"

"Hmmm?" he said, distracted and did not answer.

Days later, I had finally gotten up the nerve to ask him again while he was driving, which in hindsight may have been a mistake. It was harder for me to read his face, since it was turned toward the road and not toward me.

"When? Oh, yeah, I remember. I was driving by and I saw

her walking home from school, so I stopped to give her a ride. No

big deal," he finished in a case-closed tone of voice. I got the

message. I didn't ask him anymore questions about it, even

though I still had plenty of them. It was pretty clear that he had

said all that he was going to say about it. It was moot now

anyway, since he'd dropped off the face of the earth. I would

eventually find out what happened to Buddy, but it would take a

while.

Years in Fact. I happened to run into him in the DiSanto's

parking lot one night. Surprise! He was unexpectedly in town.

Buddy did some fast talking. He got a job offer from his

company that required him to relocate to another state. He

decided not to mention it to me. He also decided that he needed a

little breathing room. He also chose not to mention this to me. He

had been seeing another girl while we were dating, and she got

pregnant, which he definitely did not want to mention to me. He

apparently did not recall his comment to me about how condoms break. It occurred to him that moving to another state sounded pretty darn good, and might solve some problems for him. So he packed up and moved north. They had a son, who they named after him. The end. The end of us.

Chapter 8: Psycho Boyfriend

Back to square one. I was older, a little wiser, and a lot sadder.

By now, I was about halfway through college. Despite all of the

crap that was going on in my personal life, I had managed to keep

my academic life on track. Still living with my parents, trying to

forget about Buddy, and also fighting to stop thinking about

David (I know, right? Pathetic!), I focused on my job. I had run

up a ton of debt. Just two years of university tuition added up to about $20,000 in loans, plus the out of pocket costs that commuting and buying books added, not to mention the daily trips to the Burger King across from the subway stop, for sustenance and refuge.

If I had some time to kill after my classes ended but before my shift at work started, I could go there and spread out my books, buy a cheap lunch, and stay until my homework was done. Since work was on the way home from school, it didn't make any sense to go home then go back to work. The commute home and back would use up most of that free time, plus cost me more in bus fares. Sometimes I just went to work early and tried to eat and do my homework there, but that often backfired. As soon as I walked through the door, more often than not, Jim would ask me to start my shift early so that he could leave. Plus, now that Kevin and Lisa were married and had the baby, I wasn't so interested in spending any time with them, and one of them was usually there working.

My life now was go to school, finishing homework and papers, reading, eating, and sleeping. I actually spent quite a bit of time sleeping. I got up a half an hour before I had to be out the door, no matter when that might be. If it was the weekend and I was working a 3pm till 11pm shift, I got up just early enough to get showered, dressed, and to the bus stop in time to catch the last bus that would still get me there on time.

I loved to read. I never went anywhere without a book. Ever. Paperbacks were my preference, since they were lighter and easier to wedge into my bag. Eating for comfort was my next favorite thing to do, after reading and sleeping: my holy trinity of escapism. They worked pretty well to keep me a couple of steps back from the edge of the black hole that I now knew lurked close by, ready to swallow me up at a moment's notice. I learned to try to give it as wide a berth as possible.

I headed to the corner store on my street one afternoon to stock up on writing supplies and munchies: red Twizzlers, a six pack of Diet Coke, and chocolate. On the way home, I could hear a vehicle slowing down on the street behind me. I kept walking at first, but when it didn't pass me I risked a look over my shoulder. It was a big, red truck. I wasn't too concerned about anything bad happening. It was broad daylight, after all, and I was within about three yards of my house.

When the car pulled up even with me, I could see the driver, and surprise! It was a man. He looked nice enough, not drop-dead gorgeous but not gag-me-with-a-spoon ugly. More of a hybrid of both.

"Candy, little girl?" he said, with a huge smile, and this transformed his features completely, bumping him up a notch in attractiveness. I was intrigued enough to overlook that stupid line. I held up my bag of newly purchased candy;

"All set," I said, and I kept walking.

"Okay, okay, that was lame, sorry!" he said. He tried again. "Hey, hi! Do you have far to go? Want a ride?" I stopped, pointed to the house just a couple of doors down.

"That's my house. I think I'll be able to make it. Thanks, though," I said, smiling brightly, and continued walking, more slowly now though, because I was thinking. Okay, now what's the definition of insanity? Doing the same thing over and over, right? I was doing the same thing that I did the same way day after day. Why not be brave for once?

I heard him say, "Let's go for a ride then." I lived on a main street, so by now there was a stack of impatient drivers behind him, queued up and pissed off. It was time to decide. Well, why *not* let him give me a ride? I felt like I had nothing to lose. What the hell.

"Okay, fine, but just for a half an hour. I told my parents that I'd be right back," I said, hopefully sending the message that there were people that would notice if I disappeared. I circled around to the passenger door, which he had leaned over to open for me, and jumped in.

And just like that, I had crossed that line. I was in a car with a stranger. All of the warning bells going off in my head were deafening. All of the red flags were flying. If there was one thing that I had internalized from a tender age, in addition to the "no one who was surrounded by free milk would be buying any cows" maxim, it was the "don't talk to, never-mind-get-into-a-car-with, strangers" rule.

My mother wasn't the only adult in my life banging *that* drum in my childhood. Teachers and nuns did as well, not to mention Nana See.Nana See's nickname came about because apparently I couldn't say our last name "Segretti" so in toddler-ease, it morphed into "See."

I remembered when I was about twelve, sitting on the front porch at her house one Sunday morning. Nana came out holding the newspaper with a page folded back. "Here, read this," she said, handing it to me. Then she went back into the house to the kitchen. I looked at the page and saw a picture of a little Italian girl with curly dark hair, wearing a white Communion dress and a delicate necklace with a little cross at her throat. The picture was just a little grainy, but clear enough.

I started reading, thinking that it would be a story about her First Holy Communion, something boring like that. Wrong. It was a story about how this unfortunate girl, Maria, had been killed. Killed. She was walking home from school and the route took her past the proverbial wooded area, which was very convenient for the bad man who was lurking there, looking for a little girl to lure close enough to abduct, rape, strangle to death, and bury in a shallow grave. Crap; Maria's luck was even worse than mine.

"See that?" Nana had come back out and was pointing to the article. "See what happens when you talk to strangers?" she said. I nodded solemnly. "She was twelve too, same as you," she said. I nodded again. It was almost too terrible even to think about. All these years later, I can still see her face in my mind, and her white dress, and her little necklace. I'm not sure if it was a good thing that Nana See made me read that or not. I guess she felt that it was a way to help prevent the same tragic fate from befalling me, and I guess it worked.

Up until now.

Because now, not only I was Talking to a Stranger, but I was also Getting into a Car with a Stranger. Although I thought of it as "doing things differently", what I was actually doing was being reckless. Drinking booze had been an overtly reckless behavior, and I had put that aside after Buddy disappeared into thin air, but I had replaced it with something potentially even more dangerous: risking life and limb. I was feeling so bad since getting dumped without warning or explanation that I had even less self-esteem than I had before, which was already practically none. Bring it, I thought.

After I got in, he eased the car away from the curb and we drove around the block. I studied his profile. He had a mustache, and he was blond. Not my usual type, but what had my type gotten me so far? Pain and suffering. Time to see what a blond would bring. Hopefully I would live to find out.

"So, what's your name?" he asked.

"Beatrice. Bebe. Yours?"

"Steven," he replied, smiling. His smile really did improve his looks, by about a thousand percent. He had very blue eyes. I could now see that his hair was more brown than blond, but still different from what I usually thought was attractive. At this point, different was good. I *wanted* different. He was dressed in jeans, work boots, and a flannel shirt, sleeves rolled up.

"Where were you going?" I asked him, more for want of something to say than anything else. My heart was thudding away with the fright that came from realizing that I really had put myself in harm's way. He could be a psycho killer, or on his way to becoming one. What the hell was I thinking? Panic began edging its way in.

"I was on my way home from visiting my mother. She lives on the street behind yours. I stopped by to see her on my way home from work," he said. The palpitations slowed some; his mother lived near me. He was just visiting her. Visiting his *mother*. That was probably a good sign. Plus, he had a *job*; gainful employment shifted him a little further to the left on the 'psycho killer' spectrum. I took a big breath in and let it out slowly. *Relax*, I thought. Nothing bad is going to happen. Nothing bad is going to happen. Nothing bad is--

"How old are you?" he said, interrupting my thoughts.

"Me? I'm twenty. How old are you?" I asked him, and I suddenly wanted to know. He looked like he was older than me, definitely not early twenties, but maybe a little older?

"I'm twenty-eight", he said.

"Wow, you look younger than that," I said.

"I know; everyone says that," he grinned. I was starting to like him, but the age difference concerned me a little. I was used to thinking that a three year age difference was stretching it some, but eight? Forget about it.

"What do you do? Are you in school" he asked.

"Yes. I'm going to college, and I work full time," I said, careful not to give away too much information, just in case.

"Where do *you* work?" I asked him, to distract my thoughts from the "He's *way* too old for you! Hell, he's just plain way *too old*!" that was coursing through my brain, as well as to divert the conversation away from traceable information about me.

"I work in the family business," he said, blue eyes sparkling in the sunlight that was streaming in through the car's moon roof. "I have four brothers and we *all* work in the family business." Just then I realized that we were back to my house. I was still alive! My person was still intact! No crime had been committed! I had met a new man that I liked. He had done just what he said he was going to do. He'd driven me around the block, we talked a little, and he'd brought me back home. Safe.

This time, he put the car in park. He hopped out and ran out into the street to open my door for me, extending his hand to help me, as if I wasn't perfectly capable of exiting a parked car on my own. I did take his hand though, and let him pull me out of his truck. Maybe an eight year age difference had some fringe benefits. Like, you know, manners. I could get used to that. I smiled at him, saying, "Thanks for the ride," lingering for a minute.

"Give me your phone number," he said. I might as well. He already knows where I live. I told him my number. He said, "I'll remember that! Can I call you in a couple of days?" and I nodded.

It wasn't until I was back up in my room, reviewing the events and the conversation we'd had that afternoon, that I realized that apart from telling me he worked in the family business, he never actually told me what that business *was*.

Chapter 9: Butter Would Melt in his Mouth

He did call in a couple of days; exactly two days later, true to his word. He invited me out for dinner at an Italian restaurant. Hello? He had me at Italian. I'd never been there, but I'd certainly heard of it. The Olive Garden, it was not. Mario's was a higher end restaurant, the kind I never got to go to. We Segrettis frequented the local HoJo's or, if it was a really special occasion, we got

Chinese. Plus, out for dinner? Like, on a real date? Despite his

sketchy initial overture, things were looking up. He was racking

up points left and right, since anything Italian was automatically

my favorite.

Okay, so maybe *he* wasn't Italian, but he could make it

up to me by plying me with all things Italian.

"That sounds great," I said, with enthusiasm, and without

any of my social small talk angst that typically would have been

in full swing if I even thought about talking with a guy. I realized

that I actually felt okay about going out with him. Nervous, but

okay. Maybe all that I had to do was change my approach. Could

it really be that easy?

"Great. I'll pick you up after work. When do you get

done?" he asked. "Around five," I said. "See you then," he said,

and then with a laugh he added, "I already know where you live!"

and hung up. I was smiling. Wow! I had a date for dinner the next night! Yay! I took a chance and somehow it was paying off. Things seemed to be going my way, for once.

I actually got home by four o'clock and immediately started getting ready. I wasn't sure about what to wear, so I did what self-conscious women with no fashion sense everywhere have done since the beginning of time: I put on a little black dress, added black tights and black boots and called it done. I was calmer until I realized that it would be difficult to avoid having him meet my parents now that I had agreed to be picked up at my house.

Crap.

Okay, in the spirit of Doing Things Differently, I decided to go with it. Let him meet the fam. Might as well shoot the relationship dead right now if the family was going to be a deal-breaker. Time was a-wastin'. I was twenty going on thirty-five; I needed to get settled. More importantly, I needed to get a room of my own before I got old, or went completely out of my mind. If Steven was going to give me that, then the faster the better.

He arrived a few minutes early. I love it when people are not late, but when they are early? That puts me over the moon. I heard my mother let him in. They were talking too softly for me to make out the words. I was waiting upstairs, hoping to avoid any questions. I headed downstairs in a hurry, anxious to rescue him from my mother, and rescue us both from my father, who might at any moment burst into a spew of negativity. As was his way.

"Hi, ready to go?" I said, as I grabbed his arm and spun him around to face the door.

"Okay, sure. Nice meeting you, Mrs. Segretti," he said smiling, and she smiled right back, saying, "Nice meeting you, too. Have fun tonight. Where are you going again? Oh, Mario's?

Mario's is great. Great food." How the hell does she know that? We'd only been to HoJo's and Yu Wok Inn in all of the years I'd known her. This mystery would have to be solved another day. I wanted to leave as fast as possible.

"Bye!" I called, and practically pulled him out the door. Okay, maybe I overdid it but even though my mother could be civil, my father was definitely a wild card. Plus, I didn't even want to think about how much damage the sib was capable of doing even in a short period of time. We had to get out of there. He said, "Hey, I made a reservation for six o'clock, so we have plenty of time." He totally misinterpreted my urgency, but that was fine. At least he attributed it to a normal impulse not to be late for our reservation rather than an urgent need to avoid making small talk with my family and having them ruin everything.

Steven took my arm and steered me toward the passenger side of his big, shiny red truck. He opened the door for me, and then boosted me up by putting his hands on either side of my waist so that I could reach the step to get in. I was soaking this up; courtly manners were a new phenomenon for me. I was more than capable of opening a car door for God's sake, but what my inner feminist had always failed to appreciate was this: it's not about strength or ability. It's about caring and respect. Like only a really secure man can wear pink, I came to believe that only a really secure woman can let a man hold the door for her. It wasn't an affront; it was a compliment, if you could open your eyes and see it.

My eyes were now open.

That was only the beginning. When I got into the car I noticed a vase wedged into the console between the seats that contained one long-stemmed red rose, complete with a sprig of baby's breath. "Wow," I said, "it's beautiful." He smiled. "So are you," he said. As he pulled away from the curb, I was pinching myself, thinking, "Is he for real?"

When we arrived at Mario's, he pulled into a "Reserved for VIP" parking spot. When he saw my questioning look, he said, "It's okay; I'm friends with the owner."

Really? Yeah, baby.

I started looking around the floor of the car for my bag when he said, "Hey, wait a minute, I have something else for you," and he reached around and pulled out an ice bucket from behind his seat. There was a bottle peeking out from the bucket with a white towel wrapping around it.

"What's that?" I asked, as he reached again behind his seat and this time retrieved two champagne flutes. Mystery solved.

"Let's have a toast before we go in," he said. I was speechless, possibly for the first time ever.

I watched him uncork the bottle, then half fill our glasses. "To our first of many nights together," he said, and I wondered if the double entendre was intentional or if it was just my own dirty mind in overdrive. Whatever. I liked it. I raised my glass. "To us," I said, and we sipped our champagne, with me smiling like a fool, until it was gone.

"Let's go eat," he said, and I started again to get my bag, and located it on the floor half under my seat. I was about to open the door when there he was, opening it for me. "Give me your hand," he said, and I did. I felt like a queen. There are good guys out there after all, and one of them finally found me.

Our first date went extremely well. I was never one of those girls who ate salad like a sparrow on a date. I often ate more than my guy did, and I made no apologies. I was all about the food. Steven didn't mind; in fact, he encouraged me to eat more. After we had finished our salads and our meals, he insisted we order dessert and coffee. I never ordered dessert and coffee when eating out, mostly due to the cost. "I'm fine!" I protested. "I had plenty to eat." He ignored me.

He signaled to the waiter to come, and then ordered two coffees and a Tiramsu. "Fine, we'll split one dessert then," he said. I smiled. I secretly was dying for dessert, but since there were no prices on the menu, and since I wasn't sure if we might be splitting the bill, I was being cautious. Well, what the hell; he really wasn't giving me any choice. I decided to just sit back and enjoy it all. I was glad that I did. That tiramisu was amazing.

When the bill came, I almost didn't notice. The waiter handed him a black padded folder. He opened it, signed the bill, and then handed it back to the waiter. That was it. There was never any question for him that he would be paying. I should have realized. What was I thinking? On a date, the man pays.

I was feeling pretty great. The champagne and the rose before we entered the restaurant was really over the top. I was thrilled that he put all that thought and planning into our night out. I also thought it was one of the best meals I'd ever had. Now we were on the way home, and I wondered what was next.

"Want to see my apartment?" he said. Uh-oh, here it comes. He took me to his place, which was about a twenty minutes from the restaurant. The house was dark, so he said, "Wait here," and he ran inside, turned on some lights, came back out and got my door for me. "Sorry about that; I usually leave a light on, but I must have forgotten today. I was distracted, thinking about you all day," he teased.

"Oh, I can understand that," I said, smiling. He stood back so that I could precede him up the now brightly lit pathway to his doorway. He leaned in and brushed against me as he unlocked the door, then stood back to let me go first.

His place was amazing. First of all, it was my favorite kind of apartment: the first floor of a two family house. It just seemed so much homier than apartment building apartments. It also was on a corner lot. Back when I was a ten year old kid, it was a point of pride for my dad that he snagged a house with a corner lot for us. Making it clear, a corner lot was like the holy grail of lots, something toward which to aspire. So even though it was his apartment and not his own home, I felt like it showed that he had good taste and good judgment.

So far, other than this corner lot thing, nothing about Steven reminded me of my father, which I took as a good sign. He wasn't Italian. He was blond-haired and blue-eyed. He drove a big-ass expensive truck. He had many siblings. He also seemed to have plenty of discretionary income. Maybe this was a sign that of good things to come. I could go slowly. I had time. Maybe he would be worth it.

He showed me his small, neat apartment. There were three rooms total, kitchen, living room, bedroom, plus a bathroom off the kitchen. One nice surprise was a screened in back porch, with a wicker love seat and a little coffee table tucked into one end of it. I stopped at the door of the bedroom and took a peek in. The bed was very large; it had to be king-sized. It also had what looked like bumpers around the bed's frame. I didn't want to seem naïve, but I had to ask him about those. "Um, why does the bed have bumpers?" I asked, a bit embarrassed.

"Come here, sit on it," he said, and he grabbed my hand and pulled me over to the side of the bed. "Put your hand on it," he said. I leaned over and placed my palm down on the comforter, and it was met with warmth and movement. Huh? I pressed down again, and noticed the rippling of the surface. I looked up, all questions. He laughed. "It's a water bed." Oh my God, how did I not figure that out?

"Oh," I said, "a waterbed, right."

He just laughed and put his arms around me and gave me a squeeze. "Come on, it's getting late; let me get you home," he said.

I was starting to suspect that my mother had given him the curfew talk.

Chapter 10: Domestic Violence

Well, yes, she mentioned that you should be home by midnight, so I thought we'd shoot for 11:30 this first night, so I can kind of, you know, win her over," he told me, grinning. I noticed that he didn't bother to ask if this was okay with me, then I swept that little niggling distress signal to the back of my mind.

"Oh, okay," I said, and we went back out to the car to go

home. I got up my nerve up to revisit the "What do you do for a living" question, so I asked him what the family business was that he described when we first met.

"We sell cars," he said. "Maybe you've seen some of our commercials on TV? Bernie Locke?" Oh my God! Duh! They were only the biggest car dealership in the state; in all of New England for all I knew. They specialized in selling utility trucks, industrial vans, tow trucks, dump trucks, and who knew what else.

"Of course I have!" I said.

"Well, he's my father. We all work for him in one way or another. I sell cars, one of my brother does the books, stuff like that," he explained.

For a minute, I didn't know what to say. I'd never met anyone so rich before. "So, is that why you're driving this awesome truck?" I asked.

"It is," he said, grinning, "and it's also why I have a

sports car," he added. "It's good advertising for the business."

We were just pulling up to my house at 11:28PM. After all of those nights of coming home after curfew and sometimes making good on their threat to lock me out, leaving me to fend for myself, my parents might faint from shock when they heard me at the door a half hour earlier than the deadline.

"I had a great time," I said.

"Me too. Can I see you again tomorrow night?" he asked.

"Um, yes. Yes, tomorrow would be fine," I said. With that settled, he leaned over to kiss me, a short, chaste, tongue-less version, appropriate for a first date with the possibility of parental eyes viewing from the front window. He then jumped out and came around to open my door. "Thanks, I really had a great time," I said, smiling, then turning to run up the stairs.

He was right behind me. "I'll walk you up," he said.

"Oh, that's really not necessary," I said. I really didn't want him to see that I didn't have a key to my own house. He ignored me and came up anyway. Once I had opened the door (which was pretty quick since no key was required. "What do you need a key for?" my father said. "We're always home. It will be unlocked until midnight."), I turned to wave to him, "Goodnight! Thanks!" and went in. He waved back and left.

I mentally replayed the events of the evening after I'd gone to bed. I was a little uneasy with Steven coming up the stairs after I'd told him he didn't need to, but I wasn't sure why, so I dismissed it. Other than that, he seemed like a dream.

He did call me to go out the next night, and we went to another expensive restaurant. It was obvious that he was very well known to the staff there too, since they immediately ushered us to their best table, near the fireplace, but also close to the windows. This gave us a fabulous view of the city. Just like at Mario's, the menu didn't list the prices, and when the bill came, he just signed for it like they did in the movies, and that was the end of it.

Not that I never saw him with cash. Once we stopped at a convenience store to pick up some newspapers before heading to one of Steven's favorite places to have Belgian waffles. When we got to the register, he opened up his wallet and pulled a huge wad of bills. From what I could see, they were mostly tens and twenties, not ones and fives. It was the largest clump of bills I'd ever seen, other than my tip pile at the end of a double shift. I was stunned by how cavalierly he wielded that money-glutted wallet.

Then I thought, hey, I could get used to this.

We went out a lot.

Another fringe benefit of dating Steven was that he insisted on driving me everywhere. I had told him about an incident that occurred at the bus stop a while back, and he decided that it wasn't safe for me to take the bus alone. Ever.

Before Steven, I always took the bus to and from work. One night as I was waiting for the bus, a carload of scary men approached, slowing down when they saw me sitting on the wall. Waiting for the bus. Alone. In the dark. Did I mention, by myself? I felt the adrenalin rush from pure fear when I realized my situation. There was no one within ear or eye shot. I couldn't outrun three or four *people*, never mind a car. If they were up to no good, there was no one around to stop them, or to save me. I started to move away as the car approached, but they slowed to a crawl and followed me.

"Hey, whachoo doin' out so late, huh?" one crooned. "Hey, we need die-rec-shuns," called out another. There was a lot of laughing and hooting. Maybe I had no common sense, like my father always said, but I knew enough to know that I was in big trouble. I was trying to decide if I should just break into a run through backyards and take my chances when I heard the rumble of the bus bearing down on the car. It pulled up beside me. This was a very near miss. My heart was in my throat for hours after that. Bad luck was following me now.

I asked him how he could always be free to drive me to and from work. I mean, what about his own work schedule? Without going into any details, he said, "Don't worry; I've got it covered," and the case, as it was so often, was closed. Anyway, I wasn't sorry to leave behind the public transportation for the comfort and time saving attributes of getting chauffeured everywhere, so I let this go, too.

Steve liked to go away for the weekend, and one day mentioned that he wanted me to come with him next time. I was thrilled and said, "Yes!" I hadn't been on a trip overnight, like, ever. Except for Florida with Buddy. And when I was sleeping in my brother's car after being locked out of the house when I didn't make it home before my midnight curfew. Does that count? I couldn't wait to go. I realized after I hung up that I would have to figure out what to do about work. I worked every weekend, often double shifts, so I had to get someone to cover me. After everything that had happened, I would never ask my sister. It was a little tricky, since I had to get someone who could do all of the jobs that I could do.

I asked Amanda. I was a bit closer to her than I was to any of the others. We lived on the same street, so we often ran into each other on the bus coming home, before Steven entered the picture, and walked together from the bus stop to her house, then I'd continue on to mine. I had occasionally covered for her when she had a soccer game on a weekend that she was working. She reluctantly agreed to cover for me. I didn't realize until after we were halfway through our weekend away that I had neglected to erase my name on the schedule and write in Amanda's name for those weekend shifts to make the swap official. By then, writing the schedule every week was another one of the jobs that I had taken on to relieve the owner of that burden. Any supervisor could make changes to the schedule, though, so after a brief moment of worry, I decided that Amanda would do it. Of course she would. I let it go and stopped worrying about it so that I could enjoy our trip.

And how could I not enjoy it? We had a suite of rooms at The Inn, and The Inn itself had everything: a large, heated indoor pool, a fancy restaurant, and a weight room, not that we ever used that. It was near a little village with shops and more restaurants. I still loved to read; I never went anywhere without my book and so especially enjoyed checking out the book shops nearby.

One thing I noticed was that Steven had begun to subtly discourage me from reading. When he noticed me slipping my book into my bag on our way out some place, he'd say, "Oh, why do you need that?" Or if he ran into a store for something and I waited in the car, I would make the most of a few minutes and pull out my book to read. When he returned and found me with the book, he would make a point of sighing loudly and pointedly in my direction. Okay, maybe he wasn't so subtle. I got the message. I put the book away.

At the time, I couldn't think of any reason why the presence of a book should bother him so much, but in hindsight, I think it's because if I was paying attention to a book, then I wasn't paying attention to him. I didn't protest much though, and after a while, I just stopped ever letting him see me with a book. It seemed like a small price to pay at the time.

I was so grateful for my trip, which was excellent; I hadn't known how badly I needed a vacation until I was on one. I was so happy that Steven had invited me and so pleased with myself for accepting, that whenever the doubt about the scheduling oversight popped up in my thoughts, I bashed it right back down into a back corner of my mind.

When we returned late Sunday night, he helped me carry my bag up the stairs to my house, then he left, saying he would call me tomorrow. It was just as well, because as I entered the house, my mother was immediately all over me. "Have you talked to your boss? He's been calling here all weekend," she said. "No, I haven't," I answered, and that funny feeling that I had been beating into oblivion all weekend returned full force.

"Um, did he say what he wanted?" I asked casually, not wanting to hear the answer. "He wanted to know why you weren't at work on Saturday or Sunday, and why you didn't call to tell him you weren't coming," she said. I started to explain that I'd covered those shifts, but then I thought better of it and just stopped. Why bother? It wasn't my mother that I had to tell this to. "Did he say anything else?" I asked, and she said, "Yes. He said that you can just bring in your uniforms when you get back and he'll give you your last paycheck. Bebe, he said that you're fired."

"What?" I said, suddenly nauseous. "That can't be right! I switched with Amanda!" I told her. "Well, Amanda called here on Sunday too, looking for you and wanting to know why you didn't come to work." I couldn't believe this! What the hell was going on? Why would she have been calling when she said she'd work for me?

What I had failed to appreciate was how jealous both Amanda and Jim had become of me and my new, rich boyfriend. Prior to Steven's arrival, I had always been available to work on a moment's notice. Whenever I wasn't in school, I could be counted on to work. I could also be counted on to work all of the crappy shifts that no one else wanted, and to do all of the crappy jobs that no one else wanted to do. After Steven showed up everything was different. Since we went out so much, I was less at their beck and call and they didn't like that very much.

The rest of the story was not pretty. When I called to speak to the owner, Jim, I could hear the anger in his voice right away. He said that at seven o'clock on Saturday morning, someone called him to say that the restaurant wasn't open yet. He tried calling me at home, and of course I wasn't there. "I covered my shifts because I went away for the weekend," I told him, but by now my voice was shaky. "Amanda was supposed to be working, not me. Didn't she come in?"

"No, she didn't. She didn't know anything about it. I called her in when you didn't show up; she never said a word about you asking her to work for her," he said. After that, he pretty much said what my mother had already told me. "I'm sorry, but I have to let you go. That's the policy for not showing up for a scheduled shift and not calling to tell us that you weren't coming," he said. Somewhere in the back of my mind, it registered that he didn't sound sorry. I was horrified.

"No! Just let me talk to Amanda!" I said. He said no, that wouldn't change things. I was the one on the schedule therefore it was my responsibility to be there. I couldn't believe it! Why had Amanda betrayed me like that? I was crushed. Fired from the only job I'd ever had! What would happen when I tried to get another job? How could things have gotten so messed up?

Chapter 11: Job lost and job gained

In the end, I stopped pleading and hung up. I learned a hard

lesson: when push comes to shove, the coworker who you

thought was your friend will betray you in a heartbeat to get your

job that she covets. I guess she figured that with my rich

boyfriend, I didn't need the job as much as she did. Shame on me for trusting her. Of course, it was my mistake to have not changed the schedule, and I paid for it big time, not only with my livelihood, but also with my ego. I *was* my job. What would I say was my reason for leaving when I applied for a new job? It wasn't like I could just leave it off the application, since it was the only job I'd ever had.

Steven wasn't very sympathetic to my distress over this situation. On the contrary, he was very pleased with this turn of events. He looked at my job, like he looked at my going to college, like he looked at my reading, as something that distracted my attention from him. He was happy to have less competition.

"You'll have more time for me now," he said. "We can go away every weekend, since you won't have to worry about getting someone to work for you," he continued, warming to his topic. How did he not get it that I felt like the four years I'd invested working for that company were now worth nothing? In the back of my mind, I always sort of thought that if things didn't work out for me career-wise as a social worker, what I was majoring in, I could always have a career managing a restaurant. This was a job that I already knew how to do, was already doing. In my capacity as assistant manager, I was often expected to stand in for the manager, so I had to know how to do everything that he did. Now, I had no Plan B.

"I'll be your Plan B," Steven said, and I could see that he was serious. This was a little comforting in a short-term, superficial kind of way, but ultimately I wanted to be responsible for and able to support myself. I didn't want to end up like my mother: stuck with no job skills, no driver's license; a prisoner in her own home.

I started looking for a new job right away. I applied the formula that had proven to be successful for me in the past. I now had access to a car sometimes. Steven let me take the little sports car from time to time if he wasn't free to drive me or pick me up. But still. I wanted to be working some place that I could get to and from under my own power, you know, just in case. That meant that I needed to be on a bus line or within walking distance of my job.

I wasn't interested in staying in the same strip mall that contained my former employer. The embarrassment and anger I felt when I thought about what happened there made me want to avoid the shop and anyone associated with it at all costs. That narrowed the field quite a bit. There was a new shopping mall that I could get to, but it was about a fifteen or 20 minute walk from the bus stop. I felt like I had very little choice. The upside was that I probably wouldn't have to take the bus much, since Steven would surely insist on dropping me off and picking me up, but knowing that I could get there on my own gave me peace of mind.

So, I prowled the mall, scouting out what was available. The anchor stores were department stores. I wasn't interested in a job making minimum wage. After working as a waitress for so many years, I was used to going home at the end of my shift with a pocketful of cash. This was especially useful for bus and train fares to and from work or school, parking meters everywhere, and toll booths when travelling to go away for the weekend. I didn't want to give that up. I sighed and decided first to take a walk through to see if anyone had a "Now Hiring" sign up.

Two stores did: the drug store and the book store. Hoping that my successful college application strategy-apply to two; get chosen by both- would hold true for employment seeking as well, I applied to both. Applying to the book store was a no-brainer. I started fantasizing about how great it would be to work there, and started to feel a little bit better about things. After I finished up it was getting close to lunch time, and I realized that I was hungry.

The food court was my next stop. Papa Gino's had been one of my favorite places to go since I used to sneak out of class to go for lunch when I was in high school. I got my slice of pizza and my soda and sat at a small table facing out into the mall. Across the way I could see a restaurant. It must have been new, because I came here a lot but hadn't ever noticed it before. I finished my pizza and walked over to check it out.

I decided to get a coffee from the takeout window so that I could get a look inside. It was set up very much like the shop where I was formerly employed. There was a bench immediately to the left as I entered the restaurant for people waiting to be seated, so I sat down to watch.

It was pretty busy, with several waitresses running around plus a man, probably the manager, seating people and handing out the menus. In addition, there were at least two people working the grill. A person washing dishes appeared from time to time, picking up dirty ones and dropping off clean ones. I could do this, I thought. It's on a larger scale than what I was used to, but definitely doable. I finished my coffee and decided to walk around the mall some more to think about it.

After a couple of laps, my decision was made: go for it. I had nothing to lose really. What's the worst that could happen? The worst had already happened. I was already unemployed. I couldn't afford not to take a chance.

I walked with a purpose back to the restaurant, and asked the cashier for a job application. The crowds had thinned a lot, so I was pretty conspicuous sitting at the counter. I hadn't included my former job on the other two applications I'd filled out earlier in the day, but on impulse, this time I did. It seemed stupid not to include the four years of experience I had in the field in which I was applying.

Just as I was finishing up, the man I'd seen earlier

approached me.

"How ya doin'?" he said, extending his hand. I stood up

and shook it. He had a great handshake. Really, there was nothing

worse than a limp handshake. Well, okay, there was one thing

that is worse than a handshake if it's limp, but I couldn't be

concerned with that. I needed a job!

"All done?" he said. I nodded. I signed it and handed it to

him. I thanked him and got up to leave, but he said, "I've got a

few minutes now. Do you have time for an interview?" He caught

me off guard, as I'm sure he'd intended.

"Sure," I said, and plastered a big smile on my face, one

that would have made my former customer, Al, proud. I took a

breath and sat back down.

He was reading over my application, so I waited for what

was inevitably coming. "So, you worked for Jim, huh? Why'd ya leave?" I had intentionally left blank the "reason for leaving" line, hoping that the explanation would sound better than it might look. I told him the truth. "I went away for the weekend, and the person who agreed to cover me didn't, and so I got in trouble," I said. Just then I realized what he'd said about me working for Jim. Did he know him? I had to ask. "Oh, yeah, I know him; we go way back," he replied. "I'm Dan by the way. What'd you do there?" he asked and before I stopped to think, I blurted out, "Everything!" Dan laughed.

"Good. That's what you'll do here too. When can you start?" he asked, and I almost fainted.

"Now!" I said, jumping up.

"Tomorrow's fine," he said. "Follow me," and so I followed him down the long service aisle to the office in the back. There was a small, very round woman in there, smoking a cigarette. "Mags, this is Bebe. Get her set up to start work tomorrow," he said, and then he left.

She reached into drawer that looked like a miracle of organization and after combing through them with a long, manicured fingernail, she extracted a file. "Here, fill out these forms," she said, "both sides. I can't believe how many times I have to hand these back to people who don't have the sense to turn over the page." She handed me a manila folder and a pen. I opened up the folder and filled out the forms quickly, then handed them back. "What dress size are you?" she asked next.

"A six or an eight," I said.

"That figures, you're one of those skinny malinkas who has a distorted sense of their size," she said. "You're a four. Follow me," and we went out of the office and around the corner where there was a storage closet. She opened the door, reached in, and pulled out a large box. She rummaged around the contents before extracting two hideous green and white print dresses and two white ruffled aprons. "Here you go. Wash them after every time you work," she said. That was unnecessary, I thought. She must have read the look on my face because she said, "Hey, you'd be surprised how many people don't. Disgusting."

Maggie came across as a no-nonsense person, a "Don't mess with me!" kind of gal. I decided to like her. As I got to know her and Dan, I saw that they had a good cop/bad cop routine going, and it worked well for them as a tool for getting people to do what they needed them to do. As time went on, it became obvious that Maggie had a massive crush on Dan.

They were about the same age, but Dan was a silver fox kind of a ladies' man who resembled Kenny Rogers. Maggie was a plain, overweight, middle aged mother and former wife. She was officially his bookkeeper, but in reality, she kept the place running and kept him out of trouble as much as possible by making sure he got to mandatory meetings on time, completing his weekly schedule for him, and covering any sick calls that came in during the week, in addition to all of the administrative tasks involved in running the business. If she liked you, you were all set; she had your back. If Dan got mad at you -which, with his quick temper happened a lot-she'd buffer you from harm. If she didn't like you, watch out. You might as well just quit because she could make your work life miserable.

I was a very fast learner and quickly proved to Dan that he'd made the right decision in hiring me. Within three months I could do any job he gave me, and he gave me them all, often all at once. I was asked to be a supervisor, and I accepted. By the time six months had passed, I was promoted again, to Assistant Manager. I was ecstatic, and more importantly, I felt vindicated. In six months I had regained all that I had lost at my prior job, and then some. I had better hours, better working conditions, made more money, and worked with nicer people. I had landed

on my feet.

Chapter 12: Underwhelmed

Meanwhile, I was spending a lot of time at Steven's apartment. For the most part, we got along fine. When we disagreed about something, like with the reading thing, I just stopped doing it. Better to keep the peace. He was charming most of the time. I could overlook a few quirks, right? No one is a perfect match for anyone. Every couple has their disagreements.

Maybe he was even mellowing some, I thought, because the drama that I expected after I told him I had gotten another job never materialized. He didn't offer to celebrate with me or anything, but he didn't give me a hard time, either.

He had been dropping hints lately that he was thinking about marriage. Things like, "Someday, when we're living together…." and "Someday, we'll go look at rings…" and "Do you like kids? How many do you want to have?" I didn't want to mess up another shot at matrimony. After all, I was getting older every day. I did want to marry and I did want to have kids. Just because I didn't want those things at that very moment was no reason not to get set up for the future.

The other thing that I was rationalizing was how we were getting along physically. We had our first night together when we took our first weekend trip away overnight. Probably that was why I had been so distracted before we went away, wondering about whether we'd be having sex, which led to that fatal mistake of not correcting the schedule before departing. I figured he had to be planning to get physical with me on the trip. I doubted that he'd be reserving separate rooms for us. Finally, I thought.

I was right. We had one room with one, very large bed. His bed at his apartment was king-sized as well. I knew this because he'd made a point of telling me that it was a custom-made king-sized waterbed. They don't usually come in that size, he told me. I briefly wondered if he was, um, overcompensating for some perceived masculine shortfall. If he was, I'd know soon enough.

He had reserved a suite, so in addition to the main bedroom, there was a living room with a TV and a small kitchen with a refrigerator and microwave. We were on the first floor and close to the indoor pool. He told me that he always goes to the same inn and takes the same suite whenever he goes away. Of course, I started wondering who the hell he usually took with him when he usually came here. I knew better than to ask. I had met his former girlfriend, Shelly. Shelly was a total skank. If I had met her before my first date with him, I might have declined.

During the day, we went to the little village to shop, and we ate all of our meals out. That night at dinner, he alluded that our first night alone together was fast approaching, and told me how much he'd been looking forward to it. "I have been, too," I said, of course, and it was the truth. After Buddy disappeared, I had been living without carnal companionship. Now I had another chance, and I wanted it to work.

This time, I was trying to keep things as low key as possible. I didn't want a huge let down, and I didn't want any big surprises. I was excited to think we were advancing our relationship, but not over the top about it. "Three times burned, four times shy," echoed in the recesses of my mind.

We finished dinner and then took a short ride. "I want to pick up some champagne; this is a special night," he said. Great. I mentally toasted: Here's to our bodies being as compatible as our thoughts are tonight. He hopped out, told me to "Sit tight; I'll be right back!" and so I did. I was thinking about how lovely it would be to slip my book out of my bag and read a few words, but I did not. The drama would so not be worth it. He was back pretty quickly, and we drove back to the inn.

It was about eight o'clock by then, and we set about getting ready for bed. I was nervous, but not debilitated, which I took as a good sign. I didn't have that wild, lust-filled physical attraction to Steven that I now realized had characterized my relationship with Buddy, so I was calmer with him. I thought that this also must be a good sign. I was cautiously optimistic.

"Do you want the bathroom first?" he offered, and I said, "No, you go ahead, but thanks," and I smiled at him. He smiled back, saying, "Okay, I'm going to jump in the shower," and he went into the bathroom, leaving the door ajar. As soon as I heard

him turn the water on, I finished getting what I needed. He was

out in ten minutes, wearing just his boxers and a white t-shirt.

Then it was my turn. "I won't be too long," I said as I

passed by him to get to the bathroom. I shut the door firmly

behind me. When I finished, I put my bathrobe on to cover most

of me up. I had always been modest about my body, ever since I

was a little girl. The message was drilled into me from about the

age of four that girls are always supposed to keep their private

parts covered. Cover them I did.

He was already in bed with the TV turned on when I

emerged. I thought he'd shut it off right away when I entered the

room but he just looked up, smiled, and continued watching the

TV, not me, as he patted a spot on the bed beside him. Okay,

that's fine, I thought, and walked quickly over to the bed and

joined him under the covers.

He put his arm around me and I snuggled into the crook

of it as I looked to see what he was watching. I recognized it as a rerun of "*The Love Boat*". Oh well, I thought, maybe he was a little nervous about our first time too and was distracting himself with the stupid TV show while he waited. I wasn't sure why he was still watching it though. He interrupted my thoughts, saying

"It will be over in five minutes, babe."

Oh.

I tried to follow it but wasn't that interested and after a while I just closed my eyes. Soon enough he said, "It's over. Babe, why don't you get up and shut off the TV while I pour the champagne?" he said. Even though I was a little annoyed to be the one getting up to shut the TV while he just reached over to pull the bottle from the ice bucket, I did it. "And grab the two glasses on the counter while you're up," he called after me.

I went to get them, grateful that I'd kept my robe on, and trying to focus on how nice it was that he had thought of champagne and not on the darker thoughts gathering around the edges of my mind, like "Why don't you do it yourself?" Get a grip! I was here with the man that I was thinking of marrying, and was definitely about to sleep with; focus on that.

I returned to the room with the glasses. "I'm surprised there would be such nice crystal in the kitchen of an inn suite," I remarked as I got back into bed. "Oh, those weren't here; I brought them. I rinsed them out while you were in the shower and left them to dry so they would be ready for us," he said. I immediately felt contrite. Of course he did! That sounded just like something he would do. I felt the warm feelings that I had for him bubble back up as he poured the champagne into the glasses.

He handed one to me. "To us," he said, as he clinked his glass against mine, and we each took a sip. I put my glass aside after the toast, but I noticed that he drained his glass, immediately refilled it and took another sip. I'd seen him drink socially, and we'd certainly shared a glass of champagne before, but I realized that I never thought about what happened to the rest of the bottle after I'd had my one half glass of it.

Soon I forgot this train of thought, because he leaned over and began kissing me, driving away these thoughts, and replacing them with other equally distressing thoughts. His kisses were…nice enough. I waited for the internal sparks that I'd felt when kissing David and Buddy, but they weren't happening. Why not? He stopped kissing me as his hands began to travel from my shoulders down to areas heretofore unexplored by him. I hugged my body into his, and shifted so that when he started to untie my robe, it fell way easily. When his hands made contact with my bare skin, I was again surprised that I wasn't feeling any heat, neither from his hands nor from my nether regions. Okay, this was weird. Too soon, he took off his T shirt to reveal a nicely proportioned, lightly muscled body and still, I waited. No zing. He pushed open my robe and slid it off, then slid my underwear off.

"Lie down," he ordered, so I did. He removed his boxers-

No, wait! Wasn't that my job?-and then got on top of me. I barely had a second to catch my breath when I could feel him trying to maneuver his still oh-so-small dick into me. Already? I hadn't even really gotten a good look at it! He began pushing: one, two, three, and that was it. He was finished. He rolled off. "Good night, hon," he said, and rolled to face away from me.

Really? Really? I said, "Oh, good night," and started looking for my underwear in the not-really-tangled-up-at-all bed sheets. Once found, I put them back on, found my flannel nightshirt in my overnight bag, donned that, and then rejoined him in bed, spooning behind him. I tried not to think about the phrase that was stuck in my mind now, but there it was: It was like having sex with my brother.

Chapter 13: Bad Sex

At least the relationship had finally been consummated. It would

get better in time, right? Sometimes passion had to

be...cultivated in a relationship, right? Holy crap, it had to get

better because there was very little room for it to get worse.

Sexual chemistry wasn't always going to be there when you first

start sleeping with someone, like a light switch just waiting to be

flipped. As we spent more naked time together, the physical

relationship would bloom. Right?

Most likely.

Eventually.

When I was in high school, I liked to wear buttons with slogans on them pinned to my denim jacket. I had dozens of them. One of them was a cheerful yellow button with red lettering that read, "Everybody likes it." Now, I had no friggin' clue what this meant. Worse, I didn't know that I didn't know. I remember wondering what 'it' was, and concluding that 'it' might be something different for different people. Like, I liked reading. Maybe that's what 'it' was?

What's important to know is that I didn't let a pesky thing like not being sure of the meaning of it stop me from wearing it.

One day, my dad commented on the button. "So, do you know what that button means?" he asked. I hemmed. I hawed. Busted. I didn't.

"Sure," I said.

"Well, I don't think you should be wearing it," he said. "I don't think it's appropriate." Okay, so now I'm pretty sure that 'it' isn't referring to reading. "Okay, so maybe I am not exactly positive what it means," I admitted. He said, "I didn't think so." Then he added, "'It' means sex. 'Everybody likes sex." I immediately died a thousand deaths. "So, I think maybe since you don't really know what it means, maybe you are too young to be wearing it," he finished. I was so embarrassed. I removed it and put it away.

I thought of the slogan now and how wouldn't be putting on that button any time soon. I so wasn't liking 'it'. My goal was to turn that around. Could that be done? Just like it couldn't be love at first sight for everyone, it followed that it couldn't be lust at first coitus for everyone either, right? So maybe there was hope. Only one way to find out.

So I forged ahead with my new relationship, focusing on all of the positive things, like his politeness, his gentlemanly manners, his willingness to pick up the tab every time. I was acting 'as if'.

One afternoon he picked me up from work and said, "My mother wants to meet you." "Oh, okay," I replied. "When?" "Now," he said, pulling away from the curb. "We can't go now!" I said. He looked at me coolly, and asked, "Why not?"

"Because I just got out of work! My uniform isn't clean! I at least have to change," I said, hearing and hating the pleading tone of my voice.

"You look fine," he said. "Besides, she wants me to bring you now, so we're going now." Once again, case closed. I was starting to notice a pattern that I did not appreciate, a 'my way or no way' pattern. It sucked.

Resigned, I sat back in the passenger seat, pouting. Not the most auspicious circumstances under which to meet my potential future mother-in-law. I also didn't like feeling like I had no say in the matter, but the truth was that *I had no say in the matter*. Whatever; might as well get it over with. At least there was no agonizing over what to wear when I met her for the first time; that decision had been made for me. I was wearing the uniform and apron that showed every minute of the ten hour shift that I had just finished working. If that's how he wanted to present me to his mother, so be it.

We pulled up in front of her house and parked. He got out and came around to open up the door for me. He extended his hand and helped me out down from the truck. My pockets were bulging with tips and I jingled like sleigh bells when I hit the ground. I walked in front of him to the front door, which he opened for me, and we entered. He brushed by me through a dark hallway which deposited us in a bright, sunny kitchen. A woman who was more elderly than I expected was sitting at the kitchen table, a teacup before her.

She had blonde and silver perfectly coiffed hair, exquisitely manicured fingernails with blood red polish; it was the middle of the afternoon and she was clearly at an age where she was no longer reporting to a job every day (and I suspected that she had *never* been at *that* age), she was wearing a bright blue, dressy pantsuit. The fingers of both hands sported so many sparkly rings that it was amazing that she could lift them up to hold that teacup. I had a flash that maybe her being dressed to the nines while I was dressed in my grubby work garb was a power thing. Her turf, her terms, her advantage.

"This must be Beatrice," she said in a strong, gravelly voice, clearly ruined by years of cigarette smoking, evidence of which was overflowing in the ashtray on the table to the right of the teacup. Beatrice? Really? I approached her slowly, carefully. "Right. Well, call me Bebe. Hi," I said, and extended my hand. She took it, shaking my hand with only her fingertips. Check, I thought. Not forthcoming, weak, partial handshake. A pussy handshake.

This thought fired me up. I wasn't going to let her walk all over me, even if Steven was her baby. "I'm sorry that I'm such a mess," I apologized, "but Steven insisted we come straight here after I finished working, so I didn't have time to go home and change."

"Don't worry about it," she said, waving her hand dismissively.

"Come here and sit down," she said. "Will you have a cup of tea?" Now, I was a die-hard black coffee girl, but I knew that being a gracious guest meant accepting any and all libations offered.

"I'd love a cup of tea, thanks," I smiled as best I could and sat down. Steven, meanwhile, had disappeared somewhere, maybe into the living room, since I heard the sound of the TV snapping to life. I thought I'd get shown around the house first, but apparently that's not what Mother Locke, who was running the show, had in mind.

"So," she began, "where do you work?" "At the coffee shop in the mall," I said.

"How long have you been working there?" she asked.

"Oh, a few months now," I replied.

"How do you like it?" she asked next.

"Oh, it's fine," I said.

"I noticed that your pockets seem to be overflowing!" she asked. "Well, the tips are usually pretty good. We have to give ten percent to a hostess if there was one working, but today there wasn't. Usually, when I get home from work I dump it all out on the floor and roll what I can, and then I put the rolls into a jar until the next shift. On the day I get my paycheck, I take that plus the rolled money to the bank and deposit it in my bank account. I keep out enough for spending money for the week though," I added hastily. Why the hell was I talking so much? My mouth runneth over when I'm nervous so I guess I was way-over-the-top nervous. Plus, I didn't want her to think that Steven was paying for *everything*, like I was a kept woman or something.

"That sounds like a good system you have worked out there," she nodded approvingly, smiling with a little of what looked like sincerity for the first time that afternoon. "Why don't you go ahead and do that now? I have coin wrappers that you can use," she said, getting up presumably to retrieve them.

"Oh, no," I protested, "I can do that when I get home later!"

"Nonsense," she said. "Go ahead. I'll even help you," she said. "I was a waitress myself, years ago," she said, remembering. I didn't correct her assumption that I was only a waitress at the shop, even though I was now the assistant manager. I had a feeling that she would not be impressed by this, and instead would potentially think less of me than perhaps she did already if she knew.

"Okay, I guess," I said, and stood up. I usually inverted the pocket by pushing up underneath the money from under the dress on the inside of it; this was no small feat to accomplish modestly, but I did manage it somehow. "Wow," she said. I

smiled, a little smugly. "It was a good day," I said. Plus, I'm an

excellent waitress, I added silently. We started dividing up the

coins: quarters into ten dollar stacks, dimes into five dollar

stacks, and so on. I had the dollar bills separated already into my

other pocket, which I decided not to volunteer. Why should she

know how exactly how much I'd made that day? I realized once

we started counting that was probably her motive all along, and

even though I was on to her, I didn't see how I could say, "No,"

to her when she invited me to count it. It didn't mean that I had to

tell her everything.

So, we sipped our tea, counted my money, and chatted

about nothing much. I was a little annoyed that Steven still had

not made an appearance in the kitchen but I didn't feel like there

was anything at all that I could do about it. We finished our tea,

and then finished rolling the coins. She got up, saying, "I'll get

you a zipper lock bag to put the rolls in," she said. She did, and I filled the bag up then sealed it, and put it into my tote bag that I had dropped by the door with my pocketbook when I entered, then went back to the table and sat down. I noticed Steven as I walked past the living room, and there he was, passed out cold on the couch. Well, at least now I knew what happened to him.

"So, Steven tells me that you are a full time student as well," she began. "I am," I said. "Do you live in the dorms?" she asked.

"No, I commute back and forth," I said. "

But you don't have a car…how" she started, and I interrupted her saying, "Oh, I go on public transportation; two buses and two trains," I explained.

"And you work full time too?" she asked, surprised. "How do you fit in any time for studying with all that?" she asked, looking genuinely puzzled.

"Oh, it works out okay. My job isn't far from one of the bus lines, so I go straight to work from school. If I'm early for my shift, I'll go sit in a booth and do my homework until I have to get changed and start working," I say.

"How are your grades, though?" she asked, dubious.

"Fine; I've made the Dean's List every semester so far," I said, hoping that I didn't sound too much like I was bragging.

Finally, thankfully, I could hear Steven stirring in the other room. He emerged a moment later, hair rumpled up on the side where his head had lain against the couch, looking a little sheepish. I forgave him everything; he just looked so sweet standing there in the doorway, wearing that slightly bewildered expression, like a child who has just awakened from his afternoon nap.

"Hi," he said, entering the kitchen. He pulled out a chair then and sat down next to me at the table. "Ready to get going?" he said."

Yes," I said. I stood up. "Thank you for the tea, Mrs. Locke, oh, and the help with the coin rolling!" I added.

"You're welcome," she said. "Coming this Sunday for dinner, Steven?" which was more of a statement than a question.

"Yeah, I'll be here," he said. "And bring Bebe with you," she clarified, nodding in my direction. "Yeah, we'll come," he said. "See you Sunday. 'Bye, Ma," he said, kissing her on the cheek and ushering me out the door.

After we reached the car, I turned to him. "You know that I work on Sundays, right?" I said, annoyed. "It's too late to take the day off," I added. "You go and have fun, but I can't go."

"Calm down," he said. "I'll pick you up after work and we'll go then."

"What time is dinner?" I said.

"At noon," he said, with a "duh" look on his face, like, "When else would Sunday dinner be?"

"Okay, so you're going to pick me up from work at 3PM to bring me to dinner at noon?" I ask. Clearly, I was missing something here because how the fuck was that possible?

"Hey, I said don't worry about it!" came the response, edgier this time. I keep quiet after that.

Now *I* was feeling edgy. I sure wasn't used to a guy being so controlling. I wasn't sure how to respond to him. I was feeling more and more uncomfortable with his behavior, but nothing concrete had happened, nothing that I could put my finger on to explain my uneasiness.

And then suddenly, something *did* happen. It was almost a relief at first. I knew there was something off about him. I just didn't know what.

And then I did.

I had gotten out of work early that day. It was a holiday weekend coming up so I had no pressing homework. I decided to make dinner for Steven. By then, we'd been going out for about three months, and he'd given me a key to his apartment. I'd gotten together with Nana See for a cooking lesson and she'd tried to teach me how to make gravy and meatballs. At the end of the afternoon I had a quart of gravy and four meatballs that were mostly made by her so, you know, they were excellent. I froze it all until I was ready to cook for Steven. All I had left to do was to make a salad and boil the spaghetti. I was ready.

Chapter 14: Wolf in Sheep's Clothing

I had the whole afternoon to myself to get ready, so I took my time. I had shopped on my way home from school at a little ethnic market I passed by for the salad supplies and a box of spaghetti. There were so many different brands and types of spaghetti that it was mind boggling. With relief, my eyes landed on the box of the one that I remember seeing in Nana's kitchen, so I grabbed it..

I was a little disappointed that things hadn't improved

much from my vantage point in the intimacy department. I was

irrationally pinning my hopes on this dinner to heat things up

some in the passion department. If "The way to a man's heart is

through his stomach", maybe "The way to a woman's passion

was through filling said man's stomach." What the hell; it was

worth a shot.

As soon as I got home, I got to work making the salad:

iceberg and romaine lettuce, tomato, red bell pepper, cucumber. I

decided to use the pink Depression glass bowl that Nana See had

given me for the salad. I was excited and happy. I cut the

vegetables into thin slices, then arranged them artfully over the

bowl filled with the shredded lettuce. Even I was impressed with

how it turned out. It was beautiful! I covered it with Saran wrap

and put it in the fridge for later. Then I filled the largest pot that I

could find with water, put on the lid, and then set it on the stove.

Ready.

I located another, smaller pot for the gravy, and placed

that on the stove as well. I found a larger spoon that I could use as a ladle. Finally, I located a colander, which I placed in the sink, ready to receive and drain the cooked spaghetti. I opened the box of angel hair spaghetti, and then emptied the pasta into my hand. I aligned all the strands and then broke them in half, just as I'd seen my mother and grandmother do hundreds of times in the past, then I placed the now shorter spaghetti strands onto a plate, ready to be cooked. The fully thawed container of gravy and meatballs was in the fridge, ready to go.

I set the table with the dishes, silverware, and napkins that I found rummaging around in the cabinets, and found two wine glasses, which I rinsed and set out as well. Martha Stewart would be proud, I thought. Heck, I was proud! The table looked great!

I decided to go read some of my current book, since I had about an hour before I had to put the pot on for the spaghetti.

I had bought a kitchen timer and brought it with me, since

I knew that he didn't have one, and at this point, I certainly did not have the cooking confidence to guess on the timing of anything. I used the timer now, setting it to go off in an hour, so I'd have time to finish up getting dinner ready before Steven got home from work. He wouldn't be surprised that I was there, or even that I was cooking. I'd asked his permission to do so in advance. What would be a surprise was the dinner itself; I hadn't told him what I was going to make. I couldn't wait for him to try it; I knew that my family's recipe for Italian gravy and meatballs was spectacular, the best. I wanted him to know it, too.

The timer went off, startling me off the couch. The time had flown by, and the distraction of the book was helpful; I didn't have a chance to feel too worried about my cooking debut since I was mostly not thinking about it.

I shook off my reading reverie and got down to business. I turned on the gas burner under the spaghetti pot. I removed the container with the gravy and meatballs from the fridge, then carefully emptied it into the saucepan on the stove, using a rubber spatula to carefully scrape every last drop of the precious gravy into the pot, covered it, and turned the burner on a low flame.

I had splurged at the market on one more thing: a block of Parmigiano-Reggiano cheese: the good--no, the best--stuff. I bought the largest block that I could afford, about the size of a deck of cards. I found a small hand grater in the back of one of the kitchen drawers, fortunately, because I hadn't thought to bring one of those with me. I got a small bowl down from the cabinet, then grated most of the block of cheese into the bowl. I placed a small spoon next to the bowl on the table for serving.

Just then I realized that Steven was home, and that the water was boiling. I put in a good pinch of salt, then slid the angel hair spaghetti into the pot. I stirred it with a wooden spoon, and then ran back to the living room to grab the timer from the coffee table, hurriedly setting it for four minutes. I knew he would want to eat as soon as he got in the door. He had made that plain to me when we first talked about me cooking.

I heard his key in the door just as the timer went off. Yes! I thought to myself. Perfect timing. I extracted a strand of spaghetti from the pot, tasted it; thank God it was done. I grabbed a dishtowel to hold the hot pan, then brought it over to the sink to dump the spaghetti into the colander. I let it drain for a quick minute, ran to the hall to say, "Welcome home! Dinner is ready!" and giving him a kiss, I ran back to the kitchen. He smiled, saying "I'll be right in," and headed into the bathroom.

I ran back to the kitchen, picked up the colander and, after giving it one shake for good luck, transferred the spaghetti back to the pot. I put a few spoonfuls of the gravy into the pot and stirred it into the spaghetti, and then retrieved the salad from the fridge and placed it in the center of the table. Instead of the red wine vinegar and oil dressing that we would have had at home, I placed a bottle of the creamy Italian salad dressing that I knew was his favorite on the table next to the salad bowl.

He emerged from the bathroom and sat down at the table. He seemed irritated for some reason. "Is everything okay?" I asked him, and he said, "I just hate it that I have to work until six o'clock when my brother Mitchell gets to leave at four!" he said.

This was a familiar complaint. I heard often enough about how his older brother was in charge of the business and, since he had more status, he got to work the earlier shift and it completely pissed Steven off. He took every opportunity to remind me of this. "Oh, well, at least you're home now. And look! I made spaghetti with the famous Segretti secret family recipe for the gravy and the meatballs!" I said, all the words coming out in a rush, betraying my increasing nervousness. Once again: my mouth runneth over. I didn't like that he brought this trait out in me so often. This was not feeling like the warm romantic dinner that I'd been envisioning all day. Hell, all week. This was feeling tense. Anxious.

I started to plate up the spaghetti. "Why are you putting

the spaghetti out now? I haven't even eaten my salad yet!" he said, his voice terse, rising. "Um, we usually eat the salad after the spaghetti," I said, hearing my voice faltering, cowering.

"Who's 'we'?" he asked. "Your other boyfriends?"

"Oh! No! I meant my family, my grandmother…um, it's an Italian custom to…" I trailed off.

"So what?" he interrupted me. "Normal people eat their salad first!" he said, even more loudly.

What was this bullshit? "Okay, that's fine. We can eat our salads first," I said, placating him. Hating it. Hating him.

"Why aren't there any bowls for the salad?" I had planned on us eating our salad from the same plates when we'd finished the spaghetti, but now I scrambled to get some bowls. I grabbed them and put them on the table, then filled them both from the beautiful bowl of salad that I'd worked so hard to create earlier, but he didn't even notice this. He just drowned it in the dressing, scarfed it down, and then pushed the bowl away.

I jumped up to put the salad bowls in the sink, then grabbed the spaghetti pot and portioned out a generous amount on his plate. I got the pot with the gravy that had been staying hot on the stove and placed two meatballs on the spaghetti, then covered everything with more gravy. After giving myself a much smaller amount, having suddenly lost my appetite, I put the pot back on the stove and shut the burner off.

I sat back down at the table with him. I got the bowl of grated cheese and offered it to him, but he shook his head, no, he didn't want it. Really? How could he not want it? I sprinkled some on my own spaghetti and tried hard not to let the tears that were now filling my eyes spill over. He had just started eating, then began shaking his head. "The spaghetti is way too mushy, and it's cold!" I tried mine. It *was* overcooked now, and it had cooled off a little, but the hot gravy made up for that, didn't it?

Then I got even madder.

"Well, it's only cold because you insisted on eating the

salad first! I had planned for us to eat the spaghetti first!" I was talking quite loudly now. Okay, yelling. He was ruining everything! Why was he being like this? What a fucking asshole! I had gone to so much trouble to make sure everything was beautiful, was perfect, and he hadn't even noticed any of it! The tears started, and I tried to discreetly brush them away with the back of my hand, but he saw me. And then he really exploded.

"What the hell are you crying about?" he yelled. He stood up fast, knocking his chair to the floor behind him with a loud clatter. He had two yellow cats that had been sleeping in the corner windowsill in the kitchen, but the loud noise sent them running. What did they know that I didn't?

"Why are you yelling? Why are you so mad?" I cried, looking up at him.

His face was dark red, full of rage; his fists were clenched. I was suddenly afraid. In one quick movement he picked up his plate and threw it against the wall of the kitchen, where it broke into three pieces, sending food and gravy flying

everywhere. It was shocking. He was yelling now, out of control.

"You overcooked the spaghetti! What's the matter with you?

Can't you even cook a fucking pot of spaghetti, for Chrissakes?!"

he spat, then he left the room. I heard him grab his keys and coat,

then I heard the door slam and the car engine start up, tires

screeching out of the driveway. I was relieved for just a second,

and then I was petrified.

What the hell had just happened?

Chapter 15: Goodbye to You

I sat for several seconds, trying to regulate my breathing. I was

glad he'd left, but what if he came right back? I was frozen. I

didn't know what triggered his outburst. I went over what

happened in my mind. I glanced up at the clock; he'd only been

home for about a half an hour! I surveyed the room: plate shards

on the floor, spaghetti stuck to the wall and hanging from the ceiling fan blades, gravy everywhere. Like blood spatter. It looked like a crime scene. Hell, it *was* a crime scene.

I should have just started cleaning up the mess, but I resisted. After all, he did it; he should have to clean up. I thought I should have just get my stuff and leave, but I didn't. I got up, got the dustpan and the waste barrel, and started picking up all of the pieces of glass that I could see. There were three large pieces, but as I crouched down closer to the floor I could see that there were many small glass slivers mixed in with the spaghetti. I got back up and looked around in the back hall for something to use to push the mess onto the dustpan. I found a cardboard box, tore off the side, and used that as a kind of a shovel. I tore off another piece and used it to scrape the food from the wall.

Working to clean up distracted me for a while; I focused just on the task in front of me, and then the next one, and then the next one. Pick up glass. Pick up food. Scrape off walls. Scrape off fan. Get dishpan; fill with water and dish soap. Get sponge.

Wash gravy off the wall.

After I had cleaned up, I sat back down again. Now what? The yellow curtains that I had picked out for this kitchen and that I loved so much were ruined. Should I take them down? Try to wash them? I didn't want to do even one more thing. Suddenly, I felt exhausted. I put my face in my hands and finally let the tears come.

How could this happen to me? For a moment during his tirade, I was afraid that he was going to hit me. With this thought, I was transported back to my childhood and my father's drunken rages, running like hell from him, hoping to make it to my room and slam the door before he could get to me.

Could that be it? Could he have been drinking? Drunk?

I'd only seen him drinking socially when he was with me, and I had noticed that he drank sort of fast, sometimes in gulps. I never paid any attention to the actual quantity of alcohol that he was consuming, but after what happened tonight, maybe I should have.

Now that I was thinking about it, I saw other similarities between Steven's behavior and the behavior of my alcoholic parent. He was always irritated. I also found many bottles of whiskey stashed in the different cupboards in the kitchen as I was looking for pots and dishes to make dinner. There was even a bottle in the back hall, behind the cardboard box I grabbed that awful evening. Duh. What else could the stashed bottles mean? The last thing that I needed or wanted was another alcoholic in my life.

In the end, I decided to just stay put. I wanted to see how he would explain himself. I lay down on the couch, pulled a quilt up around me, and at some point must have dozed off. The sound of his car pulling into the driveway woke me up; a quick glance at the clock showed it was now almost midnight. I sat up and waited. The door opened. His keys hit the tray on top of the radiator. He turned the corner from the hall and stood in the doorway of the living room.

His eyes were red, swollen. His hair was a mess. His clothes were askew. "I'm going to bed," he said, and he went in his room and closed the door. I heard him fumbling around for a few moments, then it got quiet and the light went out.

This night totally sucked! Now I was stuck. Clearly he wasn't taking me home. Steven the gentleman was gone and there was a psycho bastard in his place. It was too late to take the bus home; they inconveniently stopped running at midnight.

I lay back down, pulled the quilt back up, and tried to sleep.

In the morning, I got up early. My plan was to get out before he woke up. I didn't want to see him and the time for talking had come and gone, and gone was all I wanted to be now. I was almost ready to leave when I heard him calling me. "Bebe? Beebe...." I didn't answer, but I heard him getting out of the bed and then there he was, standing in the doorway. I stood silent, not looking at him. He walked over to me, said, "Look, I'm sorry about last night," and put his arms around me. I stood there stiffly, not accepting the embrace. He persisted. "I didn't mean it. I'm really sorry," he said. I softened, just a little.

"Why did you act that way?" I asked. "Do you know how hard I worked on that dinner? And now the curtains have stains all over them!"

"Thank you for cooking for me. I am so sorry; I didn't mean for that to happen. I have a condition," he began, and taking my hand, led me to the couch. We both sat.

"What do you mean, 'a condition'?" I asked.

"It's a kind of epilepsy," he said. "I saw all kinds of specialists a few years ago. It just comes on me all of a sudden. I lose my temper, then I fall asleep for a long time. When I wake up I know something has happened, but I don't really remember the details," he said. "There's even a name for that, but I forget what they called it.

I knew what they called it: post-ictal. Besides being an alcoholic, my father was also something else: an epileptic. I was very well versed in seizures and post-ictal states. This wasn't that.

"Post-ictal, right, that's right. That's what they called it. I guess it's pretty common," he continued. "You know, like, post-coital, right?" His joke fell flat.

"So, you're telling me that you don't remember what you did last night?" I asked him, unbelieving.

"Not really," he said.

"Well, let me fill you in," I said, sarcastically, and I did. He listened quietly until I was finished. "Beebes, really, I mean it. I'm very sorry. Let me make it up to you," he said. "I'll take you out to dinner tonight," he said.

"No thanks; I'm good," I replied. "I have to get going," I lied. "See you later." I picked up my tote bag and my pocketbook, and without looking at him, I left.

I went home, up to my room, dropped my bags, and sprawled face down on the bed. Now what? I was still reeling from the violence of it. Even though it was an attack on my dinner, it felt like a physical assault on my self. My efforts to please him twenty four hours ago felt ridiculous now. Plus, I didn't believe his story about the seizures. All those years growing up that I watched my father have seizures, I never saw one that looked anything like what Steven had done. Alcoholic outbursts? Yes. Seizures? No. No.

Did I say no?

I was exhausted. I mostly had passed the night staring at the ceiling, trying to will myself to sleep. I dozed off now, grateful that I had the room to myself, for once.

The phone rang, and I heard my mother calling me. "Take a message," I yelled down to her. I didn't bother to ask who it was. After a little while, I got up and changed into a T shirt and sweat pants, my pajama equivalent, and got back into bed. Later on I heard the phone ring again, and again I told my mother to take a message. "Is everything okay?" she called up to me, sounding concerned now. "I'm fine, I'm just really tired. I'm going to sleep now."

Early the next morning, the doorbell rang. I heard my mother's animated voice in the entryway and I knew it was him right away. I resigned myself to the fact that I would have to go down and see him. I got up and quickly threw on a pair of jeans and a flannel shirt over my t-shirt and went downstairs, not even bothering to wash up first. What did I care? He had thrown my gravy against a wall, on to my curtains. My *gravy*. The food of my ancestors.

"Hi," he said. My mother excused herself and went back to the kitchen to her tea and toast, the perpetual mom breakfast. I didn't invite him in.

"So, what? What do you want?" I asked him.

"I brought you these," he said, and he pulled a bouquet of

roses out from behind his back. Twelve long-stemmed red roses.

What a joke. It was a shame that my first occasion of receiving a

dozen roses was tarnished by the circumstances under which they

were proffered. I made no move to take them.

"Is that it?" I asked, starting to close the door.

"No, I want to take you out for breakfast," he said.

"Oh, I thought you said you wanted to take me out for

dinner," I said sarcastically, closing the door a little more.

"Bebe, come on. Let's talk, okay?" My mother looked out from

the kitchen, questioning, but said nothing.

"Fine. I'll meet you outside," I said, still unwilling to

invite him in. "Okay," he said, looking confused, but he put the

roses down on the wicker chair on the porch and headed to his

car. I closed the door behind him. I ran back upstairs, washed my

face, brushed my teeth, grabbed my denim jacket, and ran back

down, pissed that red roses were forever ruined for me by this

asshole.

"I'm going, but I'll be back in an hour or so," I called to my mother, and without sticking around to answer any questions, I ran out the door, down the fourteen stairs to the street where his car was parked; the fourteen concrete stairs that I felt like pushing him down. His habit of holding the car door for me felt ridiculous now. Oxymoronic.

I looked at him. "Where are we going?" I asked. "I thought we'd go to the Golden Egg," he said. It was my favorite place to go for breakfast, as he well knew. Manipulator! Usually I was all about the food. Usually. Not today. "Fine," I said, and he pulled the car away from the curb. He attempted to engage me in conversation several times, but I didn't respond. I didn't give a shit about his small talk. Throw my food? Fuck his small talk. Fuck him.

When we arrived at the restaurant, and I didn't wait for him to come around. "Let me get your door," he said.

"Not necessary. Got it," I said, and jumped out. I strode

straight for the door to the restaurant and opened it, then as an afterthought, I held it open for him. He gave me a look as he walked past me but made no comment. I fantasized about the satisfactory crunch I might hear if I slammed that door on his left hand. His plate throwing hand.

"Two?" the waitress said, and I nodded, and she brought us over to the table, left the menus, and said, "Coffee?" and when I nodded, she added, I'll be right back." I sat down, opened the menu, and then closed it again.

"Why are we here, Steven?" I asked.

"I just wanted to apologize for yesterday," he said.

"You did already," I said, impatient. I didn't have time for his bullshit anymore. "I know, but I want to apologize officially."

"That's really not necessary," I said, and as the words left my mouth, I realized that it was true. It didn't matter what he had to say now. I had no interest in hearing it.

And just like that, I was over him.

After his tirade the night before, I had no respect for him. He was a fraud. More than that, though, was that I didn't feel safe with him anymore. What he really was, I was now convinced, was an alcoholic with an explosive temper that he couldn't control. In the past, I'd had no choice but to live with that crap.

Now, I did have a choice. Now, it was up to me. I did not choose this. I told him that we were over. We never ordered breakfast. I drank my coffee, then said "I can find my own way home, thanks. Goodbye, Steven," and I left.

Chapter 16: Onward

So now, I was back to square one. Again. Still living with my parents. I decided to concentrate on finishing school. Despite all the drama along the way, I had somehow managed to make it to my senior year of college. I was doing okay, still making Dean's List, if by the skin of my teeth. As I was always a wait-until-the-last-moment paper writer, so was I always a last minute studier.

I screwed up a couple of exams during my finals junior year. I'd mixed up the dates for Calculus and Psych, so when I showed up to take my Psychology final and no one was there, I hurried to go to double check the schedule. I was horrified to see that it was actually the Calculus final that was being given that day, not Psych. I had just enough time to get to class before the exam began and, just as when I missed curfew at my parents' house, I would be locked out. That was the good news.

The bad news was that now I would have to take the Calculus exam cold; I hadn't studied for it at all yet because I was a wait until the last minute and then stay up all night the night before the exam sort of studier. I was screwed and I knew it. There were some complicated theorems that had to be worked out to pass the final. When it was handed out, I saw that there were only two questions. I was completely disgusted with myself because it would have been such an easy test if I had studied! They were familiar but, without any time to review the material, I couldn't quite figure them out. I did what I could, reasoning that just putting my name on the paper would likely give me more points than not showing up at all would have. I left the room with a heavy heart.

Under the best of circumstances, I'm a worrier and an awfulizer, but in this case, I knew I had blown it big time. I loved Calculus so much that I had chosen to take this, my fourth calculus class in college, as an elective. I had a straight A going into the final, but I finished the course with a C, confirming that I must have failed the final. After that happened, I resented Calculus, even though it was my own goddamned fault that I failed it. I never took another calculus class after that.

I never made that particular mistake again. For my senior year, I only took classes that gave essay finals. English Lit, Sociology, Anthropology, Philosophy, and Psychology. The other bonus with these courses was that they only required one day a week of class time; the rest was "independent study". This meant that I could work more hours, which I wholeheartedly did. I needed the money, and I needed the escape from my home life. At this point, I felt like a total loser. I wanted to spend as little time as possible at home. I basically slept and occasionally ate there, otherwise I was always on my way to or from somewhere, usually to work or to school.

The semester flew by, and next thing I knew, it was time to graduate. I hadn't seen much of David that final semester, although now that I was back on the buses and trains every day (no more rides or car borrowing from Steven), we did run into each other occasionally in transit. When this happened, we'd sit together and talk about what we were planning for after graduation. He had a job already lined up at an accounting firm in town that had been courting him. He had been doing some part time work for them and he already knew that he liked the people who worked there. He was anxious to be done with school and start his real life, and to start stashing some money away toward paying off his loans before the payments came due in six months.

I, on the other hand, was planning nothing. A recent talk with David convinced me that maybe it would be a good idea to start, since I'd be graduating in a month or so. I set up a meeting with my advisor to talk about job prospects.

I loved my advisor, whom I'd just met toward the end of my junior year. It had taken me that long to figure out what to major in. She was a tiny peanut of a woman, barely five feet tall, with a long, more-salt-than-pepper braid falling down her back. She was interesting to talk to, with a quick wit and innovative ideas. The classes she taught were by far the most interesting of any that I took during all of my college years. I was thrilled when Ms. DePaola, PhD agreed to become my advisor.

Our meeting began with a sort of an "exit interview". She said she liked to do this with her graduating students so she could get better at her job. "So, what kind of job do you think you might want to do?" she asked in her thick French accent.

"Actually, I really haven't thought much about that," I said sheepishly. I swallowed my pride and asked, "What kinds of jobs are there that I could do with my degree?"

"Well, you could work in a hospital as a medical social worker, or for DHHS in protective services, or you could teach, like me!" she said, laughing. "Well, which one pays the most?" I asked her, only half joking. My school loans were staggering; I would owe about forty grand when I finally got out, and I needed to make enough money not only to pay them back, but also to hopefully buy a car and pay rent some place, so that I wouldn't still be living with my parents all of my adult life. This was something that I did think about. A lot.

"Well, if you are a man, your starting pay will be much higher," she said.

"What? Are you kidding me? Why?" I asked.

"It's like this: in a field that is predominantly female, the men stand out. They are an anomaly. As such, their starting pay is higher, and they tend to get the jobs with more responsibility more quickly. They also tend to get promoted more regularly," she added, hammering a few more nails into my career coffin. "Now, if you want to go into research, you could do some studies on this phenomenon," she said, smiling, finished.

I was pissed. This would have been an excellent thing to share with me before I finished school, I thought, but did not say. "So, how much can I expect to make for starting pay? You know, just a ballpark figure," I asked, afraid to hear the answer. "Oh, about eighteen thousand a year, maybe," she said. My heart fell. Eighteen thousand? That's not enough! Why didn't I think to ask about this sooner? Or to check into it myself? It was stupid of me to be so shortsighted.

"Don't worry," Ms. DePaula said, patting my shoulder sympathetically, seeing my face. "It will all work out, dear," she said. I nodded, but what I was thinking was this: fat chance.

So, although I was on track to graduate in a month, my

career prospects were now feeling very bleak, in the toilet, even. After talking to my advisor, I couldn't stop beating myself up for not thinking about this prior to deciding on a major.

My job was taking off though. The manager, Dan, and I met once a week to go over things like promotions, store specials, scheduling issues, things like that. One day, he said that the district manager wanted to sit in on our meeting. I was enjoying being second in command at the restaurant. Dan told me all the time that I was doing a great job, so I wasn't particularly worried about Jim sitting in, but still asked, "Okay. Do you know why?" "Yes. He wants to ask you about your plans after you graduate," he said. "Oh, okay. But, just so you know, I have none, so it's going to be a short conversation!" I said, laughing. "Maybe not…" he said mysteriously, then left to go seat people; the line of customers at the door had been getting increasingly longer while we were talking.

I was backing up the grill, working the sandwich board,

jumping on the make wheel at the fountain when needed, so the time flew by. The meeting was at three o'clock, and the rush had fortunately slowed down enough for me to go clean myself up a little before the meeting.

Jim arrived about fifteen minutes early. I said, "Hi, how are you?" and flashed a big smile at him. What the hell? I had nothing to lose. I was still thinking about Dan's mysterious remark about how the conversation might not be short, wondering what he meant.

"Bebe, hello! How are you?" he boomed, extending his hand. Good handshake, good omen?

"I'll let Dan know you're here. We usually meet in that last booth over by the service aisle," I said, pointing.

"Fine. I'll meet you there when you're ready," he beamed. What the heck was he up to? I wondered. I ran to tell Dan that Jim was waiting for us. "Thanks, be right there," he said, taking off his apron and exiting the grill area from the back. He reappeared in a few minutes, wearing a clean shirt that he must have had stashed in an office drawer; it looked nothing like the one he'd been wearing that showed every bit of the two hours he'd spent cooking, scooping, and seating through the lunch hour. I was glad that I'd taken a few minutes to wash up at least, and that I always tried to keep my uniform as clean as possible while I worked. I decided that it couldn't hurt to follow Dan's lead. I ran in back to grab a new apron from the closet.

We all sat down, and instead of Dan beginning with his usual "state of the shop" schpiel, Jim folded his hands together and said, "So. I guess you're wondering why I'm here," he said. I nodded. "I understand that you're graduating," he said. I nodded again. "Well, Bebe, let me get right to the point. What will you be doing after college?" I said, "I haven't made any definite plans yet," I said, which was true enough. "Good. We'd like to offer you a position as a store manager. What would you say to that?" he asked, eyes twinkling.

What? I didn't know *what* to say. I'd never considered a career as a restaurant manager. I decided to stick with the truth. "I've never thought about that," I said. If he only knew how many things that I'd never thought about before and during college.

"Well, before you say anything, let me tell you a little about the job. Usually there is a training program that our future managers must complete before being promoted. In your case, though, we've decided to waive that requirement. We know that you've been working for us here for two years, plus you have four years with our competitor. That, together with a college degree, will be adequate. We would start you in June," he said.

I breathed. "Do you have a particular store in mind?" I asked. Since I didn't have a car, it needed to be some place I could get to on public transportation. I didn't say this out loud, but Dan certainly knew. "We'll have an opening for a manager in Malden in June," he said. What a break! Malden was the next town over, so no deal-breaker there.

"Before you decide, you should know that we'd start you at thirty thousand a year, plus bonus, plus full benefits," he added. That was one third more than I'd be starting at if I sought a job in my field, which I had no guarantee that I'd even get! "That sounds great!" I blurted.

Note from future self: beware when you don't know what you don't know.

Chapter 17: Taking Charge

Even though it sounded too good to be true, I decided to go for it. What did I have to lose? I wasn't going to have to go through their training program. I'd basically be doing what I was already doing, only getting paid (much!) more for my trouble. Malden was about as close to where I lived as I could get; the transportation piece I'd figure out later.

"I accept!" I said. I had no significant other with whom to consult. Since school would be finished, I'd have no prior commitments. If I'd slowed down long enough to really think it through, I might say 'No', so I didn't slow down. I didn't think. Fear can be paralyzing, but denial? Denial is energizing.

May came, and I graduated, saying goodbye not only to my years of formal education, but to my years of unrequited love for David. Chances that I'd be seeing him anymore were slim to none. He'd be going to work every day in Boston, and I'd be going to work every day in Malden. Most likely, never the twain would meet.

Time to start looking forward. Even though I was skipping official training program, I was still going to need some training. I had all of the worker positions down pat, and scheduling I'd certainly done before, though on a smaller scale. Still, I was confident that I could handle that. Ordering and budgeting, though, would be uncharted territory. I'd never done any budgeting in my personal life; sad but true. Monthly inventory? Housekeeping inspections? Board of Health? Performance reviews? Maintenance and repair? Uh, nope. If you asked my dad, he'd tell you that I'm a breaker of things, not a fixer of things. I decided to figure it out as I went along.

I trained with Dan for a month, following him around like a puppy, and then I went to take over the Malden store as the manager. It turned out that I was replacing no one; they had fired that manager weeks ago, and while the cat was away, all of those mice were certainly playing. Big time. No one was officially in charge of the store, so the small number of people that still worked there that were honest was dwarfed by the large number of people that still worked there that were crooks.

It was anarchy.

I had no idea what I had signed up for, but I took a deep breath and jumped in with both feet, at least one of which typically ended up in my mouth.

The first few weeks were a blur of sorting through the mess of paperwork in the office that the prior fired manager had left. One of the good people that still worked there was my bookkeeper, Charity. I was lucky that she lived within walking distance of the store, and that she didn't have a car, because I found out later that those were the only reasons she hadn't quit already.

"I'd have left a long time ago, honey, if I had any other options. I'm glad I stayed though, since you're here now!" Charity said. I was glad too; not only was she a great bookkeeper, but she was caring, kind, generous, funny and, as far as I could tell, trustworthy. She knew everything about everyone, and, more importantly, she was happy to share everything she knew with me. She was a good judge of character and I came to rely on her assessment of people. She was always right on with her impressions of people. I often wasn't. I could tell if they were competent employees from a performance standpoint, but Charity could tell if they were putting the money into the register with one hand and taking it out with the other.

The best part about it was that nobody knew. Charity looked so unassuming. A not very tall, pleasingly plump, late middle-aged woman, with short blonde hair that she set and teased and hair-sprayed into a helmet, she looked like she spent most of her time baking cookies for the grandchildren.

Not so. Charity had no kids, no grandkids. She was her own person, and she did what she wanted, when she wanted. I'd never met anyone like her, and even though I was her boss, we quickly became friends. She handled everything administrative in the back of the house so that I could concentrate on cleaning up the disaster in the front of the house. Besides the bookkeeping, she did most of the banking for the store, set the schedules up every week and filled in the hours of people that didn't change, and then went through all of the requests for days off for the upcoming week and blocked them out, saving me at least an hour when I wrote the schedule. I'm sure that, without Charity, I would have sunk like a lead balloon in the first month.

In addition to helping figure things out at work, she helped me with another problem that I had: I needed a car.

One of the first orders of business by Jim, who was my district manager here as well as at my original store, was to harangue me into buying a car. The arrangements I had made for getting to and from work was this: my father was driving me. Jim felt that it undermined my authority as manager for people to see that my dad was my transportation, and he wasted no opportunity to tell me this. "You're making a good salary now; you can afford to buy a car," he said. I was in no hurry to take on any additional debt, since the crushing weight of the school loans was looming large. Ultimately, though, I could see his point and even thought he might be right, but I had something else holding me back: I had no idea *how* to buy a car.

"Can your parents help you?" Charity asked me, when we were talking about it in the office one day. "Are you kidding me? They wouldn't even help me get my driver's license! I would never ask them to help me with this," I replied, my bitterness over this issue still alive and well.

"Well, do you have a boyfriend that you could bring along with you?" she asked.

"No," I said, shaking my head.

"A pretty girl like you? Why don't you have a boyfriend?" she asked, as always, saying just what was on her mind. God, if I had a nickel for every time I'd been asked that question.

"It's a long story," I said.

"Well, let's get some coffee then! I've got plenty of time!" she said, and with that, she went to the service aisle and came back with two cups of coffee on a tray, lots of cream and sugar in hers.

And so I told her everything: David's complete denial of our relationship for years, Buddy's disappearing act, Kevin's betrayal, Steven's violent temper. "You have bad luck. We all have bad luck," as Nana See would say. True enough. With men, anyway.

Well, don't you worry, honey. Everything happens for a reason. You'll meet your guy. Those other ones were just there to teach you something, or else you were there to teach them. You'll meet the right one when it's the right time for you, honey," she said with conviction.

"Well, my mother has been telling me for years that things happen for a reason, but I don't believe it when she says it either," I said wryly.

"That's because you're young; someday you'll know it's true," she said, unconcerned by my lack of enthusiasm. "That doesn't mean you can't have some fun between now and then!" she continued, with a twinkle in her eye.

"Charity!" I said, laughing. "Hey, I was young once too," she said, "but enough about that. We've got to get you a car."

"I know! But I still don't know how to make that happen," I said, feeling worried again. "Don't worry. It's not hard. And I'm going to help you," she said.

"Not for nothing, Charity, but you when's the last time you bought a car?" I pointed out. She waved her hand dismissively, saying, "That doesn't mean that I don't remember how to do it, dear. Haven't you learned not to underestimate me?" she asked.

"I think I just did," I said. "Is there anything you can't do?" I ask.

"Not much, dear; not much," she said. "Now let's get out our calendars and figure out when we can go get you a car," she said, like she was making an appointment for a manicure.

We picked a date, and when it arrived, she met me at the store and we drove off. "What kind of car do you want?" she asked me. Surprise! I hadn't thought about that.

"I don't know, really," I said. She showed none of the exasperation that she had every right to show.

Instead, she nodded and said, "Okay, well, I like Buicks so let's go there first. If you don't see anything you like, then we'll go somewhere else, and keep looking till you do. There are plenty of car dealerships on Route One, so not to worry, dear."

I'd always been annoyed by sayings like "not to worry". Coming from Charity, though, the words were somehow comforting. It made me feel safe, like she was taking care of me. And all of a sudden, I realized that I wasn't worried. I had this overwhelming feeling of calm. I leaned back in the seat, somehow knowing that everything was going to work out.

And it did. It turned out that there was a Buick that I liked: the Skyhawk. I knew nothing about this car in particular, or any car in general. Fortunately, Charity wasn't kidding when she said she did. "How much is it?" I asked, and she said, "Oh, we don't know how much it really costs yet, but we will soon enough," she said, and then the salesman came over and

Charity's gloves came off. When he tried to patronize her, saying that the price on the sticker on the car's windshield was the lowest he could go, her claws came out.

Within a half an hour, she'd talked him down by about three thousand dollars, and got him to double the warranty and throw in free oil changes for a year. My head was still spinning just from listening to the whole exchange. I knew Charity's exterior belied her interior, but even I was impressed watching her negotiate this sale. "You are amazing!" I said, and I meant it.

"Oh, not really, dear. It's just not my first time up at bat. By the time you need another car, you'll be doing it for yourself," she assured me.

I did not believe this for a second, but hey, now I had a car! All I had to do now was sit down with the finance guy and find out if I could get a loan. I was a little nervous about this, but soon these fears were also put to rest. Turns out, a young single woman with a high paying job and only school loans for debt is someone to whom they couldn't wait to give a car loan. An hour later, I had signed all of the documents and had the keys in my hand.

"Congratulations, honey. Your first car!" she said, and I noticed that she had tears in her eyes. Then I noticed that I did too.

Chapter 18: The First Bob

As a manager, I was expected to attend the weekly meetings held
at one of the other district stores, and business attire was
required. The standard issue uniform was okay when working on
the floor, but at all other times the expectation was that a
manager be in a business suit. At first, I resisted this; I certainly
didn't own any, and a business suit? That's going to cost you.

After a while though, I embraced the idea. Why not? I decided I'd look great in a business suit, plus it was almost as good as a uniform. I always knew what I'd be wearing in advance, since I decided to only buy two suits at first: one to wear, and one for the closet. Soon I increased that number to three: one for the dry cleaner.

I found a store at the mall that sold women's suits. I opened a charge account and never looked back. My first suit was a traditional (read: boring) navy. My second one was another traditional (read: also boring) grey. Those first two were for the job. My third suit though? That one was for me. That was my break out suit. My third suit was red (read: power!). I loved it. It turned out that suits suited me. I actually did look great in all of them, which helped increase my confidence at work. I was feeling pretty good about everything at that point.

I had gotten my hair cut into long layers. The style was more professional but not a nightmare to maintain. I ditched the glasses for contacts. I was migrating away from the ugly duckling end of the spectrum toward the swan side.

I became the first woman in my family to finish college. Against the odds, I had managed to land a great paying job. I had a brand new car. Charity felt that I had to buy new, not used, so that if anything went wrong with it, it would be under warranty and I wouldn't have to worry about paying to get it fixed, and that sounded good to me. I deferred to Charity on all things "car" and anyway, I didn't want any financial surprises.

All in all, life was going pretty well. I decided that it was time to pick my head up, look around, and see what male prospects there might be for me now. There were ten managers in the district, eight of which were male. Possibilities abounded.

I was lucky because the other female manager and I hit it off right away. Like me, Susan was a relatively new manager, but *un*like me, she had grown up in the company and knew everything about the politics. Susan was enormously helpful by keeping me from saying the wrong thing to the wrong person at the wrong time, which I had a penchant for doing.

There were three managers paying an inordinate amount of attention to me. One of them was interesting, largely because, unlike the other two, he was not married. He was older, in his late twenties. He had a gregarious personality, so at first I wasn't sure if he was really interested in me, or if that was how he acted with everybody.

His name was Bob, and the more I saw him, the more I liked him. He was very tall, over six feet. He had glasses like me, and often wore contacts instead, like me. He had a lot of energy and enthusiasm, and was always smiling. I felt good when I was around him. I decided that I wanted to know him better and stayed open to any potential opportunity to do so.

I got my chance when Jim announced at one of our weekly meetings that our presence would be required at a Friday night "Manager Outing" at (wait for it…) the TGIF. He had been doing some reading about team building strategies and decided that monthly social outings were non-negotiable. This stressed me out at first, because I had no idea where this restaurant was located, and I hated to drive any place that I didn't know how to get to already, especially at night. I asked Susan if we could ride together, but she had a commitment that night already and couldn't go.

Fortunately for me, Bob overheard this. "You can ride with me, Bebe," he said. I smiled sweetly, looking up at him.

"That sounds great, Bob," I said. I meant every word. Because it was a business outing, even though it was social, apparently we were still supposed to wear a suit. Thank God Susan clued me in about that. I decided I'd get a new suit. Just in case this might turn into a date, I was determined to look good. I went shopping.

Nothing was grabbing me at first, so when the salesperson came over, I didn't avoid her like I normally did. "Do you need any help?" she asked.

"Actually, I do. I'm looking for kind of a 'date' suit. Got anything like that?" I asked. "Sure, on the back wall. Follow me," she said, and she took me over to see them.

I saw it immediately. It was pale pink, and I loved it. I couldn't believe my luck. They had it in my size, and the blouse they displayed with it was beautiful. Done. I was all set. I was looking forward to the outing, but with controlled enthusiasm. I had been through a lot recently in my dealings with the opposite sex, and was not interested in repeating any of my myriad mistakes. I was not interested in a serious relationship. Enough was enough. I was hoping that Bob, with his great sense of fun, would be my transitional boyfriend. I was now the girl who just wanted to have fun.

All of those months with Steven were filled with such unimaginative couplings: roll on, roll off, never initiating, only tolerating, lying back and thinking of England. I missed the excitement, the chemistry that I had with prior boyfriends. I did have some favorites among my mistakes, and I wanted some of that back, but I decided I would do better this time. I was hoping that Bob might be my ticket back to boyfriend excitement.

When the Friday night came, I was ready. I looked hot. I knew it and soon he would know it. I told him just to beep when he arrived, and I'd run out. I told my parents that he was a colleague who offered to let me ride with him since I didn't know the way, which was the truth. No need to get their curiosity up.

He was right on time. I hated it when people were late, especially if it would result in making me late. I ran down the stairs to meet him. I was inordinately pleased to see him smiling out the window at me. I came around to the passenger door, which he leaned across to open for me. "Hi," I said, settling in, buckling my seatbelt.

"Hi to you," he said. "You look amazing in that suit!" he added, leaving me no doubt that I was not the only one in the car who was looking at the world through date-colored glasses.

He also looked amazing. He had on a dark suit, a pale blue shirt, and a dark navy tie. He had just gotten a haircut, and he had just the right amount of cologne on. Subtle, but effective. "Thanks again for picking me up," I began, suddenly shy.

"No problem; I've been hoping for a chance to get some time alone with you," he said, making my heart flutter in a nice way. Great, I thought, we *are* in this together.

"Me too," I said.

"There are always so many people around at the meetings, and there's never enough time to talk," he said. "So, are you seeing anyone right now?" he asked with a sidelong glance, jumping right in.

"Um, no, I'm not," I replied. "What about you?" I asked, not looking at him.

"Nope," he said, and I could see him shaking his head.

"Well, that's good!" I said. "Maybe we can work something out," I added, half joking, but he said, "Good. I was thinking the same thing." The future was looking very promising, and we hadn't yet arrived at the restaurant.

Usually I had trouble making small talk, but with Bob, once we'd established our mutual interest, I felt completely at ease. I laughed and talked easily with him. We ended up standing together at the bar. We each ordered a drink and a couple of appetizers to split. The evening flew by. By the end of the night, I was hooked.

Chapter 19: Moving Out

When Steven and I were together, I'd spent most of my time at his apartment. Now that I was back living with my parents, I felt stifled. Steven spent a lot of time at work, so I had extended periods of time when I had his apartment to myself. I got used to having my own food in my own (okay, his own) fridge. I liked sitting on the couch and watching whatever I felt like watching on TV, with no negotiation required.

Steven also had two cats that I loved. On days when he

was coming home late from work, I'd lay down on the couch and pull the quilt that my grandmother made me up to my chin. I kept my quilt there for just such occasions. One cat would settle on my chest, and the other would wiggle under the covers and curl up on my thighs. I'd pull out my current book in progress and read and doze, snuggled up with the cats. Bliss.

Anyway, I decided that I liked a quiet house. I loved not listening to anyone else's noise. I loved doing writing in my journal and reading my book without having to listen to anyone yelling at anyone else. I wasn't sure how long I was going to last back in my parents' house, so when my sister casually mentioned one day that the tenant in the apartment under hers was moving out, I was immediately interested.

She was living on the second floor of a two family on a quiet side street. I'd been to her apartment many times, and I loved the neighborhood. The grocery store was close enough to walk to, and there were a couple of parks that also were within walking distance, as well as the holy grail: a Dunkin Donuts.

"How many rooms?" I asked her.

"Let me think," she said. "I've been down there a couple of times…there are two bedrooms, living room, dining room, kitchen," she said. "Oh, and we split the basement, and share the backyard," she finished. "Why, are you interested?" she asked.

"I'm definitely interested," I say firmly. "Can you talk to the landlord, do you think?" I ventured.

"Sure; I see him every month when he comes for the rent. I'll see him next on Monday," she said.

"Find out when I can see the apartment," I said. "Do you know how much he's asking for it?" I asked. "Well, I know he was getting nine hundred a month from the person who's leaving, but who knows? He's so greedy. I'll just ask him and see what he says," she said.

I got a call from her that Monday. "He said that you can come over anytime and see it," she told me. "Can you come now?" she asked. "He's still here, and he said he'll wait." I was off from work that day, so I said, "Sure, I'll be right over," and grabbing my bag, I headed out the door. I took a moment to appreciate having a car as I drove over to meet them.

I couldn't believe my luck. The rooms were all big, open and airy, and had many large windows that took up much of the wall space. Every room was bright and sunny. The dining room had a built in china cabinet which would come in handy since I had very little (well, actually, no) furniture of my own. The kitchen had a little pantry area, and the front door had an entryway, like a foyer, that opened up to the living room or could be closed off with French doors.

And there was a driveway. Parking could be a huge issue for apartment dwellers. I had found this out over the years, as I listened to people complaining about how there was no street parking near their apartments, and it was especially bad on snowy days. They sometimes had to walk several blocks from whatever space they had finally found to park their car to get back to their apartment. I wouldn't have to worry about this at all. Plus, my nearest neighbors would be my family!

"I'll take it!" I said to the landlord, as soon as the tour was finished. "How much is the rent?" I asked.

"Well, since I didn't have to advertise for you, and since Lisa is vouching for you, I'll knock fifty bucks off. So, seven fifty a month, plus deposit. I usually get last month's rent up front too, but since you're Lisa's sister, I'll waive that. I trust you," he added. "Great. When can I move in?" I asked. "The first of the month is the official date, but you can move in whenever the tenant leaves, if that's sooner." I was ecstatic.

I couldn't think of a more ideal place for my first apartment. I'd be living alone, in my own place, but also with my family, not strangers, right upstairs. I had long since made peace with my sister and her husband, especially since there were two babies to love now. I could tolerate Kevin in small doses, and fortunately, that was all that was required. He worked six or seven days a week now. Since becoming a husband and father, he'd left the store he was managing for Jim and now he had his own restaurant. Most of the time, thankfully, he wasn't home.

So, finally, finally, I was getting my first place. In my haste to get away from Steven, I had left some of my things behind at his apartment that I really wish I had now. My grandmother's quilt, my mother's sewing basket, not to mention some of my favorite clothes and jewelry were still there, as well as some of my mother's pans, my grandmother's dishes. I hated that he still had these things, but the thought of having to talk to him or see him again made retrieving them highly not worth it. I was still pretty pissed about the Depression era glass bowl that he broke when he had his temper tantrum the night I'd made him dinner. No, nothing was worth getting back in contact with him again. I thought it was best to cut my losses and start over.

I couldn't wait to move in. Nana See came through with

some furniture for me: a dining room set, a bed, and mattress. I guess my father told her that I had a big empty dining room to fill, and she had an extra dining room table and chairs on her enclosed front porch. "It was just collecting dust! I just use it to hold plants! Better that you should eat off it," she said, practical as always. Besides, never argue with an Italian grandmother about eating. Or, you know, anything else.

Knowing that I was renting a U-Haul, which was a terrifying prospect, by the way, she decided to throw in "just a few other things I might need," which turned out to be sheer white lace curtain panels that miraculously were the right size for my windows, and there were enough of them for every window in every room. She also had some pans, dishes, silverware, drinking glasses, blankets, a couch, a coffee table, a couple of small end tables that she wasn't using and so she decided to send those things, too.

When Lisa saw the apartment for the first time, she was

speechless. "What's all this stuff?" she asked.

"Oh, you know Nana! She thought maybe I'd be needing a few more things, where it's my first apartment and all," I said, laughing, "and come on, you know she was right. I needed everything!"

After we got everything into the apartment, I called Nana. "You shouldn't have given me so much stuff," I began.

"Of course I should! Who else would I give it to?" she asked.

"Thanks, Nana," I said. "I can't wait for you to see the apartment once it's all set up," I said, and after talking a bit more about how well everything was coming together, we hung up.

Now, things were really coming together. A month earlier I was still living with my parents, and today I had my own place that was only two rooms short of being fully furnished. All that was left was the kitchen and the extra bedroom. I found a small kitchen table with four chairs on QVC that was very inexpensive, and a friend of a friend offered up a futon she no longer needed. I found an old desk and chair in my half of the basement and the landlord said that he didn't know who it belonged to so I was welcome to use it. I moved it up to my apartment with some help from my sister. I found a rocking chair at a yard sale that I put on my back porch. Voila. My first apartment was furnished.

Chapter 20: Self-improvement

Now that I had my own place, I also had my own kitchen. Now that I had my own kitchen, I started eating better. I didn't feel compelled to stop for cheap eats at Burger King or to grab something quick at Dunkin Donuts on my way home from work anymore. Now I could buy food, cook it, and leave it in my fridge, where it would still be when I got home. I started making more salads; I was anxious to replace the memory of that awful night when I'd made such a beautiful salad in the beautiful bowl Nana gave me, and then seen it smashed on the floor. I made more beautiful salads in my new salad bowl, a clear Pyrex version, a housewarming present, courtesy of Lisa. Even if this one was dropped, or God Forbid, thrown, it was highly unlikely to break-although it probably would leave a mark.

There was a barbecue grill on Lisa's back porch, and whenever she was cooking out, she made an extra piece of chicken, pork, or whatever, and sent one of the kids down with it for me. The nearby supermarket had a large health food section and the fruits and vegetables always looked so good that I couldn't resist buying them. I started losing a little weight without even trying. I felt good. I looked good.

I must have been radiating this, because suddenly Bob seemed to be around me all the time. After that night at TGIF, he asked me if I'd go out with him sometime. "Absolutely!" I replied. I thought, this is what happiness feels like. I told him that I was usually off on Wednesdays and Sundays. Since we wrote our own schedules, we could take off whatever days we wanted. He said that he'd take off Wednesday next week. He would pick me up and we could spend the day together. "Sounds like fun," I agreed.

He picked me up early in the morning. Ever the overachiever, I had been ready for about half an hour and was sitting on the front steps waiting for him.

I was wearing jeans and a T shirt. At the last minute, I decided to pull a sweatshirt over it. He'd told me to dress casual, but other than that gave me no information about what we would be doing or where we would be going. I was excited to see him, and a little off balance, not knowing where we were headed. When he arrived, I was happy to see that he was dressed the same as me. It was the first time I'd seen him dressed in something other than a business suit or a work uniform, and I was impressed. I liked him more every minute that I spent with him. I never paid too much attention to the kind of car a guy drove, but Bob had a black Camaro Convertible that he loved so much that I ended up loving it too. We zipped all over the place in that car, and he had the top down any time the sun was out and it wasn't raining or snowing.

"Coffee first?" he asked, and I nodded.

"A man after my own heart," I said, and then immediately realized the double entendre I'd inadvertently put out there. I felt the heat rushing to my face.

"I am that," he said, laughing, "but first: caffeination!" That was fine with me. I loved Dunkin Donuts. Before I'd gotten my apartment, I'd spent many quality hours there. A coffee and a chocolate croissant were basically my go-to meal, so when we got there, I didn't hesitate to order. He got a couple of glazed donuts and he drank his coffee black, like me.

He had gotten on the highway and headed north. "Where's your apartment?" I asked. He said, "Uh, actually, I have a house." Wow! I was excited that I'd finally gotten up the nerve to get my own apartment, and here *he* was owning a home! We were sitting in the parking lot in front of Dunkin Donuts, eating our breakfast and sipping our coffees. This is going very well, I thought. I can't wait to see his house. I hoped that was where we were going.

"So, how long have you lived there?" I asked him.

"Oh, for a couple of years now," he said. "It's in a good location; I can just hop on the highway and I'm at work in about twenty minutes," he added. "Plus, all of the other stores in the district are right off the interstate, so I'm all set even if I get transferred," he added. Good plan, I thought. I could do worse than to hook up with him. He's got a lot going for him. First, he's gainfully employed. Second, he owns a home. Third, he's got a cool car. Finally, he's a big, handsome guy with a rockin' bod! What else? He sure smelled good. I wondered if he's a good kisser.

"Hello, Bebe? Did you hear me?" he asked.

"Oh, sorry. What?" I asked, pulled out of my reverie. Back to reality. "We can swing by the house for a few minutes, if you want to see it."

"Yes, please," I said.

So I did get to see his house. He pulled into the driveway. "Well, this is it," he said, waving his hand in the general direction of his house. It was on the coveted corner lot, which enamored me of it immediately. It was slate blue, and had an enclosed back porch. We entered through the porch to the back door, which led into kitchen. It was a very cluttery kitchen, but good cluttery; it felt homey and comfortable.

The living room was straight ahead as you passed through the kitchen, and it was a very dark room, with dark carpeting, filled with dark furniture. This room was stuffed with what I imagined were the necessities of bachelor life: a large TV and a big comfy couch…and a black cat. Not that I believed in bad omens or anything, but really? Shoot.

The room was so dark that the cat was almost invisible. "Oh, it belonged to a former girlfriend," he explained when he saw me staring at the cat. "She didn't want it anymore, and he kind of grew on me. He's outside most of the time; it's rare for him to be in the house. He must have wanted to meet you!" he teased. I smiled. Hey, I don't mind if he lives with a cat, I thought. I can deal with that.

To the left of the living room was his bedroom. "Want to see it?" he asked. Yeah, baby, I thought, but did not say. I nodded. The door was shut; he leaned past me to open it, and said, "After you," with a wicked grin. I went in.

The room was large compared to the other rooms. It had what looked to be a king size bed, and there was a dark blue comforter on it, and at least four pillows, maybe more. There was a dresser, a chest of drawers, and two nightstands. This room, like the living room, was packed with furniture; there was barely space enough to squeeze in. The bed definitely dominated, and I wondered if it was intentional, influenced by something Freudian.

"It's bigger than I thought," I said, talking about the room, but aware that I had put my foot squarely in my mouth again. What was it about him that brought out the double entendre in me? He laughed, "Oh, you're right about that! How'd you know?" He came over and puts his arms around me. "I'm so glad you came," he said, and we both laughed again.

"So, is the end of the tour?" I asked.

"Well, there's an upstairs, but I have a tenant up there, so yeah, that's it for today. So, what should we do now?" he asked, lowering his voice and smiling suggestively. "Well, what did you have in mind, Bob?" I asked, knowing full well exactly what he had in mind.

"How about this?" he asked, leaning in to kiss me. By way of answering him, I kissed him back. Hard. This just in: Excellent. Kisser. Thank God. I felt myself getting excited by the thought of connecting with a man that I actually did want to connect with. And the more that I kissed him, the more that I was sure that I wanted him. He smelled even better really close up. I ran my hands over him. This was tricky, because he was so tall, but I gave it my best shot. He was moaning now, as into this as I was.

We pulled apart, took a breath. "So, what did you want to do now?" he asked again.

"More of this," I said, breathless. We moved to his bed, his very large bed. There was plenty of room. There was also plenty of time. He backed up and sat on the edge, and I was right there with him. I straddled him. He didn't have a gym body, so I was a little surprised by the strength in his arms and hands, and I said as much. "From years of scooping ice cream, baby," he murmured with a little smirk, squeezing my butt, looking at me with half-closed eyes.

"Well, it was totally worth it," I told him. He pulled me in closer, and we fell back across the bed, a pillow falling over our heads. I pulled back, laughing while he flung the pillow onto the floor, and reeled me back in. "How'm I doing so far?" he asked, and I held him tighter in response, kissed him more aggressively. My tongue entered his mouth, strong and sure. Now I was moaning. Man, he tasted so good! I couldn't stop kissing him. His hands started roaming freely now, and I made no move to stop them. It felt good to be having fun with someone that I was attracted to physically, and so far, he'd given every indication that he knew exactly what he was doing, where he was going, and how he was going to get there, and get me there too.

A thought flashed through my mind: maybe I should have taken the idea of a soul mate off the table years ago. Bob and I got along really well, and we had an evolving physical relationship that was exciting and fun. Our first date that brought us to his apartment was contained to kissing and above-the-clothes exploration, and every inch of me was on fire. I knew from what we'd done so far that I definitely wanted to more, and I also knew that when we did, it was going to be great. I loved his size, his scent, his face, his touch. He was strong and gentle. He was fun both in and out of the bedroom. He made jokes and teased and laughed all the time, but he also was full of compliments for me. He was going to be next, and I was feeling pretty lucky to have found him. I was nervous about seeing anyone again after what happened so far with my boyfriends; nothing had gone the way I hoped or expected, and I was a little gun shy. Maybe this time would be different.

I could hope.

Chapter 21: New Friend

After that first date, things progressed pretty quickly with Bob.

We saw each other several times a week. Our paths crossed at

work frequently, and we went to each other's houses at least once

a week. I loved being with him, his quirky personality made me

happy. Because we had the same job, I felt like I was his equal and had nothing to prove. I came out ahead of him sometimes with our weekly sales and profit figures, and sometimes he beat me. We had a friendly competition going and we were each equally pleased for the other no matter who came out on top that week. He seemed like a great guy, but I was keeping my options open. I didn't want to be so naïve this time, not hopeless and pathetic, not waiting by the phone. It was nice to be a girl with options for a change, to be the pursuee and not the pursuer.

At my job, things were moving pretty fast as well. I did so well managing my first store that I was offered a move to another, bigger store which, as luck would have it, just so happened to be on the same road as Bob's, one town over. I jumped at the chance; this would mean more prestige, more money, and more proximity to Bob. The hours were tougher though. This store opened at the ungodly hour of six in the morning and closed at midnight, but I didn't mind very much, since there were so many good reasons to make the change.

I had expanded the staffing at my new store as the first order of business, and because Bob's store was busier but had fewer employees, I was in a position to send my employees down to work at his store to help out. This was a win for everyone, because he could afford to pay them an extra dollar an hour to do this. That made the employees happy, which made me happy. Happy, well-compensated employees are good for business, and as it turned out, were also good for my love life.

Because I wasn't sitting by the phone, I had more time to do stuff. Not only had my new store brought me increasing financial security and self-confidence, but it also brought me a new friend. She was a regular customer who came to the restaurant first thing in the morning. I liked to work the early shift and she was always there already when I opened up.

One day I asked her why she was always up so early. "Is it for work? I asked one day

. "No, for school," she said, "but I'm a morning person anyway; I love to get up early to watch the sun rise."

"So, you're saying that you get up at dawn even when you don't have to?" I asked, incredulous.

"Yep," she nodded.

"I would never do that in a million years!" I said.

"Why not? It's great! Almost everyone else is still sleeping, so it's quiet. You get to see the sunrise, which is beautiful! That alone makes it worth it," she said, sighing.

"I'm sorry, but I couldn't care less about that," I told her. I was a night owl. I only got up early for work because I had to, and I only chose the opening shift instead of closing because then I could set everything up for the day the way I wanted it.

Lorraine and I were so unlike each other on the surface that it surprised us at first that we liked each other so much. She came in for her breakfast every day. I rarely ate breakfast, unless several cups of black coffee counts. Actually, we did sort of have that semi 'in common', because her daily breakfast also included black coffee, but then that's where the similarities ended. She would order a whole wheat English muffin, drowning in butter, with extra butter on the side. In a word: gross. I didn't put butter on anything. I had my toast, English muffins, bagels, whatever, dry, thank you very much.

I asked her why she came here to eat. She said, "Oh, habit I guess. I used to work here. It's close to my house. I could walk here if I wanted to. In fact, I always did when I worked here and I still do sometimes. Plus, you make good coffee here," she said, grinning.

My ears perked up when she said that she was a former employee. I was always on the lookout for good people to expand my staff. In my view, there was always room for another employee, especially a former one, who may still possess some latent skills that would translate into being cheaper for me to train.

I made my pitch. "Well, why don't you work here again?" She looked at me and laughed. "Oh, you're serious?" she asked.

"Sure! Why not?" I asked.

"Because that phase of my life is long over," she replied.

"Besides, I have a work study job through school."

"Oh, doing what?" I asked, but no longer that interested now that I was pretty sure she wasn't going to be swayed.

"I teach some classes," she said. I became interested again.

"So, you don't get paid?" I asked, and she shook her head, "No." "Then you do need a job!" I said. "What position did you do when you worked here before?" I queried.

"I did everything. I was even a supervisor for a while. Waitressing was what I preferred though; I liked the tips. You couldn't pay me enough to do that now, though," she said, smiling. "Well, maybe you'll think about it," I said, finally dropping it.

I figured that I had lost that battle, but every so often I'd remind her, "There's a job here for you any time you want it…" and she'd just nod, and that was it. After several weeks of this, however, she said there was one job she might be interested in doing after all. "Name it!" I said. "I heard your bookkeeper was leaving," she said. He was. "How'd you know? I didn't know anyone knew yet," I asked, puzzled. "Because he and I know each other. I hate to say it, but I think he told me before he told you," she continued. I let this pass.

"Do you want the bookkeeper job?" I asked, daring to hope. "I do, believe it or not. I think it would work great for both of us. As long as I could make my own hours during the week, then I could work around my school and teaching schedule. I would be here Monday mornings for payroll, of course. Would you be okay with that?"

Uh, yeah! I couldn't believe my good luck. I was totally bereft when I lost Charity in the move to the new store. She was the one person that I missed after being promoted. I'd tried to get her to come with me, offering to find a reason to ditch whoever was doing the books there already, but she wouldn't hear of it. "No, that's okay. It would be hard for me to get back and forth every day. Anyway, it's getting to be about time for me to retire," she said. "I would have retired already, but you know how much I like you," she said, smiling.

The bookkeeper that I had was competent, but his responsibilities often required us to spend time together in the office working, and while I enjoyed this time very much with Charity, I did not with Mark. He often ate strongly spiced ethnic foods at meals and sometimes the smell was lingering, overwhelming. At the least, it was very distracting while I tried to concentrate on whatever I was doing. I would have to leave the room frequently just to clear my head, and I'd have a headache for hours afterward. I couldn't wait to get rid of him. To replace him with Lorraine would be a dream come true. If I couldn't have Charity, I could have someone just as good, and maybe even better.

Chapter 22: Lorraine, BFF

Lo and I started going out for coffee. We discovered that our

romantic pasts were very similar. She had a long history of failed

relationships, just as I did, but she was currently with someone

for several months and they had just decided to live together.

Since he already had a house and she lived with her parents, it was a no-brainer that she would move in with him. His house was within walking distance of the beach, which would have made Lorraine my new best friend, if she hadn't been that already.

I was in need of a bookkeeper and of a best friend. Lorraine stepped into both of these roles with ease. We shared the office like it was a dorm room. We were excellent multitaskers. We got each other coffee refills. We brought each other snacks. We traded gossip about the customers and the other store managers. Life was good.

We started to go out for suppers. We'd meet up at the store, and one of us, usually Lorraine, would drive to one of the many restaurants on the main drag and we'd grab something to eat. Eventually, we expanded our territory. Someone had given her a book with discount coupons to local restaurants. We took turns choosing which restaurant we'd visit. I was a wimp about driving when I didn't know where I was going. Lorraine, fearless, was happy to drive. We probably visited half of the restaurants on the North Shore before we'd finished that book. It was so much fun! We bonded over potato skins and nachos, Mexican pizza and Margaritas.

Knowing how much I loved the ocean, she invited me to visit her at her new house, her boyfriend's old house, on a day when he was at work. We met at the restaurant and she took the long way, so that we could get the best view of the ocean. After we arrived, she parked the truck and said, "Want the grand tour?" "Of course!" I responded.

It was a beautiful house, small, but every room was filled with light. The breezes were so redolent of sea air it made me feel giddy. The main floor was comprised of a living room, dining room, and kitchen, and there were two bedrooms upstairs, one of which had been outfitted as an office. The furniture was dark and heavy, not my preference typically, but here, it worked. It was

Mission Style, plain and simple. Her house had such a nice ambience; I immediately felt at home there.

After the tour, we went out walking, first down to the ocean, and then to the village, which was filled with little shops and great restaurants. The delicious aromas of food wafted by us. There were artists painting. Their easels set up on the water front, and their paintings were for sale in the shops in the village. We had a great time walking, talking, and eating all afternoon.

The ride home seemed much too short. We stowed our purchases in the back of her little white pick up truck, and settled in to chat some more. I told her about how Bob had chased me until I caught him. She'd been around the company long enough to know everything about everybody.

"Be careful," she said. "What for?" I asked. "He's got a reputation of being sort of a playboy-type," she said. "He's a nice enough guy, but just, you know, watch out," she repeated.

"Playboy-type is just what I'm looking for right now, so it's all good," I said.

"Okay, okay; I'm not against having fun," she said, laughing. "I just wanted you to know what you were getting yourself into, and now that I know you do, I'll shut up."

"Well, I'd love to hear what you know, if you care to share," I said.

"There's nothing recent that I know of," she said, "and some of it may not be anything that's actually *true*…but did you know that he was engaged before? He was living with his fiancé for a couple of years, and then they split up."

"Actually, I didn't know that, but it's over now, right?"

"Right," she said

. "Fine, what else?"

"You know how all the girls that work for him follow him around like puppies? Well, there were rumors that he was spending a lot of time outside of work with some of them. Oh, and he was dating someone for a while that works higher up in the company, but as far as I know that's over. Everyone likes him so that's probably a good sign," she finished.

"Okay, so now I have to ask: did *you* go out with him?" I said, and I was only half kidding. "No! He's not my type, believe me. I don't go for the big, tall, handsome, busy types," she laughed. "I like them thin, and with blonde hair, not brown, and with lots of time for me."

"Well, I'm not getting into anything heavy with him right now; we're just having some fun —tame fun."

"Good. As long as your eyes are open, girl," she finished.

I'd actually decided that since I was no longer Desperately Seeking, I could take a break from The Pill. If my mother was right, and "No one marries the town pump" (you know, unless they're pregnant) then I was going to be a virgin again. Why not? Emotionally, I most certainly still was. Plus, who would know? I was busy concentrating on my job. I really had very little discretionary time now, and the supper dates with Lorraine were more than enough social life for the time being. Bob was fun, and that was all. I liked it that he had a reputation of being a party guy; that should keep things light. I didn't want a heavy relationship; been there, done that. I wanted to work, make as much money as I could so that I could keep up with my car loan and student loan payments, not to mention the rent and utilities that now were also on my plate.

Except for the bills, I loved having my own apartment. I was no Ms Fix-it though, so when things went wrong, I would have to call someone. For the first time, I thought how great it would be if I could fix the flushometer (what the hell was that damn thing called, anyway?) in the toilet tank that sometimes spontaneously ran for no reason except to drive me crazy and exponentially increase my water bill. When the tub upstairs in my sister's apartment starting leaking through into my bathroom, that was something that required attention from a professional. I was so not into the Chinese water torture.

Because we were renters, Lisa called the landlord who told her to call a plumber and deduct the bill from the next month's rent. The day that he could come was, of course, a day when she couldn't be there to let him in. It happened to be a Wednesday so I was off, and said I'd do it. I had planned to do some errands that day, but it was worth it to me to stop the incessant dripping that followed every bath or shower up there, and with two adults and two toddlers, there was a *lot* of tub time.

The scheduled arrival time came and went; no plumber. As I was beginning to learn about tradesmen, they almost never show up when they say they will. I was faintly annoyed, but not surprised. I had a good book to read, and the couch was right by the window where I had a good view of the road, so I was distracted from the time passing until the sound of loud motor broke the silence of my quiet street. I looked out to see a vehicle turning into the driveway. One hour past due; right on time. I went around to the back of the house where he'd pulled up, opened the door, and stepped out onto the porch.

I was surprised by the man that emerged. He was no grizzled old guy with drooping chinos that exposed half his butt when he crouched. This was a handsome man with curly dark hair, blue jeans stuffed carelessly into well-worn brown work boots, and a white T shirt.

Hel-lo. He was gorgeous.

He picked up his bag of tools as he swung himself out of the truck. I stood mesmerized. He moved like a cat, surprisingly lithe for such a big man. His looked around, saw me on the porch, and headed my way. His eyes met mine and he smiled, a big grin that almost knocked me over. He really was gorgeous, in a take-your-breath-away sort of way. I breathed him in.

"Got a call to fix the second floor bathtub leak," he said.

"Follow me," I said, barely managing to get the words out. Get a grip, I thought. Good thing I'd taken myself off the market for a while, otherwise I'd be in big trouble with this one.

"What's your name?" I asked.

"Bob," he said, "Bobby," he corrected, and flashed a million dollar smile. I was glad I had lost a little weight and was wearing my tight jeans as he followed me up the narrow stairwell to my sister's apartment. She'd left the door unlocked, so I didn't have to fumble with keys, thank God.

"Up here?" he asked.

Huh? Um yes…that's where the second floor is located? Hel-lo? I thought, but did not say. "Yes, right up here."

"You still with me?" I ask, smiling, when we entered the kitchen. "It's right through here," I motion to the hallway which opened to the bathroom. I stood aside so that he could squeeze past me to enter. He was just close enough to make me take notice, but not so close as to be inappropriate. As he moved past me I caught his scent. His pheromones-or mine- must have been working overtime, because he smelled so good. "Where's my spoon?" I thought; "I could just eat him up." Except that I'm not doing that right now, I reminded myself. I'm just concentrating on my job. Concentrating on my job. Concentrating on my job…

"So, do you need anything?" I asked him.

"No, I'm all set. I'll just get started then," he said, and when he crouched down to look at the tub drain, I found myself wishing that half of his butt *was* exposed. Wasn't he a real plumber? Why was it all covered up? My disappointment was palpable.

"I'll be in the kitchen," I said, and went to the fridge to grab a Diet Coke to drink while I waited. I had forgotten my book downstairs, so I positioned my chair so that I could see some of him from the doorway. Something about watching a man working with tools who knew how to use them totally made me hot. I moved my chair a little closer to the door. Wow, just…wow. He was definitely more interesting than my book, and that was saying something because, you know, my book was riveting.

After about fifteen minutes or so, he stood up and came back into the kitchen. "I just have to run out the truck for a minute," he said, and brushed by me, a little closer this time, but I did not mind in the least. "Fine. Want a Coke?" I offered, always a gracious hostess.

"Sure, thanks," he said, and flashed that grin again. I grabbed a can of Coke for him. I was acutely aware of him watching me bend over, and I realized that now his eyes were now on *my* butt.

I handed it to him. "Thanks," he said, as he took it, turned, and ran back out to the truck. I watched him from the kitchen window where I was sure he couldn't see me. He rummaged around in the truck, apparently found what he was looking for, and then shut the door. He leaned against the back and lit a cigarette. Ugh! So, the honeymoon was over, having lasted exactly thirty-two minutes. I ran back down to my apartment, grabbed my book, and then went back upstairs to wait for him to come back, resuming my place at the kitchen table. I barely looked up when he returned, no longer interested. No matter now about his physical attributes, since he smoked. He'd be dead soon.

He came back up the stairs and returned to the bathroom. The smell of cigarette smoke clung to him now, erasing the pleasant scent with which he had first entered. After about another fifteen minutes, he packed up his tools and started cleaning up the area where he had been working. He came back into the kitchen.

"It should be all set, but it would help if I could take a quick look in the bathroom downstairs. Is that possible?" he asked. Nodding, I turned and went back down the stairs. He followed at my heels. I let us into my apartment, a mirror image of the upstairs apartment, minus a bedroom. Still, he had to ask me for directions to the bathroom. Are you kidding me? The phrase "dumb but pretty" flashed through my mind. Must be all that nicotine strangling his poor brain cells.

"Right there," I said, gesturing to the hallway. I couldn't resist adding, "You know, directly below the one upstairs bathroom?" He didn't catch my subtle sarcasm, or if he did, he chose to ignore it.

"Right, thanks," he said, flashed The Smile, then disappeared into the bathroom. Thank God I'd cleaned it up a little today.

Chapter 23: Bobby Kicks the Habit

After he checked out the ceiling, he pronounced the problem

"Fixed!" and started back out the door. He stopped and turned to

me in the kitchen and said, "They'll send the bill out from the

office." He hesitated.

"Did you forget something?" I asked, ready for him to be on his way. I'd wasted enough time on this. I wanted to get back to my book.

"Well, how about going out with me sometime?" he asked, all eyes, getting a few steps closer to me. I could smell the cigarettes still.

"You smoke, so sorry. I have this policy of not going out with people who smoke. Thanks anyway," I say, ushering to the door.

"Wait, I'll quit," he says.

I laughed, and then I realized that he was not. "What, are you kidding?" I said.

He comes another step closer, shaking his head.

"No. I'll quit. So how about it; will you go out with me?" I figured I had nothing to lose. I mean, what were the odds?

"Sure. You quit smoking right now, and I'll go out with you sometime," I say.

"I'll call you in a week. Give me your phone number."

Yeah, right, I think. "How about you give me yours, and I'll call you in a week. Then you can tell me how well your efforts are going."

"Okay, fine. Got something to write it on? I wouldn't want you forgetting it," he says, smiling now.

"Okay," I say, and grab the pad that I kept in the junk drawer. "What is it?" I ask him, a little impatiently now. He tells me; I write it down. "Okay, 'bye!" I say.

"Talk to you in a week," he says, and heads out to the truck. He gets in and I see him fumbling around at the dash, then he comes back in.

"Here," he says, putting his hand out.

"What's that?" I asked.

"The cigarettes. I won't be needing them anymore," he said. With two fingers, I gingerly took them. What else could I do? I sure didn't *want* to take the gross things.

"Okay. Fine. 'Bye now," I said, and he left. As soon as I closed the door, I walked straight to the trash and dropped them into it. So what if he made a grand gesture? It didn't impress me at all. I'd grown up with two smoking parents. I knew that he probably had a carton of cigarettes out there in his van, and for all I knew, had a case of them at home. I stopped thinking about it after that. I was just glad that my bathroom ceiling would no longer be dripping water on me.

At work, I was doing my best to win the weekly friendly "productivity competitions" and usually, I did. This got the attention of the upper management. In a business where it was all about the numbers and the bottom line (and let's face it: what business isn't?), being the best was something that got noticed.

I had a meeting with my district manager every month, and this time he had an interesting question for me. "So, where do you see yourself in five years, Bebe?" he asked.

"Well, I haven't thought that far ahead, to tell you the truth," I answered. As we've already established, I was more of a 'here and now' kind of gal.

"Well, start thinking. There's going to be a Training Supervisor position opening up soon," he continued. "I think you'd be the perfect person for it. I talked with Chuck and he agrees with me," he said. Chuck was his boss, the Division Manager, so that was saying something. I could appreciate the irony that this move would present: if I was hired to be the district's Training Supervisor, then I'd be in charge of the training program for new managers. The training program that I myself had never taken. I said to Jim, "Don't you think that it might present a credibility issue for a person who'd never gone through the program to be in charge of administering it to others?"

"No, not at all," Jim said. One thing about Jim: nothing got in the way when he was committed to a course of action, not even logic. "You've been training new staff since started working for us; you certainly know how to do that," he said.

"I don't know…" I began. "Well, just think about it for a few days," he finished, and I said that I would.

I didn't know how I felt about his idea, actually. After a rocky start in this new store, I was pretty comfortable now. My job in any new store was to staff it, clean it up, and make it profitable, preferably all at once, but if not possible, then at least in that order. I had gotten things to the point where I no longer had to work six or seven days a week, ten or twelve or fourteen hours a day to get it all done. Now I worked my ten hour days, five days a week, with only a small portion of those hours actually spent on the floor with customers or working one on one with trainees. The rest of the time was filled with meetings, planning, prepping, whatever. I lived close enough to work so my commute wasn't too bad: maybe fifteen or twenty minutes, depending on the time of day.

I also liked my staff. They worked hard and they had my back in emergencies; they now knew what to do, when to do it, and they were willing to do whatever I asked them to do. Why fix what wasn't broken? Jim was all about shaking up your comfort zone, otherwise growth and advancement, in his opinion, wasn't possible. Since I wasn't so sure that I wanted growth or advancement, I was more committed to holding onto the comfort zone that I had so painstakingly created. After all, it was comfy in the comfort zone.

This was exactly what happened with my first store. I cleaned up that mess after about six months of hard labor, and then decided to take on this second store because, after all, anyone could do something *once*. What if it was just a fluke, and not my skills, that had produced the dramatic change? This was what some of the older, more experienced managers were saying, and I certainly was aware of their comments. I wanted to prove them wrong, and make sure everyone knew that it *was* my hard work that accomplished those changes; it wasn't luck. I knew this for sure because, after all, hadn't I heard all of my life from my father and grandmother that we only have bad luck?

Plus, I liked the other managers in this district. Especially Bob. I did really like him and liked being around him. I didn't want to lose that proximity. On the other hand, one of the things that concerned me about seeing him was that "don't shit where you eat" philosophy. If I got the TS job, then I'd be in a much better position to quietly see him. We wouldn't have to act natural under the probing gazes of our colleagues (not to mention our district manager) who had already witnessed our public flirting and were asking questions about what the hell we might have going on in our off hours. I was still in the do-not-get-serious mode, but at least it would be more my decision about if and when to advance things, and less decided by circumstances and geography.

Another advantage of taking the job was that it paid better. I was only a couple of years into my decade of payback for my college education and anything that could increase the amount I could keep from my take home pay was hugely attractive to me. This position would afford me more freedom as well; I would have the use of an office at the district headquarters, and would no longer spend much, if any, time on the front lines. I would teach workshops for division personnel. The thought of this terrified me. It wouldn't just be manager trainees; I would apparently be expected to lead workshops for existing managers and upper management at times as well.

There would also be a fair amount of travel involved. Our division covered about a hundred square miles, and at one time or another I would be expected to visit every store within it at which manager trainees were working. This was potentially very upsetting; I had zero sense of direction and was known to have panic attacks when driving in Boston and getting lost. I could drive around in circles for an hour and have nothing look familiar enough to tip me off. I was not anxious to put myself in any position that would increase the chances of me getting lost while driving.

I was leaning toward staying put when I found out exactly how much more money I'd be making; it was a *lot* more. A. Lot. More. Suddenly, the Training Supervisor job was calling my name.

I couldn't turn it down. I heard myself saying, "Okay. I'll apply." At first, I was very nervous, but after I thought about it, I told myself that applying and accepting were two different things. There was such a small chance that I would be chosen that I stopped worrying. Hey, at least I was going through the motions of advancement. Hopefully, this would get Jim off my back for a while, and I could continue to enjoy my comfy comfort zone for a few more years.

Jim started coaching me on how to ace the interview. As his protégé, he wanted me to do him proud. He liked to say that he was my mentor and he told anyone who would listen, so it would not reflect well on him if I bombed.

"First, you want to have a good, firm handshake, make eye contact, and smile when you walk in," he began. "Of course, it goes without saying that you should wear your best suit," he added. "Next, look around the room and find something to compliment. Maybe you notice a picture on the desk. You can say 'What a handsome family!' or something like that. You want to break the ice with a neutral comment that is not about work," he said. "Just try to be yourself, and answer the questions succinctly," he finished. Is that all? I thought, but did not say.

"Thanks for the advice. I'll do my best," I promised.

When the interview day came, I was a little nervous, but not paralyzingly so. I was able to put all of his advice to practical good use. I left the interview feeling sure that I'd done well enough not to have embarrassed my mentor, and glad I went. It gave me an entire morning off from actually having to work, however I was still getting paid. Not a bad way to spend the morning.

No one was more surprised than I was when I got the call from Jim that Chuck was offering me the job. What, were there no other applicants? "Me?" I asked, stupidly.

"Yes! Congratulations!" he effused. "I knew you could do it!"

I was in shock. I hadn't allowed myself to contemplate what might happen if I actually did get the job. Now I was stuck. That nice story that I told myself-about how applying for a job didn't mean getting it-wasn't worth shit now that I had been offered it. How the hell could I say no? I felt like my credibility would be jeopardized if I said no thanks to it now that I'd basically *asked* for it. I was worried that they'd look at the situation and think that I was wasting everybody's time if I turned it down.

So I didn't. "Wow, that's great," is what I said. "What happens now?" I managed to choke out.

Well, things happened pretty quickly after that. A new manager came to replace me and I oriented him over a period of two weeks, then I was sprung. My new job would afford me a month of orientations, workshops, and meetings with the goal of getting me up and running independently. I was feeling excited, but also scared to death. I had so many challenges right off the bat, with the travel to parts unknown number one on the list, and my fear of public speaking a close second.

I had certainly given talks in front of groups before, but my deep-seated fear came from a Public Speaking class that we were all required to take in junior high school. I still break out into a cold sweat just thinking about sitting there in the auditorium, speech in hand, hoping that an act of God would necessitate the evacuation of the premises before my name was called and I had to get up on that stage and not only read my speech, but also make eye contact with the teacher and my fellow students. Social skills were never my strong suit under the best of circumstances, and that was definitely not the best of circumstances. I was petrified to the point of hyperventilation and lightheadedness. Let's just say that some of the students were not kind to each other before, during, or after speeches.

Fast forward fifteen years to my first presentation as a Training Supervisor. Unfortunately, I had to present a workshop to the entire division of managers, district managers, and managers-in-training, and a hotel function room had been arranged for this purpose. I was a wreck. Did I mention that I was a wreck? I was immediately that thirteen-year-old girl again, shaking in my sneakers, dreading for my name to be called. The situation was made worse by the travel involved in getting to the hotel. It was several states away, and I had to be there by 9am.

Because I was in uncharted territory, I left my house at dawn, and I was happy to have found the hotel without getting lost, but I got there two hours early, earlier than the hotel staff had anticipated anyone would be arriving, as evidenced by the room still being locked up tight. There I was, with my easel, my over-large pad that had my posters on it, my brief case, stuck leaning up against the door, waiting for someone to let me in. I liked being early, but that was over the top, even for me.

The presentation went fine. Once I started speaking the jitters faded away pretty quickly. I got through the material and even got some strong applause at the end. There were other speakers after me, so I sat at the table with the district managers, roughly the level that my TS position put me on now. Oh my God, these people were so boring!

I was in serious need of a distraction.

I found the table where the managers from my former district had congregated and joined them. Now that we had some professional space between us, I was putting up less of a fight when Bob made advances. I needed to have some fun with somebody, and he was looking better by the minute. Even though Lorraine wasn't especially fond of him, and even though he may have been carrying on with his female staff while he was pursuing me, I missed having a man around that I actually liked.

One night, I was closing up the shop, which was my least favorite thing to do. I heard a tap on the window and looked up. There was Bob, smiling and waving. I was surprised and happy to see him. I was alone in the shop and very glad to let him in.

"Hey, where's your crew?" he asked. The last of the crew had left a little earlier. Usually we all left together, but tonight the last two had asked to leave a bit early because they were driving out of town early the next morning, so I said they could. Fate at work.

After I told him this, he said, "Well, what do you have left? I'll help you finish up," and he did. We finished up quickly, and then he said, "Well, looks like we have a little time now, right? In case there's anything else you might want to do together." He smiled expectantly.

We were sitting side by side in a booth by the door, where we had just finished the night's paperwork. I felt his hand on my knee, then start sliding up my leg. Really? This smacked way too much of a demand for payment after services had been rendered. Even though I knew he didn't mean it that way. Even though I knew he just saw a chance and figured, "What the hell? Why not take it?" I picked up his hand and put it on his own leg.

"As appealing as that sounds, I have to take a rain check," I told him. He didn't blink. "That is the best news I've heard all day!" he said, still smiling. Nice. I liked how he'd handled the way that I had handled his advance.

And then he asked me to do him a favor. He wanted me to help him figure out why his store was losing money. He thought someone was stealing from him and was hoping that I'd help him catch whoever it was. He devised a secret shopper operation and he wanted me to participate. I was more than willing.

Chapter 24: Bob and Bobby

In the meantime, I called the other Bob, because my curiosity got the better of me and I was dying to say "I knew it!" when he told me he hadn't really given up cigarettes.

"Hi, this is Bebe," I began

. "Hi! I'm glad to hear from you. I was wondering when you'd call," he said. Hearing him say when, not if, annoyed the crap out of me. Just knowing that he expected me to call him made me wish that I didn't. Who the hell did he think he was, anyway? I was just about to say, "Well, okay. Bye!" but before I got the words out, he said, "I was hoping you would call, is all." This deflated me

. "Okay, so did you quit?" I asked, getting right to the point.

"I said that I would, didn't I? So yes, I did." I couldn't believe it.

"You did? How do I know that you're telling me the truth?" I asked.

"I guess you'll have to take my word for it, at least until you see me, then you can see if I pass your sniff test and decide for yourself if I'm lying or not," he said.

He sounded confident. I remembered how good-looking he was, and then I had an idea. "Fine. You can pick me up at 5 o'clock on Thursday night; I promised a friend I'd help him with something and you can take me," I said.

"That sounds great. See you then," he said, no questions asked. Wow, he's pretty uncomplicated. There weren't many guys who would have just agreed to that without any discussion. Could it be this easy?

I called Manager Bob, as I'd come to think of him when differentiating between the two Bobs in my mind, to tell him that I'd be visiting his store Thursday as the mystery shopper like he'd asked. I decided not to mention that I wasn't going to be alone. Let him wonder about that. He was effusive in his thanks, and I finally said, "Okay! Wait and see if this even works!"

Now I had a dilemma, however, since Plumber Bob (the younger, prettier Bob) said he did stop smoking. What if it was really true? I had arranged this "date" with him just to keep up my end of the bargain, but if he really had kept up his end, then what? I remembered how hot I thought he was until I saw him with the cigarette.

Uh-oh.

Thursday loomed large. I had to dress down, so as not to attract any attention to myself at the store visit. Anyway, I wasn't out to impress him. I showered, dressed in jeans and T-shirt, and waited for Bob. He pulled up five minutes early, and I thanked him for it. "Well, it's not like I don't know where you live," he joked.

God, it was a pleasure to look at him. He leaned in to give me a quick peck on the cheek, and being caught off guard, I didn't have time to deflect him. After getting over my surprise that he would be so familiar with me on the first pseudo-date, I realized something: he smelled good. Not a whiff of tobacco.

Could it be true? Could he really have quit smoking in just a week? He not only smelled good, he looked fucking great. He was rocking jeans and a T shirt. His smile dazzled me. I was going to have to be very careful.

I gave a quick prayer of thanks that sex was off the table. I wasn't on any birth control anymore. I decided not to have sex again for a long time. What good had it done me? I'd had sex and no cows had been bought, just like my mother warned.

Damn it.

I deserved a do-over. If I wanted to, um, revert, it was nobody's business but my own. I could be a virgin again. Madonna did it. If past experience had taught me anything, it's that, for some men, deflowering a virgin was a burden that they did not want. Maybe that would be the case with the Bobs.

Just when I found myself wishing that I had gone to a little bit of trouble with my appearance, Bob looked right into my eyes and said, "You look beautiful," and I could see that he meant it. I was noticing that he had this disconcerting habit of stepping in just a millimeter too close to me when we talked, and it inflamed all of my nerve endings. I was struggling to keep the upper hand here. Breathe. Breathe. Oh my God, his scent is overwhelmingly sexy...focus! Breathe!

"Ready to go?" he said, and when I nodded, he took my arm and guided me toward the door. I was not used to all this...*physicality*. It kept me off balance. He'd touched me more times in the last five minutes than Steven had during our entire relationship. I shook my head, trying to clear it. "Yes, let's go," I said.

He opened the passenger door for me, and that was a nice surprise. I hadn't expected much from him. I guess when you set the bar low, everything is gravy. He had a nice way of moving through space. He had a strong physical presence, due to his height, not to mention his large biceps. I realized that I was looking forward to the evening, and would have to make an effort to focus on what Bob needed me to do at his store.

"So, where to?" he asked, and I gave him directions.

"Tonight, we're going to catch thief," I said.

"We are?" he questioned.

"Hopefully we are," I amended. I explained to him what had been going on and how now I was on mission to help a friend figure out where a significant chunk of his profits were going.

"So, we're going undercover?" he said, giving me a sidelong glance. I laughed.

"We are," I said.

"Sounds fun," he proclaimed, "and by the way, call me Bobby."

"Okay, Bobby," I said. That certainly simplified the name thing. Why the hell hadn't I thought of that? "Bobby, it's really important that we don't look like we're studying everyone. We need to blend," I said, thinking how impossible it would be for the women not to notice him. Besides the fact that he took up a lot of space, he was *that* gorgeous.

"We need to sit in a corner booth so we can see *them*, but hopefully they won't take too much notice of *us*."

"Fine by me," he said, and then he said, "I'm starving!" Just as he said this, I realized that I was too. A man after my own heart.

"Good, because we're going to eat a lot, and eat it slowly, so we have time to figure out what's going on," I said.

We pulled up at the shop, and when I opened the car door myself, he didn't make a fuss over it, but I did notice that he beat me to the door of the restaurant and opened it for me. Score one for him. The hostess approached. "Two?" "Yes, a booth please," Bobby said. "Right this way," she said, smiling big at him, and who could blame her? She delivered us to our booth, placed the menus on the table, and with one more smile over her shoulder at Bobby, which I truly didn't begrudge her, she left.

While he studied the menu, I surreptitiously studied him. I knew the menu by heart, so why waste this opportunity? "Anything look good?" I asked him after a few minutes. He looked up at me, right into my eyes again, and even though he didn't move an inch, I felt the space between us shrink.

"Oh yes, definitely. *You* look very good to me," he said, "but first, let's talk about what we're going to order. What's the best thing they make here?"

Great question. "One of my favorite things is the mushroom burger, no cheese," I said, waiting for the "How can you eat it without cheese?!" argument to begin, but he just nodded.

"That sounds great. Let's have two of those, but I want bacon and cheese on mine. And fries. And do they have onion rings?" he continued. Wow, he was pretty slim for such a big eater. He must have been reading my mind, because he said, "Lifting weights burns a lot of calories," looking sheepish. Hey, if it ain't broke, I thought, but did not say. Instead, I just nodded. And smiled.

Chapter 25: WTF

I usually didn't go for the muscle-bound type, but he sure looked good to me. I tried not to sound too sarcastic when I asked, "So, do you spend every waking moment at the gym?"

"No, I work a lot, plus I have another job doing construction. I work for them whenever they call me. I probably only get to the gym four or five days a week," he said. I could see that he was completely serious about the 'only' part and was glad that I'd managed to hold back the laugh.

I asked him how old he was. "Twenty-two," he said.

"Did you ever go to college after high school?" I asked, then realized that I was making a huge assumption. Had he even *finished* high school? He didn't look at all pained by my question, however.

"No, I didn't like school much; couldn't wait to get out," he said, neatly side-stepping the issue of diplomas and such. "I went right to work. I was already getting a lot of construction work back then, it being summer and all. I was apprenticing with the plumber and then he offered to hire me full time, so I took it." He continued, "I wanted to save up enough money to buy a better car, which I finally did last year. Now I'm saving for first and last month's rent and a security deposit so I can move the hell out of my parents' basement."

Ambition is good. I couldn't shake the "dumb but pretty" phrase that came to mind again though. I was going to have to figure out a way to make peace with this if we were going to move forward at all as a couple. No, wait! I wasn't doing that coupling thing anymore! Old habits sure do die hard.

I decided that maybe I should reconsider this revirginization I was cultivating. Just in case. Maybe I'd overlooked something. I was willing to revisit this issue.

We sat facing each other in the booth. The waitress came, we ordered, and I switched modes. "I need to start watching the staff now," I said in a low voice. "Want to help?" "How?" he asked.

Sigh.

"If you see anyone pocketing money with the guest check rather than putting it in the register, let me know. Or if you just see anyone doing anything vaguely suspicious, point them out to me, but don't be obvious about it," I said.

"Will do," he said, as his eyes started panning the room.

"Don't stare!" I admonished, when I noticed him practically gawking at a girl on the register, as if he were a cheetah, poised to pounce. "You know what? Never mind what I said about helping. I'll keep a look out. You just relax, okay?" I said.

Geesh! Operation Catch a Thief would be sunk before we ever got away from the dock if he kept up like that. He seemed relieved as he nodded his head. "That's fine. I wouldn't make a good detective, huh?" he grinned. That's okay. He had other fine attributes which were distracting me no end.

But, oh my God, his hair! Thick, wavy black, a little long…nice teeth, full lips that should have been girly, but on him, they worked. Why was I even looking at his lips? I tried to give myself a pep talk. Bebe, what the fuck?! Get a grip! It occurred to me that I'd rather get a grope.

But I got a grip. Back to the business at hand. Bobby was talking about his day of plumbing today, which I found only marginally interesting, but interesting enough that I could sort of keep up my end of the conversation with a series of mmmmm's, nods, uh huh's and such, while still casing the joint.

I noticed Bob come out from the back. He looked at me and smiled briefly, raising his eyebrows, and then looked away. After all, we didn't want the staff to catch on to what we were doing. I hadn't let him know that I was bringing someone, so I'm sure that he was wondering about Bobby, and what I was doing there with him. I was wondering that myself, actually.

Our food arrived, and I realized that I was pretty hungry. The mushroom burger was big and messy; therefore it took most of my concentration to eat it without getting any on myself. Or on him. The need for small talk was suspended for the moment. He ate with gusto, as did I. I liked it when other people enjoy eating as much as I do.

As I debated whether or not I still had room for a brownie sundae -well, I knew that I did not, but still wanted one- I noticed Bobby push his empty plates aside and then reach for the dessert menu. Hurray! That helped me with my decision.

"How about we split a brownie sundae?" I asked.

"Sold!" he said, closing the menu. Wow; was there a more easy-going, agreeable man on the planet? I could get used to this. The waitress came back, removed our plates, took our dessert order, and left. I was disappointed that I hadn't seen anything suspicious at this point, because our meal, and therefore our time there, was winding down. We wouldn't have an excuse to linger much longer.

I could see Bob over at the wheel, making my sundae. He knew what my favorite dessert was. I'd waxed rhapsodic about it often enough. Heat up the brownie, add three four ounce scoops of mocha chip or coffee fudge swirl ice cream, then one ladle of strawberries, one ladle of hot fudge, and then generously cover it all with whipped cream. Oh! And of course, the cherry on top. I see him smirking a little as he made it, no doubt because I've told him enough times that no one can make this sundae as well as I can. Hopefully, he was out to prove me wrong, and I was about to get a spectacular dessert that was not going to cost me a dime (thank you, expense account).

Bob delivered it himself; with a flourish he placed the dessert down on the table with his right hand, then produced two soda spoons with his left hand, both of which he placed down on the table next to me.

"Enjoy!" he said, and after nodding to (and checking out) Bobby, he left us. I picked up the spoons and handed one to Bobby. "You first," he said, and that was one invitation I accepted without hesitation. I had to give it to him: Bob did one hell of a job on the sundae. Next to my own, it was the best one I'd ever had. When I make it, I cover the ice cream with the cold strawberries first, which insulates it from the hot fudge so it doesn't cause the ice cream to melt excessively by the time it gets to the table. He missed this step but, to be fair, I had invented it, so how could he have known? I gave him an A-. He did a good job. I wondered what else he might be good at.

I watched for an opportunity to catch Bob's eye, and when I did, I smiled big. He smiled back: message received. After the first bite, Bobby said, "This is excellent!" and was careful to alternate spoonfuls with me so as not to eat more than his share. We finished it fairly quickly, and it was almost time to leave. I was afraid to admit it but it was starting to look like our mission had failed.

"I know that I told you to stop watching, but did you happen to notice anything remotely suspect?" I asked him. He shook his head. "I didn't either. Oh, well. It was only our first try. I'll pay the check and we'll get going," I said. I put some cash with the check on the edge of the table. Ordinarily I would just have paid at the register, but I didn't want to risk any conversation with Bob that might blow my cover. The waitress came by and picked up the check. "Do you need change?" she asked me.

"No, it's all set," I said, smiling.

"Great, thanks! Have a nice night!" she said and bopped off. I sat and watched a little bit longer, chatting with Bobby.

Finally, I said, "Let's go," and I gathered up my things and we left.

He asked if I wanted to take a ride, but I declined, saying I had to get up early the next day, which was true. On the way home, I was distracted by something that had been niggling away at the back of my mind, just out of reach in my subconscious where I couldn't quite grasp it. What was it? My thoughts were interrupted as he pulled up in front of my house. I opened the door immediately and got right out of the car. "Hey, what's your hurry?" he asked. Um, I am desperately trying not to tear your clothes off. I am dying to kiss your face, and hey, why stop there?

"Like I said; I have to get up early, but thanks. I had a nice time tonight," and I ran up my stairs. And it was true. I did have fun. I did want to see him again.

"I'll call you," he said, and I smiled to myself.

"Great!" I called back, and closed the door.

Great.

As I hung up my coat, something clicked and I figured out what had been bothering me. The waitress had taken our check with the money to pay it, folded it into her hand, and as she walked away, rolled it into her pocket in one fluid motion. I'd just assumed that she was going to ring it into the register the first chance she got, but at least while we were still there, that didn't happen. What if it *never* happened? I had the number of our guest check written down in my log book. I'd gotten into the habit of doing this in advance because, so often, I'd forget to get a receipt, like tonight, but if I'd written down the check number and the total, I could still expense it.

I quickly called Bob, excited now. "Hey, do you know the name of the waitress that was serving me tonight?" I asked, breathless.

"Sure, Mary. Why?" he replied.

"Because I never saw her go to the register after she took my check. If I give you the check number, could you look it up?" I asked.

"Sure, go ahead." I read him the number. The wait staff was expected to come up with all of their checks to reconcile at the end of the shift, but often one or more would come up missing and nothing was ever done about it. Nothing could be proven by just the fact that a check was missing. It was well known that teenagers employed the "chew and screw" method of payment very frequently in small restaurants and it was just assumed that was what happened to it. In this case, however, if this check number came up missing, I knew *exactly* where it went, and more importantly, I could prove it.

"Is she still working?" I asked him.

"She is. She's closing tonight. I'll take it from here. I'll call you later," he said, all business now, and hung up.

Wound up now, I tried to kill time. I started getting my things ready for work the next day. I picked up the apartment. I threw in some laundry. When I still hadn't heard back from him, I found that I couldn't even read; my mind was racing with thoughts of what might be happening. I paced around the apartment, waiting for Bob to call me back. Finally, a little before midnight, he did. "Well, I have to thank you," he began. "We caught her red-handed. Because of the information you gave me, I was able to challenge her when she said she was missing a check tonight. I asked her to give me the check number, and guess what! It was your check. Big surprise, right?"

I was so thrilled to find out that he'd caught his thief, one of them, at least, since thieves often traveled in packs. As a manager, you almost had to catch someone stealing in the act, or else it became an endless nightmare of "he said, she said" and it was very difficult to prove anything. When he confronted his thief, she had just told him that the check was missing. She had already documented that in writing in the log, so there was no changing her story. When he asked her to empty her pockets, there it was…well then, no matter what she said at that point, he had her, because he had an independent eyewitness who had seen her put the check with the money into her pocket: me. There was nothing she could say. He fired her on the spot.

After that, he noticed his revenues go up about a hundred bucks a day. Either she had been making big money, or else the other thieves, after seeing what happened to Mary, had been scared straight. Either way, his profit was back up where he needed it to be. He credited me for that. I respect a guy who can share the accolades, not hog them all for himself. I was liking this side of him, and I told him as much.

"Then go out with me," he teased. I was tempted to say yes this time. Tempted, but still, my instincts said *wait*. There was no reason to rush into anything. Because I was no longer baby-proofed, it really did serve as a reminder to go slow, take my time. I could afford to really get to know him first, before making any decisions about becoming intimate with him. If we were dating, that would inevitably lead to something more, and I wanted to be as sure as I could be that I wanted to go there before starting anything.

So I said, "Bob, let's talk straight, okay? I'll meet you for coffee later this afternoon, would that work?" and we agreed to meet at four o'clock. I arrived way too early, as usual, and grabbed a corner booth. I liked to get there first, survey the place, choose a table, and seat myself in a spot that would give me the best view of the room. Maybe it was a power thing? I certainly felt more confident when I did this. I settled in to wait.

Bob arrived soon thereafter, also early, about ten minutes in advance of our agreed upon meeting time. I was liking this trend. So this what respect feels like.

"Hello," I began, and smiled. "Hello to you," he said, taking his suit jacket off and laying it over the seat, smiling back. "Thanks again for your help with that Mary thing. I should have known. She was always picking up closing shifts, and the other waitresses were complaining that they thought she was stealing their tips." "Well, as a former waitress, I am especially thrilled that she was caught, and that I helped," I said. I hated tip stealers. May they rot in Hell.

"So," Bob said, not-so-subtly shifting gears, "who was the guy that you brought with you the other night?"

"Oh, he's my plumber," I said. He laughed. "No, really; he's my plumber. He was fixing a bathtub leak in the apartment above mine, and we got to talking...anyway," I stopped, not wanting to make Bob jealous or have him question or suspect my feelings for Bobby, which were ambivalent at best at this point,

"I thought it would be nice to have an extra set of eyes from someone not connected to the store," I finished.

"Gotcha," he said, and I was grateful when he stopped asking me Bobby questions.

"So, should we talk about us now?" Bob said, leaning in closer.

"Yes," I began. "You know I really like you a lot, right?" and he said, "Well, I do now! Seriously, it's great to hear you say that. I like you a lot, too," he said.

"The thing is, I was sort of putting you off--"

He interrupted and said, "No kidding!"

"I was putting you off," I repeated, "for a couple of reasons. One is that I was just coming out of a long term relationship and it didn't end very well. I wasn't in any big hurry to start up anything with someone else." He nodded, leaning forward. Encouraged, I continued, "Also, I didn't think it was such a great idea to go out with someone that I work with, as you know." He nodded again.

"We aren't exactly in the same pond anymore, though," he objected, and I said, "Right. Things have changed, and that's part of why I asked you to meet me today," I said. "I am thinking about going out with you, but I just want to go out once in a while. I want us to have fun, to go out and do things sometimes," I said.

"I do too. So, what's the problem?" he asked. "I'm just saying that what I *don't* want is a physical relationship right away, so if that's not okay with you, I'd rather know now," I finished.

Before he'd even said anything, I was relieved. I felt proud that I'd finally asked for what I wanted in a relationship, took control before anything got out of hand, and set the terms of any future connection we might have. If he didn't agree to them, that was fine by me. He could find someone else. I wanted to save myself from any potential heartache. I wanted to keep things as uncomplicated as I possibly could.

A serious relationship meant sleeping with him. Sleeping with him meant going back on The Pill. Going back on The Pill meant worrying about taking it every day, worrying about when I forgot to take it, worrying about what I might catch from whomever else he is sleeping with if he ends up living up to his reputation. I didn't need that kind of grief. Plus, I wanted to be in charge this time. If I was sleeping with him, I would not be in charge of anything anymore. I'd be thinking about him when I set any goals, made any plans. Which means I would not be thinking about what was best for me.

I waited for him to respond. He took his time. "You know, I'm sure that we will be able to make this work," he said.

"We're both pretty busy with our jobs, and I am also just getting out of a long term relationship that didn't end well."

I didn't ask. I certainly was aware of his broken engagement. News like that travels fast. I had been trying not to think about the rumored reason for the break-up: girls on the side. If I wasn't going to bed with him, then I didn't need to concern myself with any of that. See? Uncomplicated.

"I think that taking it slow makes sense for me too. Let's do it and see how it goes," he said. I couldn't resist saying,

"Weren't you listening? That's just it; I don't want to 'do."

"I guess that was my subliminal wish coming out. Please disregard that. You know, for now," he said with a wicked grin.

That was it; I was in. Hey, he was trying to meet me halfway, or making a good show of it. Plus, he was so funny! I always had a good time when I was with him. He was always in a good mood, always laughing and joking. Oh, and did I mention, gorgeous? Now that we were reporting to different bosses in the corporate hierarchy, I wasn't worried that dating him would hurt me professionally. Well, not *as* worried.

"So are we seeing each other?" Bob asked.

"I think we are, if you agree with the terms of engagement," I said, laughing.

"I do. Great. Let's plan something right now, okay?" he said with enthusiasm. "Ever been to the Top of the Hub?" he asked. I hadn't, but I'd certainly heard of it. The Top of the Hub was the place to go if you were trying to impress someone, so I had to assume that he was trying to do that.

He was succeeding.

The Top of the Hub was a restaurant at the top of Prudential Building. No matter where you sit, you have an excellent view of the Boston skyline. Of course, it was very expensive; there was no chance of having dinner there for less than a hundred bucks, and that was without appetizers or dessert. I had always wanted to go there but I never thought it would happen. I certainly wasn't able to spend that kind of money on a dinner. Okay, so I was dying to go, but he didn't need to know that.

So, I tried to be low key and contain my excitement. "Oh, um, I think I've heard of it…" I trailed off. He smirked. He was on to me.

"Well, should we go there?" he asked.

"Um, sure, that would be okay," I said, barely containing myself. "Okay, fine. I'd love to." I admitted. "Thanks for thinking of it."

"When?" he asked. "Is next Friday night okay?"

I decided to let him work for it. "I'll check my calendar when I get home and I'll get back to you," I said sweetly.

"Fine, I'll be waiting," he laughed. "And I'll keep *my* calendar clear until I hear from you. I hope you can go." Don't worry, I thought to myself, there's no chance in the world that I'd miss going to the Hub.

"Oh, I do too," I said. "I'm glad we talked today," I said, gathering my things up to leave. "I'll call you about Friday night," I said.

"Well, what are you doing now?" he asked. "We could go grab something to eat." As much as I wanted to go, I reminded myself to go slow. Two dates in a row was fast.

"I'm meeting my friend for supper tonight, sorry," I said, and it was sort of true. I was planning to call Lorraine as soon as I got home and ask her to meet me to talk about Bob. I was hoping that she would be as excited for me as I was about where we were going, even if he might not be her first choice for the one I should be going there *with*.

"Okay, fine," he said, "let's go." He threw some cash on the check for our two coffees, then we left the shop together.

"Where's your car?" I asked him.

"Right next to yours," he said. We hugged, got in our cars, and went our separate ways.

For the time being.

Chapter 26: Donny? Not

It was a relief to have made the decision, right or wrong, to let my guard down and date Bob. I mean, it wasn't like I hadn't had any offers at all to go out since the Steven thing. Right after I'd moved into my new apartment I got a call from Lisa. "Hey, you know my friend Donny?" she asked.

"Sure, he helped us when I moved. Why?" I asked.

"Because he sure remembers you," she said, laughing.

"What? Why? What did he say?" I wondered.

"Well, he thought you were really nice and was hoping that you might want to go out sometime. I'm calling to see what you think, you know, before he puts his ego on the line and calls you himself," she replied.

"So," I said, "what you're really saying is he has no balls!"

"No, he just doesn't want to pursue you if you're not interested in being pursued. There's a difference. He knew about Steven," she added.

"How did he happen to know about Steven?"

"I told him. Why wouldn't I? Is it a secret?" she asked.

"No, I guess not. But it feels like it should be a secret. I'm surprised he'd want to get involved with me after that mess. How much did you tell him?" I asked.

"Not enough to scare him off, obviously," she said. "So, how about it? Can I tell him that it's okay to call you?" she persisted.

"I guess so. Sure," I said finally.

"Great. I'll let him know. I already gave him your number, but now I'll let him know that it's okay to use it," she said, and hung up.

Donny called the next day. He wanted to take me to Canobie Lake Park, an amusement park that was about an hour and a state away. I'd always like going to the amusement parks as a kid, so even though I'd never been to Canobie, I agreed. I had a soft spot for amusement parks for another reason: my parents had met at one. We arranged to go the following weekend, and he said he'd pick me up. I was into the whole feminist thing, but I didn't mind abdicating the driving component of it. Not because I thought that the man should be in the driver's seat, but because my lack of any semblance of a sense of direction made it impractical (not to mention fraught with peril) for me to be in charge of getting anyone anywhere.

He was nice enough. He was my sister's age, a year or so younger than I was. I knew he had a job, but I didn't know exactly what he did. He was tall and blond, on the thin side, and kind of bookish looking. When I had first met him, I remember thinking that his silver wire-rimmed aviator glasses really suited his face. I was still wearing contacts at the time, when I was out in public at least, but I felt the kinship. I had an affinity for any other people who were so nearsighted that they couldn't find their way across a room without their glasses or contacts. Like me.

He was soft spoken, and there were people who were less kind than I who would refer to him as effeminate, but after Steven and his psycho temper (like masculinity run amok), Donny was a complete relief. As I got ready to go, despite my initial reluctance, I realized that I was now sort of looking forward to it. I dressed in a practical way, suited to our destination: T-shirt, jeans, sneakers, sweatshirt in case it got cold. It was early fall, still fairly warm during the day, but the nights were more unpredictable. I watched for him from my window.

He pulled into the driveway, and I was ready. Happy to see him, even. Happy to see him until he got out of the car, that is. I couldn't believe my eyes. Now, I was no fashionista, and had never considered myself a snob about clothes. After all, I was the queen of the hand-me-downs, so I was not one to throw any stones, but oh! Oh! What was he wearing? I closed my eyes briefly, then reopened them. No, he was still wearing the same thing: brown corduroy pants, brown socks, brown sandals, long-sleeved flannel shirt, sleeves rolled up. Now, I might have been able to overlook the corduroy when it was still more early fall than late summer weather, but the sandals with socks? Unforgivable.

"Hi. Are you ready to go?" he asked in his soft voice, smiling at me. I took a deep breath and managed a half-hearted smile back. I nodded, but I wasn't ready to go at all. I was ready to turn around and go back in the house. Realizing that this was out of the question (he was my sister's friend after all), I grabbed my pocketbook, put on a brave face, and preceded to leave with him. One thing was for sure: no matter how short I was able to cut it, this was going to be a long night.

We talked a little in the car, and I tried to make the best of it. It would be dark at some point, so I shouldn't have to deal with the stares that his outfit was bound to attract as we walked around the park for the *entire* time that we were out. As we drove, I discovered that he was working as an accountant, a job that he liked well enough. He lived with his parents, which I couldn't really hold against him. After all, I was a year older and had just recently gotten my first place of my own. He was the middle of three kids in his family, and they were each a couple of years apart in age. I told him about my job managing the ice cream shop that I got after studying for four years for a completely different job at an expensive university. He was easy to talk to, and finally I started to relax a little bit. I might as well make the best of it; it would be our only date.

After we walked around some, we decided to eat some supper. We each got a burger and split an order of fries. We carried it over to a picnic table and ate our good-enough dinner, and when we'd finished, it was pretty dark. We walked around a little more, went on the mini-roller coaster and the bumper cars, and had a good-enough time. He really was a nice guy; it was a shame that his wardrobe choices left me gasping for breath. I tried to put it aside, but I just couldn't get past it. I mean, who wore socks with sandals? My God! It was just wrong! It made no sense! I might have seen him again if not for the fashion faux-pas, but instead it was all I could do to just get through the night.

When the park closed at 10PM, I could see his disappointment when I declined to his offer to "take a ride" before he took me home. "No thanks; I'm pretty tired. I have to get up early for work tomorrow, so I'd just as soon go home," I told him. I took a moment to appreciate my new BFF, the 'have to get up early for work' excuse. It made my life less complicated.

It was too bad, but I had to face facts: I was just too shallow to go out with him again. That's just how it was.

When we pulled up to my house, he parked in the driveway, turning off the motor. Uh-oh, I thought. Hello? There would be nothing going on here tonight. I certainly didn't want to mislead him in that way. He started to lean in for a kiss, and I turned my head just in time to receive it on my cheek instead of my mouth. "Thanks so much!" I said, and quickly backed away and got out of the car. "I had a nice time," I added, just to be kind, and before he could do anything unnecessary, like walk me to my door for yet another awkward moment, I booked it into the house.

As soon as I got settled, I called my sister. "So, how'd it go?" she asked.

"Oh my God! Who dresses him?" I asked.

"What do you mean?" she said. I filled her in.

"Oh," she said, "he's always been like that. No fashion sense," she said, chuckling. "You care about that?" she said.

"I'm sorry to say it, but it turns out that I do," I told her.

"How superficial of you," she said, "but hey, you tried, right? Sometimes things work out, sometimes they don't, No harm done?" she said. I agreed that there was no harm done, as long as no one had seen me with him, knowing that I was being mean but for the moment, not caring one bit.

Next up was a friend of my cousin's, and I had very mixed feelings from the start about agreeing to that one. First, it was a blind date for me, but not for him. My cousin Frank, whom I saw rarely anymore but with whom I'd used to spend a lot of time, had shown my picture to his friend at my sister's urging, and he'd been hounding Frank to set us up for weeks, or at least that's what he claimed. I hadn't ever seen his friend, and since he had no pictures of him to show me, I was completely in the dark about his appearance. I mean, come on! That's a pretty important dating detail, right? So I was at a disadvantage right off the bat.

Second, his name was Eugene. I had never known anyone with that name, and it sounded odd to even say it in my head. To me, it sounded like a small name. Don't ask me why. I told myself that I was being silly about it, but I had an uneasy feeling.

Frank was in the front seat with his girlfriend Gail, and Eugene was in the backseat when they arrived to pick me up. They beeped the horn for me to come out, as we'd agreed upon when we made the plans, but then Eugene got out of the car, meeting me halfway on the walkway. The irony of my thinking of his name as "small" was apparent to me right away, because by some strange coincidence, he turned out to be a little guy.

Little as in short. He was just barely a couple of inches taller than I was, and at five foot two, I hadn't encountered many guys that could boast that. Also, he had kinky, frizzy, dark blond hair, with freckles all over his face, and this was not a look that was appealing to me. His hands and feet were small, too. What unpleasantry might that foretell about his other body parts? I shuddered.

He opened the car door, got in, then slid over to make room for me. I got in, sitting behind Gail. I'd never even spoken to him before, because Frank and I made the plans on the phone a few days before. When he finally did speak, saying, "Hi. I'm glad you could come tonight," I was glad that at least his voice wasn't off-putting, his voice was fine. "That's *something*," I thought, thinking of the advice my friend Lorraine had given to me prior to the date.

"No matter what, find something about him to like. Anything. It just has to be one thing. His eyes. His teeth. His smile. Something. That way, if the other 99% of him is upsetting, whenever you start to have despairing thoughts that you'll never make it through the night, you can focus on that one thing about him that you decide is nice. Or nice enough." Okay, his voice was nice enough. I'd just listen to him talk as much as I could,

and avoid looking at him as much as I could. How long could it

take for us to go get pizza and sodas and get back home?

Chapter 27: Kill me

Well, it felt like it took forever, but in fact it was just three hours.

Three. Long. Hours. When it was finally over and I was home

sitting on my own couch reviewing the day, I was convinced of

one thing: I wasn't ever doing *that* again. Of course, it's possible

that there are people in the world that manage just fine on blind dates, maybe even meet their future spouses. It's just that I was sure that I was not one of them. No one who operated at the level of anxiety that I typically did had any business going out on a blind date. What was I thinking? Right now, I was thinking that desperation sure did make people do the strangest things.

Fast forward a few months, and now here I was, with two prospects that I was equally interested in, and who were both interested in me. Other than that, and of course, their name, the two Bobs couldn't really be more different. I thought that this was good. Bob from work was older than me by the largest margin of difference so far of any of the guys that I've dated. The thing was, I rarely, if ever, noticed it. He acted just like me. There were a couple of other differences, of course. I noticed that he had some grey hair at his temples, and he was the only one I'd been with that was a homeowner. Really, though, he was just a very big kid wrapped up in a GQ suit. He could be a little vain about his appearance, but it was kind of endearing, not off-putting.

Plus, if that was what it took for him to be so well put together, that was fine with me. Sometimes he could be a hyper, impulsive, driven mess, but usually I only saw that side of him at work, not in what I'd come to think of as our real lives. He was cerebral, living more in his mind than in his body most of the time, like me, and he could challenge me in ways that Bobby never could, both professionally, personally, and later, sexually. He was wooing me with words, and I loved that. He was a complicated Capricorn, sometimes kind of jaded, in a "been there, done it all" rut. The bottom line was that he could be a challenge, but this was a challenge that I was starting to feel ready to meet.

Bobby, on the other hand, was younger than I was, but only by about three years. He was calm and easy-going. He was not good at expressing himself with words, but was great at expressing himself with his body. Where Bob was great at telling me what he felt, Bobby was great at showing me. Bobby always had his hands on me somewhere: on my shoulder, taking my hand, on my back. He was simple and straightforward. He liked to be with me, and it showed in his gentle touches. He was most himself in his jeans and T shirts, and I was, too. I never had to worry about walking in heels (and potentially tripping and falling on my face) like I did most of the time when I was with Bob. Since my sneakers went great with my jeans and were all that was required, I didn't have to focus my attention so much on just remaining upright, like I did when I was with Bob. Bob liked sneakers too, it turned out, but in a different, kinkier context.

I decided that I liked the different "me's" that I became when I was with each of them, and decided to continue to see them both, but to kick it up a notch.

So, when Bob invited me to dinner at the Top of the Hub, I was nervous, but I jumped in with both heeled feet. I was so out of my element, but I was also feeling okay about it. Was this what is referred to as "growth"? I had a nice time shopping for a dress with Lorraine, who was being as supportive as she possibly could, satisfied that her continual cautions to "be careful", and "just don't believe everything he tells you" were being given the weight that they deserved. "I'll be careful, Lorraine," I patiently told her. "I know his reputation," I said another time. "It's just dinner; a big, expensive, high falutin' dinner, but dinner nonetheless," I joked. "Plus, hey, with all of the hours that I've spent commuting in and out of Boston over the years, it will be nice to get to have an aerial view of it," I say, smiling.

"Just as long as you keep your head on your shoulders," she couldn't resist admonishing me one more time, "and your face out of his pants."

"Lorraine! Really? I will. And thanks for coming with me today. Oh, and for all of the reminders," I said, letting just the tiniest hint of sarcasm creep in. She just made a face at me. "You're welcome," she says. "Come on, let's find you a dress," and she leads the way to the section marked "Petites".

We found a killer dress, a "cocktail dress", to be precise, which was a term I had never before heard but wondered if it boded well for my date.(what with the "cock" and the "tail" and all).

I suddenly felt a brief pang, a wave of nostalgia for my former ally, The Pill. Even though I was now officially re-virginized, I had a thought that it might not hurt to investigate that last frontier of pregnancy prevention that I had successfully avoided dealing with for all of these years: condoms.

We were on our way to the shoe department when I said to Lorraine, "Ever use condoms?" and she laughed right out loud.

"Are you kidding me? Of course I've used condoms. Hasn't everybody? You mean you haven't?" she says, all in one breath, before her laughter dissipated and was replaced by a look of surprise. "Wow, how have you gotten around without using condoms all of these years?" she asked, interested.

"I was on The Pill," I said, a bit defensively. "You went right to The Pill as your first choice?" she asked

"Well, yes. To be honest, it wasn't completely only *my* first choice," I said sheepishly. "My partner at the time refused to use condoms. 'It's like taking a shower with a raincoat on,' he said."

"And you slept with him anyway, even after he used that stupid old cliché on you?" she asked, incredulous.

"I did," I admitted. "I guess I had some self-esteem issues in college."

"Not to mention some self-confidence issues!" she said. I was starting to get a little irritated when she said, "Never mind; that's in the past. You're not like that anymore, thank God," she affirmed.

I'm relieved to hear her say this, because I don't think that I'm that passive girl anymore either. I was definitely stronger, and was much more in control of my life now, and hopefully, of my relationships. Graduating from college had given me not only a degree, but also, finally, thank God, some much needed confidence in my abilities. Some self-reliance. I finally felt like I'd accomplished something big, and I'd done it on my own.

Well, unless you count the large financial loans that I'd been given and would be paying back. You know, forever. I'd also gotten promoted twice at my job, based on the higher-ups noticing that I was doing good work. This gave me a huge boost.

If I could do these things, then I could certainly do other things. Like manage my personal life. Or so I hoped.

Once again, in keeping with the grand tradition, I put on my safe, little black dress for my dinner out. With Lorraine's help, I found a pair of strappy, high-enough-without-being-dangerous-for-me heeled black shoes that were comfortable enough to envision walking more than a dozen steps in before my feet started screaming in painful protest to take them off, already. I went out on a limb and bought a blue (not black! not black!) coat. Yep; living on the edge. I now considered myself edgy.

"What about makeup?" Lorraine asked.

"What about it?" I asked, truly puzzled.

"Well, you can't really get away with your sweep of blue Great Lash and the strawberry Lip Smacker at the Hub," she said. I guess she had a point, but I didn't know what to do about it. "Why don't you go to one of the department store make-up counters?" she said, a plan formulating. "They do makeovers for free to get you to buy their makeup. You don't *have* to buy it though. They'll still do the makeover."

"Sure, but what if I hate it? I don't want to look like a clown or anything," I say, worried.

"Just schedule it for the morning of the day you're going, if you can. That way, if it turns out hideously, you'll still have time to get home, wash it off, and figure out something else, but at least you gave it your best shot," she said.

That sounded like a hell of an idea to me, so I agreed to do it. "I'll go book it right now," I said. "Why not? We're here. Which one, though?" I asked her. I surveyed the makeup counters, realizing with a sinking feeling that there were at least a dozen options. "How do I pick?"

"Oh, come on," she said, and dragged me up to the Clinique counter, saying, "Excuse me…excuse me? My friend would like to schedule a makeup appointment," she said, and a lab-coated woman turned around, smiled, and said, "Sure, I'm free now, if you'd like," she said. I noted with some relief that she did not look like a clown in her makeup, and figured that, odds were, she had applied it herself. I took this as a good sign that I would not look clown-like either after she worked on me. I shook my head, "No, that won't work. "Okay, well then, when would you like to come in?" she asked.

"How about Friday morning?" I asked. I had taken the day off for the occasion, not really knowing why at the time, but now grateful that I had the foresight to realize that things come up.

"Ten o'clock?" she offered, after consulting her book.

"That would be great," I said.

"Okay, ten o'clock Friday. See you then!" she said in her cheerleader-y voice. I started to second guess this plan, when

Lorraine said, "Great! 'Bye!" as she grabbed my arm and dragged me away.

"What are you doing?" I asked, annoyed. "Getting you away from there before you cancel your appointment," she said.

"So, how did you pick the Clinique counter?" I asked.

"Well, they have a reputation for being understated, which I thought you would like," she began.

"Okay, what else?" I asked, sensing there was more to her reasoning.

"They were the closest counter to where we were, and I wanted to get you over there to schedule an appointment before you changed your mind!" she laughed, and after a moment, I laughed with her.

"Yeah, you get me. I *was* thinking of bolting," I admitted, smiling. "You got me there just in time. Seriously, though," I continued, "thanks for all of your help today. It was much more fun, and much less nerve wracking than it would have been if I'd come alone," I finish.

"Hey, don't mention it," she said, giving me a side hug.

"You can reward me by telling me every detail of your night out, and if you decide to bring home a doggie bag, I get half!" she said, laughing. "Deal," I said. "You earned it."

Chapter 28: Bob and Bobby

So, the day for my date with Bob arrived. I was completely psyched. I had gone to the mall earlier for my makeover. Not something that I would wear every day, but for a night out? It was excellent. I looked great. I made an effort with my hair. I even broke out the curling iron. It was worth it.

He picked me up at my apartment, and we started driving into Boston. I was impressed with how easily he navigated the traffic while still carrying on a conversation with me. I'd have been too busy hyperventilating to simultaneously talk if *I* was driving. We got into town pretty quickly, or else I must have been having fun, since the time did fly. Soon enough we were at our table, overlooking the city,

The date was a big success. The view was amazing. The food was incredible. He ordered fish, and I ordered filet mignon, which was my go-to meal in any fancy restaurant. We talked easily, and before I knew it the dessert menus were presented. "I couldn't eat even one more bite!" I said.

"Let's split something then," he said, smiling.

"No chance," I say, then offering a compromise, continue, "but I'll have a cup of coffee to keep you company.

"Two coffees," he said, handing back the menus to the waiter.

"See? I can be flexible," he says.

"Are you looking to score some points?" I ask, feeling the blush even as the words leave my mouth. Why would I phrase it that way? He laughed, and shot back, "Yes! Every kind of points I can get!" I appreciated his humor in rescuing me, as well as his candor in letting me know what he wanted. I wanted the same thing, but while he was on the fast track, I was on the slow track. I intended to remain there, at least for the time being.

I lowered my eyes and peered up at him through my lashes, but said nothing. Our coffees came, and I watched him put enough cream and sugar into his to rival Frosted Flakes. I raised an eyebrow. "How do you drink coffee without adding the vital nutrients?" he asked.

"Ummm, hot?" I replied.

"Cute," he said.

"Hey, I'm having a great time," he said, turning serious.

"Me too," I smile.

"Let's do this again, okay?" he said, and I nodded, "Definitely." "How about next weekend?" he asked, and even though my first impulse was to say yes, I stopped. I took a breath. Go slow, I reminded myself.

"I can't, but how about the one after that?" I countered. If one week was fast, then doubling that could be slow.

"Two weeks?" he said. "I'm not sure if I can wait that long, but yes, okay." I wasn't so sure that I could wait that long either, but I let it stand. "Okay, great. What do you want to do?" he asked.

"Surprise me," I said. If he wants me so badly, let him do the work.

After we got back to my apartment, I could tell he was dying for me to ask him in. I knew that would be a mistake. It was just too big of a temptation, too big of a risk, to be in my apartment alone with him so close to so many horizontal surfaces. "Well, thanks for tonight," I said, gathering up my things, "I loved every minute of it."

"Me too," he said, leaning over to my side of the car for a kiss. I let him kiss me, then I began to kiss him back. Wow, he can kiss, I thought. This was going to be harder than I thought. Hopefully all of this sacrifice would be worth it in the end.

"'Bye!" I said, finally, reluctantly, extracting myself from him and exiting the car. I ran to my front door and went in before I had a chance to lose my resolve, and before he had a chance to follow me.

One thing that I knew for sure was that my old way of doing things had not brought me much joy. What's Albert

Einstein's definition of insanity? Doing the same thing over and over again and expecting different results, something like that. I hoped that my new, different approach to men and relationships would produce new, different (read: better) results.

One thing was certain: The more time that we spent together, the more I liked him, so that was definitely a good thing. I liked it that he watched his alcohol intake; he kept it to one drink at the most when we were out, sometimes foregoing alcohol entirely and ordering water or a Coke. He didn't smoke, and as far as I could tell, he didn't gamble. I guess, if the rumors were to be believed, women were his only vice, emphasis on the 'were'.

The next day, I received a call from Bobby. "I've been thinking about you," he said, "and want to see you again. How's this weekend look for you?" he asked. I mentally thanked myself for the lucky foresight of putting Bob off for two weeks, leaving me free to accept Bobby's invitation.

"I'm open. What did you have in mind?" I asked him.

"How about we just take a ride down to Revere Beach, get a roast beef at Kelly's?" he asked.

"That sounds great. I'm in," I replied.

"Okay, pick you up around ten Sunday morning?" he asked. "I'll be ready," I said.

Getting ready for this date was quite a different matter from getting ready for my dinner out with Bob. For one thing, I certainly already had appropriate attire for going to the beach. It was late spring, so jeans and a long sleeved T shirt and a sweatshirt would do it. As an afterthought, I grabbed my denim jacket. It would be cold at the ocean.

No heels required for this outing; my sneakers would do the job. Also, no makeovers were required. I could just go as I was, which was a huge relief, actually. No extra time or expense required to go out with Bobby. This also meant no extra angst. I was not nervous around him the way I was sometimes with Bob. I felt relaxed, and that was sort of a new feeling for me. In the past, I was always pretty nervous before, during, and after going out with a guy. Before: What to wear? What to say? Makeup, hair…all were concerns. During: Did I look okay? What should we talk about? Is there anything in my teeth? After: Did I do or say anything stupid? Did he have fun? Will he call me again? With Bob, I had a lot of these concerns racing through my mind.

With Bobby, I did not. I had not invested much, so I had little to lose. What if he doesn't call me again after we go out? Well, so what? I was becoming more independent. I had a great job, a great apartment, a best friend. I was seeing two guys, both of whom I really liked, and who seemed to really like me. I was being pursued instead of being in pursuit. I felt like I was finally dealing with the male sex from a position of strength, not weakness. It did not exactly feel comfortable yet, but hopefully it would in time.

He picked me up Sunday morning like we planned. "Hey, nice to see you," he said. "You look great, as always," he told me. I smiled at him, saying, "So do you," and I meant it. It was true. In his jeans, his beat-up work boots, T shirt, and sweat jacket, he looked so handsome that I could burst with lust just from looking at him. Bob was handsome, but Bobby had …something, something that clicked with me. I was interested enough to keep exploring the relationship to see where it went. I was especially impressed that he had quit smoking cold turkey, just to get me to go out with him. I knew that was no easy feat. Both of my parents smoked, and both had tried and failed to quit often enough for me to see how frikkin' hard it was. He was working hard to get me. This gave me a good feeling.

We were lucky to have a sunny day on Sunday, and we headed straight for the ocean. I loved it there this time of year. The summer crowds had not arrived, so there was plenty of room to move and breathe. We could park without difficulty, and soon we had a front row seat watching the waves. He unbuckled his seatbelt, asking, "Want to get out and sit on the wall?" and I nodded. I was happy that he asked.

Being close to the ocean was a very good thing. It reminded me of when I was a little girl. In the summers, I would spend a week at Nana See's, and I always got my own room. Her house was within walking distance of the ocean. Because she used to rent out rooms back in the day to make ends meet when her husband was sick and unable to work, the rooms all were numbered and had a color theme. There were six bedrooms in all; four on the second floor and two on the third. My room was always the green room on the second floor, between the bathroom and Nana See's room. I loved going there.

One especially great thing was my hair always looked better after I'd washed it there than it ever did at home. First I thought it must be her shampoo. She used Prell, so I started using that at home, but I never got the same results. Then I heard that it was actually something about having her town having hard water or something like that. I never did find out for sure, but I enjoyed it while it lasted.

I walked down to the beach frequently when I was there, but Nana always insisted on accompanying me, to make sure that I was okay. That translated into feeling loved and protected, a feeling that ultimately I came to associate with the ocean itself.

For a while, when I was sitting on the wall with Bobby at Revere Beach looking out at the ocean, I had that sense of well-being that was so fleeting in my adult life. It was hard to know if the feeling was coming from within me, or from him. I decided finally that it didn't matter; what mattered was that I felt it. I took it as a good sign.

We sat there on the wall for a half an hour or so, with his arm around me the entire time. I was in no hurry to move. Well, I was in no hurry until he asked, "Are you getting hungry?"

I nodded, "I'm always hungry."

"Me, too. Let's go get something to eat," he said. I was up in a second, and following him across the street to Kelly's.

He studied the menu for a few minutes, then asked, "Do you know what you want?" I always got the same thing when I went there, but he didn't need to know that. We gave our orders, then I heard him add on one more thing: a black and white frappe, one of my favorite things, but he couldn't have known that. "For us to split," he said, and shrugged.

"You did good," I told him.

Yeah, baby.

.

Chapter 29: Lo weighs in

After we got our food, we took it back to the car and got inside to

eat. Seagulls love French fries (well, they love everything,

actually) and would have dive-bombed us to get our food,

making us miserable. We drove around for a while after that, and

I was having such a nice day that I was surprised when I noticed the time…almost 5pm! We'd been out for hours, and not once did I wonder what time it was, worry about what to say next, or wish I was somewhere else. Bobby was simple, straightforward, and fun to be with…"I could get used to this," I thought. "We could stop for an ice cream on the way home if you want," he offered. Ah, a man after my own heart.

"Yes, that sounds great," I said.

We stopped off at the Dairy Joy on the way home from the beach, an older, white domed building with walk up windows. Since it was the off-season there wasn't any line, so we got our cones right away. It felt completely decadent to be having an ice cream cone after a lunch that included a frappe, but I didn't care. It was fun to do something different with someone who was placing no demands on me of any sort. It was a huge relief, actually.

After that, we headed back to my apartment. "I really had a nice time today," I told him.

"Me too," he said. He got out of the car, then came around to my side and opened the door. This was a nice gesture; it didn't feel like a power struggle like it did when Steven used to do it. Bobby had nothing to prove. It was like he just suddenly thought, "Hey, why don't I open her door for her?" Like it was no big deal. I got out, smiling. He didn't talk much. He walked with me up to the door, and to my surprise I heard myself saying, "Want to come in for a minute?"

What did I just say? Oh my God! I was supposed to be treading lightly! Going slow! He might get the wrong idea about my invitation, read things into it that I didn't intend! He smiled and nodded. "Okay, sure. Just for a minute though. I have to get home," he said, but made no explanation about why. I didn't ask, but I was relieved to hear him say that. Keep it simple; keep it simple, I thought, repeating my new mantra to myself.

We entered through the back door, and went into the kitchen. He pulled out a chair at the table and sat down, legs extended. He took up a lot of space. He was over six feet, and although his legs weren't that long, he had a lot of bulk. I remembered that he'd told me that he goes to the gym, plus all that construction work. Oh yeah, it was working for him. Hell, it was working for me! Muscles looked good on him. I was not typically a fan of the muscle-bound muscle-heads but fortunately, his muscles were, um, in the right places.

"Something to drink?" I asked, but he shook his head.

"I actually want to check your bathroom," he said, getting up. "Huh?" I asked. "I wanted to check to see how my work was holding up," he said. Wow. Conscientious. How many plumbers follow up with an in-person satisfaction survey?

"Well, you know the way," I joked. "I do," he said, and with that he up. I followed him and waited in the doorway as he stood on the toilet and inspected the ceiling. "I haven't noticed any drips," I said. And I would have, because they usually hit me on the head as I was sitting on the toilet, a tidbit that I certainly wasn't going to share with him. "

Well, I do good work," he said matter-of-factly. I wondered what other things he might be good at.

I turned to leave the bathroom, and he came right up behind me, so quietly that I didn't hear him, but I sure felt him. His arms came around me, encircling me. He was so warm! I guess muscles throw off a lot of heat. It was a wonderful surprise to feel his arms around me. I turned to face him and put my arms around his neck. He stooped down until we were nose to nose, and I had a clear view of his bright blue eyes. We breathed at each other for a moment, and then he kissed me. It was a long, slow, involved affair. Did I say that I didn't have much invested in Bobby? Well, this was the moment that it changed. Right then. He was a great kisser. Better than great. The kind that made you weak in the knees. The kind that left you breathless. The kind that left you wanting more.

After the kiss ended, he pulled back, smiled, and said, "See you," and he waved and let himself out. I just stood there for a few minutes, basking in the afterglow. "Okay," I thought, "there's no going back now."

I had no experience with dating two guys at once, but I was about to acquire some on the job training. It was an interesting coincidence, I thought, that they both had the same name. I mean, what were the odds? It just made it more interesting, as far as I was concerned.

Lo thought it was hilarious. "Are you kidding me? First Bob and now Bobby? Well, at least you're consistent!" she laughed. "Seriously, though, how are you managing it?" she asked. "Well," I explained, "I sort of worked out a schedule by accident. I only have one or two days off a week, so I have to be careful with my time. When Bob took me to the Top of the Hub, he wanted to see me again the following weekend, but in the interests of not repeating past mistakes, I told him I had plans and we made a date for two weeks out. Then Bobby called, and asked me for Sunday, which I had off and since I wasn't doing anything, I said okay. I was interested to see if he was still not smoking, and as near as I could tell, or should I say 'smell'? Ha! He wasn't. Isn't. Next weekend is Bob, and if Bobby calls, I'll see him the one after that. So it turned into a weekly date with the guys on a bi-weekly rotation schedule!" I finished, triumphant.

She was looking at me quizzically. "So, do they know about each other?" she asked.

"Well, yes and no. Remember when I did that undercover job for Bob at his store when he was trying to catch his thief?" She nodded. "Well, Bobby came with me when I did that, so they have seen each other, but neither one knows that I'm going out with the other," I finished.

"Well, be careful. I bet the two of them would not be the least bit happy to find out that you are seeing the other." "Well, that's kind of too bad for them, right? I mean, there are no exclusivity agreements between me and either of them. I don't ask them who else they are going out with, and I don't really want to know anyway," I said. "As long as things are going along okay, I'm satisfied with my strategy," I felt a little on the defensive, but wasn't sure why.

"Hey, it's fine by me," Lorraine said hurriedly. "I'm not throwing any stones from *my* glass house." I gave her a look.

"Got a shady past that I don't know about?" I asked.

She just smiled. "Honey, you don't know the half of it."

"Well, I sure would like to," I said. "Maybe you can give me some pointers if I run into any trouble," I added.

"Well, I have been a man multi-tasker at times in the past," she admitted, eyes cast down, full of sorry. Then she laughed. "Nothing to worry about. Usually they're so wrapped up in themselves and what *they* have going on the side that they don't have time to wonder about what *you've* got going on the side. Know what I mean?" she said.

"I think so," I nodded."

"Plus, there's one surefire giveaway when they're up to no good," she continued. "Really? That's convenient! So, what is it? How do you know?" I ask.

"They start accusing you of stuff. They'll start asking you where you're going, what you're doing when you aren't with them. When you start getting a lot of that line of questioning, it's a pretty sure bet that they're trying to distract you from their own wrong-doing," she said.

"So, when the pot starts calling the kettle black, watch out. Is that it?" I asked.

"That's it!" she nodded. "You got it. Now you're all set. Go get 'em."

"Fine," I told her. "Thanks for the advice." "No problem," she said. "Want to know who I'm rooting for?" she asked.

"For what?" I ask, not following the question.

"Rooting for to win the Bebe race!" she said.

"Oh. Sure, I guess so. Who?" I ask.

"Bobby," she said.

"Well, I guess that doesn't surprise me much," I said. "It's no secret that Bob isn't your best friend or anything," I said. "Hey, are you sure that you never went out with Bob? Or that you don't want to go out with him now?" I asked, accusingly.

"I never did; I never do, and I never will," she assured me. "It's not because I don't like him or his past escapades that I didn't pick him to win," she said

"Well, why then?" I persisted.

"It's just that you sound more like yourself when you talk about Bobby than when you talk about Bob. You also seem more relaxed about him. It makes me think that, in the long run, you'll be happier with him," she said, shrugging her shoulders. "But, hey, what do I know?" she said. "See which one *you* choose. That's the important thing. Give yourself plenty of time," she said.

"Oh, I definitely plan to do that," I said, and I meant it. I had no agenda other than to have fun and keep it simple, sista. I had my troubleshooting info from Lorraine. I had my bi-weekly schedule. I was good to go.

Meanwhile, work was still going very well. I had just had my annual review and got gold stars. I had settled into my job so well that it didn't feel new anymore. It felt comfortable. I was enjoying the freedom of having almost complete control over not only my personal life, but my work life as well. In theory, I had the same benefit with my job as a restaurant manager, but in practice, it wasn't true. There were always the demands of the business that could dictate when I had to work. For example, if I didn't have a supervisor to cover a Friday night closing shift, then I was it. The manager was always the Plan B. If anything went wrong ever with anything, I would get a call.

As a Training Supervisor, however, there was none of this. No store opening and closing schedule that I was responsible to cover, no equipment failures that I had to respond to, so when I was off, I was off. No one would be calling me for any reason, thank God. My time really was my own. It was probably the best perk associated with this job. There was nothing like being off from work and knowing that you truly were off, not off with strings attached. It felt luxurious. It felt amazing; kind of like my personal life was shaping up to be.

I was looking forward to my next night out with Bob. And then with Bobby.

Chapter 30: Shopping with Lo

During the week, Bob called to ask if I was up for something big this weekend. My mind immediately turned to impure thoughts, as it was wont to do whenever the word "big" popped up. I found myself hesitating. Did I really want to know? I decided that I did. "What did you have in mind?" I asked. "How about we go see a

show at the Music Hall?" he asked, in a 'ta da!' tone of voice.
"What music hall, The Wang?" I asked.

"No. The New York City Music Hall," he corrected me. I laughed. "No, I'm serious. Would you like to go?" he said. I considered this for a minute.

"How would we do that? By the time we drove down there, it would be time to turn around and come back," I said, mentally calculating the commuting time from here to there.

"No," he said, patiently. "We would take the airport shuttle to the city, then a cab to the show," he explained.

Seriously? Holy shit! I thought about it for another moment, and then said, "Sure, let's go." Once again, I surprised myself. I had never been on a plane before, but I didn't admit that to him. I didn't want to call attention to our age difference in any way. Even though the years usually didn't seem like such a big deal, occasionally it did.

"Great. I'll pick you up that morning, and then we'll head to the airport," he said. "But what will you do with your car?" I asked. "I can park it there in the lot. There's a charge, but it's not that much," he said. "Well, great! See you this weekend!" I said, and hung up.

And then the worrying began. What should I wear? Oh my God, I hadn't even asked him what show we were seeing! I was so surprised by what he was proposing that it hadn't even occurred to me to ask. I guess it didn't matter that much, but I didn't want to appear completely unsophisticated. I decided to check with my worldlier friend.

"Ever been to a Broadway show?" I asked Lorraine.

"Yep. You?" she asked, and I shook my head, but added, "but you can ask me again next week."

"Oh, really? You're seeing The Female Odd Couple?" she asked, excitedly. Yay, Lorraine! I knew I could count on her!

"Perfect! Yes! I guess so. I forgot to ask him what the show was, so thanks for telling me!" I breathed. I was feeling a little better now. At least I knew the name of the show; now I could put that worry aside and concentrate fully on my fear of flying.

"When are you going?" she asked.

"Sunday. I have to find something to wear," I said.

"Oh, that's no big deal; there's no real dress code. You can't go looking like a slob or anything, but otherwise it's kind of open. 'Business casual' should cover it. Are you going with Bob?" she asked.

"I am; how'd you know?" I said, smiling.

"Well, I thought it was more likely to be him than the plumber, plus I was pretty sure that you hadn't taken on a third guy at this point," she said, smirking, "although I'm not ruling it out for the future. Are there anymore available Bobs in the area? Kidding! Kidding!" she finished, laughing. "You'll love it," she said. "I heard it was great. Sally Struthers is in it, and Rita Moreno, too, I think."

"Once I figure out what I'm wearing, I'll feel better about talking about the cast, okay?" I said.

"Fine, come on. Take me to your closet!" she said. I'll follow you to your house, because I have to be back by six." We left the shop where we had been having coffee and she followed me home.

We immediately got down to business. "Let's see what you've got," she said, and started rummaging through my closet. "You've got a ton of great stuff in here! There must be something you can wear to the show," she muttered, more to herself than to me. I stood back, keeping a respectful distance. "Hmmm. Hey, wait a minute, what's this?" she said, delicately extracting a black dress from the chaos that is my closet.

"Oh, I remember that dress!" I exclaim, happy to see it. "I haven't worn that in a while," I said, mostly because I couldn't find it, but also because I hadn't gone many places lately that called for a dress like that. It was a simple black, no sleeved, A-line dress that came right to my knee. "This is really cute," she said. "You could totally wear this. Got any shoes to go with it? Boots?"

"Um, I think so…" I trailed off.

"Are they somewhere in there?" she asked sternly, pointing toward the closet. I nodded, hanging my head. "I guess I'd better find them now, then. I have a feeling that you aren't going to be venturing in there anytime soon, right?" she asked. I nodded, sheepish. "Fine, I'll find them, but you owe me," she said.

"I know. It's worth it," I said. After she rummaged around a bit, she *did* find them. "Wow, you actually found them in two minutes flat!" I said, admiringly. "You're good!"

"You can throw those compliments around as much as you want; you still owe me!" she said.

"Okay. Next time we go out, I'll buy," I offered.

"You can buy me dessert; how's that?" she countered. "I'll even split it with you," she said. "Deal!" I said, happy to have had her help.

"Now, what about flying?" I asked her.

"What about it?" she asked. "Oh, no…haven't you ever been up in a plane?" she asked. I shook my head.

"Didn't your parents at least do the Disney thing when you were growing up?" she asked. Lorraine came from a more affluent family than I did, so I had to cut her some slack when it came to these kinds of things.

"Uh, no. Have you retained nothing that I've told you about my upbringing?" I asked. We were on food stamps, social security, and Big Nana's good graces. We were essentially homeless for the latter half of my first decade of life. Where would a plane ride to Disney fit into this picture?"

"Okay, I gotcha. Forget I said anything. What do you want to know about the plane ride?" she asked.

"Well, are you afraid at all of flying?" I began.

"No. I never think about it," she said.

"When it's time to get on the plane, then I briefly think about what can go wrong while the stewardess gives us the plan in case we have to ditch the plane, then I don't think about that anymore either. Here's a tip: get a cocktail as soon as they offer

them up. Or, call your doctor for some Valium; that works too,"
she counseled.

"I'm not calling the doctor for Valium to fly," I object.

"Well, I guess I could give you one of mine, just in case,"
she said, then started rummaging through her purse.

"Have you been flying lately?" I ask.

"No, why?" she replied.

"Well, do you just carry your pre-flight Valium around
everywhere you go?" I ask.

"Sure do," she said. "You actually never know when you
might need it! See? I need to give you one right now. What if I
didn't have it with me?" she responded, smug.

I decided to let it drop. She tapped two pills out into the
cap from the bottle. "Go get a baggie from the kitchen." I did as I
was told, wondering why. I returned from the kitchen and handed

over the requested item. She emptied the pills into the baggie and closed it up. "Why two? Should I take them both?" I asked. "No! The dose is one pill, but you have to fly home, too, don't you? You are coming back?" she joked. I nodded. "Now put those away until you need them," she said. I tucked it into my wallet, uncomfortable. I hoped I'd forget they were there.

"Anything else?" I asked.

"Now you're just looking for trouble," she said.

"What about the take off and the landing?" I asked.

"You'll be fine; stop worrying about it. People fly back and forth to New York on that shuttle a dozen times a day," she added. I nodded again, somewhat appeased. For now, at least. "Oh, bring a sweater," she said. "It can get pretty cold on the plane. Sometimes they have blankets, so if you forget it, it's not the end of the world," she finished. Blankets on the plane? That was interesting. I filed that thought away to ponder later on.

The day came, and I got up early to get ready. I showered, soaped, shampooed, moisturized, and then got into some black lingerie, black nylons, black slip. I put on my little black dress, then applied a bit of makeup. It had been a long time since I'd worn this dress, I thought. Too long. I checked my reflection in the full length mirror that hung on the back of my bedroom door, turning so I could inspect the dress from every angle. I looked good, thank God. I was a little nervous that the dress might be too tight; after all, it had been months since I'd had it on, but I guess having a job that kept me moving a lot had a side benefit: it was keeping my weight in check. If anything, it might have been a little loose on me now. Good, I thought, I'll have plenty of room to eat.

I put in my emerald stud earrings, my birthstone. These were my favorite earrings and I wore them most days. I had a gold Seiko watch that my parents gave me when I graduated from high school, and I rummaged around in my jewelry box to locate it. I was not a big jewelry wearer after the experience I'd had with Steven. He liked to give me jewelry as gifts and I associated it with that bad experience and usually would forgo it.

Tonight, I changed my mind. I found the watch and put it on. Then on impulse, I added a necklace that consisted of a single pearl that hung on a thin gold chain that my maternal grandmother had given to me. It looked perfect against the black dress. I remembered about the sweater that Sheila suggested that I bring and located a black one in a dresser drawer. The sweater came from my other grandmother, Nana See.

I loved this sweater. I had a white one just like it. I never knew where she bought them. I always looked for them whenever I went to Jordan Marsh or Gilchrist's and I never saw them. She never told me either, but she always made sure I had a black one and a white one at all times, even if it meant she was giving me hers. One thing left to do: find my evening purse and transfer my essentials to it. This only took a few minutes. I checked my watch; I had about a half an hour before he came.

I decided to try to read a little, and got my book out of the briefcase that I used for work. I had spent about ten minutes staring at the same sentence when something that had been nagging away in the back of my thoughts broke through…the Valium! I had forgotten about it! I left it in the walled I used in my everyday purse. I quickly retrieved it and slipped it into the hidden inside pocket of the evening purse. That was close, I thought. Just then, I heard Bob pull up. I ran to go to the bathroom one last time. I finished just as he was approaching the front door, which I had left open for him.

Just then I had another thought: oh no! What if I had to go to the bathroom on the plane?

Chapter 31: Bob, Mile high

I pushed that thought out of my mind; no use going there. I heard him come in the house and call to me. "Be right there!" I yelled. I took one last look in the mirror and decided that I looked damned good, and went to greet him. "Are you ready? We really should get moving if we're going to catch our flight," he said.

"I'm ready; let's go," I replied. I was in no mood to sit around here. I wanted to get the actual flight part of the date over with. I was still stressing about that whole thing, but didn't want to let him know it. A spontaneous thought came to mind: why not have a small drink after boarding? Nothing that would induce incoherence or anything. Just enough to take the edge off. I decided to take this brilliant step as soon as possible after boarding and before my anxiety attack kicked into full gear.

We got to the airport quickly. I was fairly disoriented at first, but it really didn't matter much. Bob knew where to park, what a "terminal" was and which one we needed to get to, and he also had the whole "boarding pass" thing sorted out. I basically just followed close by and let him handle things. Why not? He had invited me, after all. It was a blessing, since I had not one clue about what we were doing or how we were getting it done. Having so little up-front knowledge was a bit disconcerting, but soon I let that go. Hey, I could give up the control once in a while. I was comforted by the thought of that aperatif.

Before I knew it, we were buckled in and ready to go. I surreptitiously watched for the flight attendant. Bob was saying something about how I should have taken the window seat so that I could watch the take-off, but I just shook my head. "You seem like you are getting much more out of it than I would," I said wryly, and continued to stare at the fixed point straight in front of me, just a little to the right of where the flight attendant's head was as she gave the preflight instructions, words that I was doing my level best to Tune. The Fuck. Out. I mentally covered my ears and repeated 'lalalalalalalalalalalalalalalalala' in my head.

Finally, I ordered my drink. "That sounds great," Bob said. "I'll have the same." They were served to us shortly thereafter. After about ten minutes, I noticed a warm feeling spreading throughout my body, a liquid sort of feeling that I supposed was the alcohol doing its job. Good thing, too. I had been holding myself together but I didn't know for how long I'd be able to keep it up. Bob seemed not to realize what I was going through, which was fine with me. I didn't want him to suddenly find himself superior to me in any capacity, for any reason. I wanted him to continue to view me as an equal, which would not be possible if he were babysitting me during a panic attack on a plane ride. I was feeling much better *now* though. The edge was off and I was ready to date him. Hard. Heh, heh, heh.

A bit later, they came back around with snacks. Who knew? I love snacks. Everything was going very well. We were just chatting about the workweek that had gone by, the one that was approaching, and reviews that he had read about the show that we were going to see. I was completely relaxed. I wasn't even worried about finding the bathroom anymore. The nice flight attendant had helpfully pointed it out to me as part of her opening remarks at the beginning of the flight, just before I stopped listening. In my complacency, I had forgotten one thing: for every take off, there is a landing.

When the pilot came on the speaker to announce that landing was imminent, I was actually surprised. An hour hadn't even past yet, but then I started regretting my choice to decline that second alcoholic drink during the flight. I felt my anxiety rising, but was reassured sensing it wouldn't get out of control. I found Bob's hand and grabbed it, tightly. He misunderstood my intentions, because he leaned over, put his free hand around my waist as best he could manage under the circumstances, and kissed me. This was a good thing, as it turned out. I loved kissing him, and it was an effective distraction as well as a reminder about why I was there. We kissed for a minute more as I allowed his available hand to roam freely until I noticed the male passenger in the seat across the aisle from us glancing over, smiling big at me. Pig.

As we were landing, I hoped God would excuse the absence of hearing from me for the last, oh, ten years or so as I mentally said a few quick Our Father's until we were safely back on the ground. I was pretty happy when the direction to unbuckle and then exit the plane came over the speaker. Gladly, I thought, although I had to admit that it was not as bad as I expected it to be. I would not let myself think about the return trip until I had to. For now, I decided to just anticipate the night ahead. To concentrate on the next thing, and then the next thing, and the next thing.

He hailed a cab and we jumped in. Yeah, I could get used to this.

I was all about the food usually, and today was no exception, so I was just a tiny bit disappointed when Bob said, "I'm starving, but we don't have that much time. Do you mind if we just grab a hot dog from one of the carts? They're excellent actually. I sometimes do that when I'm in New York even if I do have other options."

Oh, well, might as well make the best of it. "Sure, why not?" I said, wondering and hoping that my little evening bag had a dozen or so napkins left in it from the last time I used it for a night out. Usually, I did remember to re-stuff it. Napkins were something that a girl who could rarely eat without getting some portion of it on her clothing needed. Napkins in great supply had a way of calming the soul.

The hot dog *was* excellent, surprisingly, and I did manage to keep it off of my clothing, and off of his as well (bonus!). The napkin safety net was not needed. "We have just enough time to make it to the theater," he said, "if you feel like walking fast." "Sure, let's walk fast. It's nice out tonight," I agreed.

We were there in no time. I'm not sure what I expected, exactly, but it was much better than my vague mental picture.

There were so many people there that I couldn't believe it. I'd certainly been in plenty of crowds over the years, but nothing approaching this magnitude. Most of the crowds that I had encountered were at concerts for rock bands…an entirely different genre of people, with an entirely different agenda, not to mention entirely different pre-event activities. These people were older, much better dressed, and probably richer.

I was excited to see a Broadway show. I was impressed with being flown to New York City for just one day, not even an entire day, to see it. I wondering how many other women he had flown to New York like this, but then pushed that thought to the back of my mind. Who cares? Keep it simple. Whatever he had done in the past had nothing to do with me in the present. I was here with him now, and I was happy about it.

Rita Moreno played "Felix" and Sally Struthers played "Oscar". I wasn't very familiar with Moreno, but I loved Sally from "All in the Family" on TV, and she gave an excellent performance as "Oscar". To say that this was one of the best nights of my life so far would not be overstating it. During the intermission, I excused myself to go to the ladies room and when I returned, I saw that he had gotten us two glasses of champagne. Nice.

He easily hailed another cab to get us to the airport. Just like in the movies: he barely had his hand up and a Yellow Cab veered out of traffic to stop for him at the curb. Somehow, I thought it would require a bit more effort in real life to do this. It made me wonder again about how practiced he was and it was unlikely to be from hailing them at home, that's for sure.

We were boarding the plane to return home. I thought I would be able to skip the cocktail. I wasn't sure if I needed it this time, since I had that glass of champagne at the show. I decided to risk skipping it. When the drink cart arrived, I opted instead for just water this time. I felt great. Expansive. Happy. Like I wanted

to do something to thank Bob for taking me, but I wasn't sure

what. After the drink cart passed another stewardess came around

asking people if they wanted a blanket or a pillow. "Why are they

offering those?" I asked Bob.

"Since it's later in the evening, sometimes people want to

try to grab a quick nap on the way back," he explained. "I never

use 'em, but go ahead if you want to," he said. And just like that,

I had an idea.

"Sure, thanks. I'll take a blanket," I said when it was

offered by the flight attendant. Bob looked over at me and

smiled, then went back to looking out the window. I had turned

him down again when he offered me the window seat for the

return trip. I was so not interested in watching the ground fall

away from us as we ascended into the air. No thanks. So, while

he scanned the exterior of the plane, I was scanning the interior of the plane. I realized that it was much less filled than the previous flight had been. Probably two-thirds of the plane was empty. Also of note was that we were in the back of the plane. I was sort of distressed by this at first, as I tried to recall plane crash statistics. Wasn't it the people over the wings that always made it, and the ones in the back that always perished?

But then I had a better thought to replace this morbid one: if we were in the back of the plane, and we had a blanket, and it was dark (they had turned the cabin lights out after they completed the rounds with the blankets and pillows), all of this added up to camouflage and a lot of privacy. Now, that was something a girl could work with. That was something that could help me formulate a "Thank you" plan.

I turned to Bob. "Ever heard of the 'Mile High Club'?" I asked, smiling sweetly.

Bob peered at me from the corner of his eye. "Um, what?" he asked.

"The Mile High Club," I repeated.

"Heard of it?" "Of course I've heard of it. Why?" he replied.

"Well, are you in it?" I persisted.

"Am I in it? No, I'm not in it!" he said, turning to squarely face me now, and he actually seemed to be a little flustered by the question.

He recovered quickly. "Are you?" he asked.

"No way. Never even considered it," I said, "until, you know, now."

He was still facing me, but his perplexed facial expression dissolved into a huge grin. "So, just so that I'm clear about this," he began, "are you proposing that we join this club together?

Like, now?" he asked, and I slowly nodded, and I opened up the blanket that I was given but had left folded up on my lap, and spread it out over both of us. Because we were in the back row, and because the plane was so sparsely occupied, there really wasn't anyone close enough to get a view of what we were doing, whatever that might be. It emboldened me. Well, *that*, plus the glass of champagne at the show may have played a role as well. I was not usually that bold sexually. Actually, I was pretty much *never* bold sexually.

Once we were covered up, I let my hand search around beneath the covers, looking for him. It didn't take long. He had thoughtfully positioned himself in a way to maximize my hand's encounter with his happily waiting member, which was swelled with enthusiasm at the thought of what was quite likely coming. I was not exactly sure of what I was doing, having never done it before, but I was willing to boldly go there. I positioned my hand over the general area that I was targeting, and began. Within a few minutes, I concluded that it didn't matter what I was doing, exactly, as long as I was doing something, which seemed to produce a big reaction. Soon enough, I felt his hand in the general vicinity of my own, and then he placed it over mine, and I realized that he was helping! I let him. Then I felt him partially lower the zipper on his pants and reposition his hips on the seat.

I gathered up my courage and unzipped it the rest of the way. I held my breath, looked around to make sure that there was still no one watching us, then I reached in. Oh. My. God. My hand made contact with his fully ready dick. I freed it, then began to manipulate him as best I could in the small space. What had seemed private and covert a minute ago, now seemed very public and overt, but there really was no turning back. Actually, I didn't want to stop. I wanted to follow through on what I'd offered, and within several minutes, his low moan, not to mention the hot, stickiness in my hand, told me that I had. I fumbled around in my purse for a napkin. I knew those napkins would come in handy at some point, but had not imagined *this* particular use for them.

I looked over at Bob. He was lying back in the seat, eyes closed. Happy. I was happy too. Finally I had initiated a sexual encounter and had been the one in control. Hell, I hadn't even removed one article of my own clothing and the mission was still accomplished. I did it! His eyes opened; he smiled. His hand found mine under the blanket, and he held it. We sat there in the dark, grinning like little kids who had gotten away with something, which of course we were, and we had. Just in time too; the cabin lights came on and the flight attendant started down the aisle to collect the blankets and pillows. I was careful to fold up the blanket with the, um, busy side facing inward.

We deplaned, found the car in the airport parking lot, and headed back to my house. For once, I had nothing much to say. I was tired but happy, and I knew that he felt the same way. He may be older and worldlier than I was, but today we met on equal ground. Well, on equal *air.*

"You know, people usually are initiated into that club in the bathroom stall," he said, laughing. "You know, with the door closed?" So, I had been even bolder than I thought!

"So, what, are you complaining?" I teased him.

"No, actually, I was hoping to get you to agree to a 'do-over'!" he said, laughing, but I could hear that he was half serious.

"Well, I guess you never know," I said. I decided to leave it at that.

Chapter 32: Party

The months passed. Bobby was invited to a party that a one of his friends was throwing for Memorial Day. He wanted me to go with him. In my mind, a party for that holiday was just an excuse to drink, and I told him so. "Well, maybe for them," he said, "but it's at the VFW and they're having a DJ, so what the hell? If we aren't having fun, we'll leave and go do something else." I couldn't really see a flaw in that plan, plus it was my weekend on with him, so I agreed.

Lately, I had been thinking about where things were going between me and the Bobs. After all, I was now in my mid-twenties, and I'd been seeing both of them for more than six months. I had tried the Going Slow thing, the Keeping It Simple thing, and I guess in the back of my mind, I was hoping that some logical resolution was going to present itself. After all, my goal was to get married at some point. Mentally, I had set the finish line at my twenty-seventh birthday. It wasn't a completely arbitrary age to choose. I decided that I should be married by that age years earlier, when I was talking to my grandmother, my mother's mother, about her wedding.

"So, how old were when you got married?" I asked her as we were looking at her wedding picture. Back in the day, brides sat for portraits in their wedding gowns and Nana was no exception. I loved Nana, but even I had to concede, if only to myself, that if this photograph was any indication, she had been sort of plain-looking. In her grandmother stage of life, I thought that she was beautiful, much better looking in her familiar flowered housecoat, with wild, graying, unruly hair than she'd been in her finest dress and coiffed hair in her youth.

"Oh, I was about twenty-seven," she said.

"Twenty-*seven*?" I repeated.

"Yes," she laughed, "I know. That was considered old to get married back then," she admitted.

That's when I first remember having the thought that twenty-seven would be my cut-off age for marriage. Whenever I started to feel hopeless about my prospects, I would remember my plain-ish grandmother. If even she could find a man to marry, then I, who was not quite as plain as she, could certainly find one too, right? This was an image that sustained me many times over the years: Nana in her simple wedding dress back in 1938. She knew what she wanted: marriage, a family, a home of her own. She made it happen; she got it done. I would too.

She didn't just sit around waiting for it though. She worked, went out with friends, and spent time with her own large family. I followed her lead in this respect as well, if not by definite intention, then by happenstance. I worked. I earned my own money, and established some independence. I had proven to myself that I could do this, but now I wanted this same success in my personal life. I wanted a husband, and I suddenly realized that I only had few years left to meet that admittedly self-imposed deadline. I was used to succeeding. I was always an honor roll student in high school, and always on the dean's list in college, with that single, tragic exception of the semester of the blown calculus final. I wanted to achieve this goal as well.

I had finally gotten smart about my approach with how I'd been managing things with the Bobs. So far, I still really liked them both, and they both seemed to really like me. No clear favorite had emerged, and neither of them had disappeared without warning, displayed any deal-breaking behaviors, like, you know, a tendency to violence, or tried to pressure me into anything that I hadn't felt ready to take on, or been dating my sister on the side. As far as I knew.

I wanted to be the one in control of my dating life, and it seemed that I had accomplished this, but too well. I was in charge, but now it was looking like I was going to have actively decide, instead of passively waiting for circumstances to present me with the right choice, like a beautifully beribboned, long awaited gift to be opened. Crap, were Dad and Nana See right? Was nothing going to come easily for me? Would I always have to do things the hard way?

So anyway, it seemed time to kick things up a notch with my personal life now that I was aware that time was short and getting shorter. Time to figure out in which direction I should (now) boldly go. So, this weekend with Bobby, I would have my new resolve firmly in mind, and this would be strongly influencing my behavior now, for better or for worse.

So when Bobby picked me up and as usual, was happy to see me, and leaned in to kiss my mouth lightly, as he always did, I was ready for him. Instead of just receiving the kiss, I shortened the distance between us to nothing; I delivered a deep, probing kiss with a full body press to accompany it. He responded to this immediately, with his own version of the full body press, replete with a large firm presence pressing into my abdomen. For the first time, I wished that we were closer in height. I was fired up by his immediate positive response and was determined to keep this heat going today.

"Hey, great to see you too!" he said, not releasing me right away. Instead, he pulled me back in and gave me another kiss, this one harder rougher, sending me another unmistakable message of his own. Message received, I thought. We kissed a little bit longer, right there on the porch, then slowly broke apart, "Come on," he said, and we walked to the truck.

He let his hand run down my back, stopping just above my bottom, intent clear. Fine with me, I thought, but let's wait a little bit longer. I pulled back, finally, and asked, "What time does the party start?"

"Oh, it started already. I knew you were kind of on the fence about going, so I figured it was okay if we got there a little late. I hope that's okay?" he questioned.

"Sure, I don't mind," I replied. They were *his* friends, after all. I sure didn't know any of them.

We arrived to a party in full swing. The music was loud enough to hear it from across the street. "That's the good thing about the VFW," he said. "It's far enough away from civilization that no one is around to complain about the noise." I laughed. "Good thing!"

There was someone out in the parking lot operating a gas grill, cooking burgers and hot dogs. I was already hungry, and the smell of the barbeque was only making me hungrier. I was starting to feel pretty good about being there, being with Bobby, everything. "Let's see what's going on inside," I said, my hand finding his, and then pulling him along with me.

"Fine! Great! Let's go!" he said, catching up to me. "Boy, I don't know what's got into you today," he said, "but I'm sure liking it." I knew what had gotten into me: urgency. Time to get things done. Time to take some affirmative action.

We entered the hall, and it was fairly dark inside. "I love the B-52's!" I said, smiling, recognizing strains of "Love Shack". Someone had rigged up a strobe light, disco ball type thing in the middle of the ceiling and turned off the lights to get the full effect of it. It reminded me of dances in high school, doing The Freak, having fun with my friends. I loved to dance, and I attended every dance I knew about when I was in school, including many that the CYO sponsored. I was mostly going because I wanted to see David, but along the way I had plenty of fun dancing with my girlfriends, as well as the occasional boy who was brave enough to dance with me in front of his peers. Most of these boys were gay, but hey, what did I care? I just wanted to dance, not have sex with them. Gay or straight, male or female, it didn't matter to me. Very, very, *very* few straight boys would dance to the fast music at these dances anyway, and of those that would, it was rare that one of them would ask me, so I took what I could get.

So imagine my shock when, after I proclaimed my excitement about hearing "Love Shack", Bobby said, "Me, too. Want to dance?" Well, I could have fainted right there and then.

"You're kidding, right?" I asked. "No, come on!" and he pulled me out to the dance floor. "*Love shack! Baby Love Shack!*" We wedged ourselves in around the edges with the others already out there dancing. I was a little hesitant at first, because he certainly didn't look like he could dance at all, but I was surprised. In a good way. He *was* dancing. He was a *good* dancer. He wasn't just standing there, moving his arms side to side. He was really moving! I was transfixed. Watching him move his hips around was making me…hot. Really hot. There is nothing like watching a man move his body that knows how to move it to turn another person on…well, to turn *me* on, anyway. I already wanted him, but watching him dance made me want him *now*. I mean really; dancing was the closest thing there was to having sex in public. I wasn't missing out on this.

At least that point was now clearly defined. I had no doubt that we'd be great together. I had no desire to postpone it any further. We danced a few more fast dances, then a slow one. Bobby was right; the DJ was excellent. More importantly, though, Bobby himself was excellent. I started thinking of ways to lure him back to my apartment, and was interested to note that these thoughts were even crowding out my thoughts about the barbeque, which was unusual for me, because hey, I am all about the food.

At least I knew that I was serious now.

I must have been throwing off big-time pheromones, because every time I looked up, his eyes were fixed intently on me, and he was pretty much glued to me, never venturing off more than an arm's length or so away before snapping back to my side as if there were an invisible bungee cord linking us together. I could feel the heat that he was throwing off, and it was making me crazier by the minute.

Now I had a new dilemma: was I ready to do it with Bobby? If I was, then wasn't that the same as making the choice between Bobby and Bob? Could I have sex with Bobby and still date Bob? I didn't think so. I also did still really like Bob, so I didn't want to jeopardize that relationship with this one until I was certain of what I really wanted. Confusion; thy name is Bebe.

We stopped dancing for the moment, both of us laughing and out of breath. "Let's find something to eat; I'm starving!" he said, and I nodded, feeling the same. Starving for food; starving for him. I needed *something* fast. We decided to each fill a plate, then we found a place inside to eat together. There were some tables and chairs set up around the periphery of the room. The food was great, and filling. We said "Hello" to a few people that

Bobby knew as they walked by, but for the most part, we could have been strangers in the crowd who had eyes only for each other.

The heat between us was intensified by the simple act of watching each other eat. His mouth was gorgeous, and I had a hard time looking away. As soon as we finished the food and cleaned up after ourselves, he grabbed my hand and said, "Let's go!" and we left. I didn't ask him where we were going. I didn't care. I didn't know where *go*ing, but I certainly knew what we'd be *do*ing.

As it turned out, we went to his parents' house. We let ourselves into the basement where his room was. Because the house had a walk out basement, we were able to enter his room unobserved by anyone who may have been home upstairs. He was not allowed to have guests of the opposite sex in his room. Little did they know. I was certain that I wasn't the first. I hoped that I was the only one currently visiting him here, but it was not a deal-breaker if I was not.

One good thing about visiting him on his home turf was that I could see first-hand that it was probably true that he was an ex-smoker. I was pretty sure that he wasn't expecting me at his place today, and yet there was no visible signs that he might be still smoking: no ashtray, no matches or lighters, no stray packs. This was encouraging.

We were all hands with each other since leaving the party. He was not allowing me to get even two steps out of his reach. We were orbiting each other. I knew that I was on fire for him now, and was confident that the feeling was mutual. This emboldened me. As soon as we rounded the corner to his room, I headed for the bed, firmly grasping his hand.

I was startled at first to see that his bed was fitted with a make-shift four poster frame, which was draped with some kind of fabric. It was slightly opaque, providing some privacy. I wouldn't have expected a bed like this in a man's room, but this wasn't the time to dissect it. I checked in with myself, realized that even though it was unexpected and unusual, it hadn't put a damper on my ardor, so I plunged ahead.

I lifted the corner of the fabric so that we could enter the bed's enclosure. He immediately began kissing me, holding me with one hand on either side of my head, fingers entwined in my hair, capturing me. He showered kisses on every inch of my face, then finally finding my mouth, he began exploring it with his tongue. Not a minute too soon, because I was about to die with wanting, waiting for him to get there. His kisses were firm enough, long enough, wet enough. Not too much of anything; everything just right.

His breath was sweet on my face when he pulled away. We shifted to get more comfortable on the bed, lying together, me on my back, him beside me, then leaning over me, partially covering my body with his. I reached up and put my arms around his neck, pulling him down to me. I was feeling very liquid-y now, and I knew that I was close to the line that I'd drawn in the sand of sexual encounters. His hands were roaming over my body, touching all the places that I wanted to be touched. Up to this point, we had confined our explorations to our clothed selves, but that was over. He was practically bulging out of his pants now, and I was rubbing up against him with my thigh and with my hand. He so clearly wanted more. Now.

I pulled back, took a breath. Was this what I really wanted to be doing? Having sex with Bobby would not only change things between us; it would also affect my relationship with Bob. I had never cheated on any of my boyfriends, and as long as there was no sex happening, I didn't feel like I was betraying either of the Bobs. Now, though, if I went where we were headed right now with Bobby, would I have to stop seeing Bob? Would I have to go here with him, too, to level the playing field? I was shocked at these crazy thoughts that were running through my mind.

Bobby, wondering about the momentary break in the action, drew a conclusion for himself. "Hey, don't worry. I have condoms," he said, then reached over to his nightstand, opened up the drawer, and pulled one out. Hmmm, maybe I really *wasn't* his only female visitor lately. Stop! I thought. This is stupid! We were never exclusive! I couldn't hold him to a standard that I wasn't living up to. Then something registered: Magnum XL? What was I getting myself into here?

"Hey, wait a minute," I said.

"Come on," he said. "Don't stop. I love you. I want to be with you like this." I was not impressed by any declarations of love offered up in bed at the point of entry. This was his first time mentioning that he loved me, so I did feel a quick little thrill of happiness, but then I regained my control. "Come on," he repeated. "We went slowly, like you wanted, but now we're here!" he said. He was persuasive. "If not now, then when?" he asked.

"When you marry me!" I blurted out, not only to his surprise, but to my own.

"Well, maybe I will then," he said, smiling, covering my body back up with his own, the foil wrapped condom placed unopened on the pillow next to my head. "I'll keep it close by, just in case you decide we need it," he smiled, then resumed kissing me.

We didn't need it that night. We stayed put at hands mostly over, but sometimes under each other's clothes while ceaselessly kissing each other. Some of the intensity ebbed after the "M" word was tossed out into the open, but not all. It was our best time together so far. He took me home just before midnight, since we both had to work in the morning. We stealthily exited his house, trying hard not to attract the attention of any parents that might have ears cocked.

I got home with more questions, feeling even more confused than I had when we left that day, which was something that I hadn't believed possible. I resolved to have a serious conversation with Bobby about any future prospects that we might have. Come to think of it, I should have that same conversation with Bob, too. Maybe it was time for everybody to put all of their cards on the table.

In my state of confusion over what to do about the Bobs, I was trying to focus on my goal of keeping it mostly celibate. Circumstances were changing though, and I thought I should take a little break, hoping that some distance would give me a little perspective and help me figure out what was the right thing to do before it I got in too deep with *both* of them and it was too late.

Chapter 33: Billy Joel

It was my weekend with Bob coming up, but then Lo called me
with an invitation. She had somehow scored two free tickets to
the Billy Joel concert at the Boston Garden, complete with
backstage passes. No way was I passing that up! I loved Billy
Joel, plus I hadn't seen her in a while. She reminded me of this

fact when she extended the invitation, probably in response to my moment of hesitation during which I was wondering how hard it was going to be to reschedule with Bob. I told her, "Don't worry; I'm in. I'm dying to see Billy Joel, and I'm dying to see you. Of course, I'm going. Thanks for inviting me," I said, then hung up to call Bob.

Well. He was none too pleased. "What do you mean, you have other plans?" he asked. "It's our weekend." Had he suspected that I was juggling him and Bobby? Uh-oh.

"Well, of course it is our usual weekend, but I haven't seen my friend in a long time and she only has *this* weekend free," I began, deciding in that moment not to share with him what our plans were. He was kind of acting like a jerk so I didn't feel like being very forthcoming with him.

He said, "Okay, fine. Whatever. It's okay," backpedaling a little. "I'll call you," he said, and hung up. For a moment, I had a little twinge of worry, then dismissed it. I had never broken a date with him before. I was not even actually breaking one now. We hadn't actually made any plans yet. Maybe it would be a good strategy to make him wait a bit to see me. That whole "absence makes the heart grow fonder" thing; maybe there was something to that? Either way, I really had no choice, since there was no way that I was going to let Lorraine down, and I certainly couldn't ask Billy Joel to reschedule. And anyway, I really thought that our relationship would benefit from a little space.

Lo and I went to the concert. She picked me up early so we could go out for coffee first. We headed for our old stomping grounds, HoJo's, which was now open twenty-four hours a day. We asked for a booth, were seated quickly, and ordered our coffees. I immediately pushed the bowl of creamers over to her side of the table. I had long ago started drinking my coffee black, since she drank her coffee extra light and since it always took forever for the waitress to bring us more creamers when we needed them, and since Lo got tired of me going into the kitchen to get it myself. It was easier this way.

"So, how've you been?" she asked.

"Pretty good; you?" I responded.

"I'm doing great. I'm so glad to be out of school, aren't you? Although working every day isn't such a great deal either," she admits.

"I know what you mean," I said, "but at least there aren't any friggin' exams!"

Lo laughed. "Seriously, though, how are you doing?" she leaned across the table. "I'm so glad you're not with Steven anymore, I can't even tell you," she said.

"I know. I'm fine. I'm glad too," I replied.

"Are you going out with anyone?" I asked.

"No, we're taking a break," she said. Seeing my concern, she said, "Don't worry; it's a good thing."

"What about you?" she countered.

"Are *you* seeing anyone now?" I nodded. "Actually, I'm seeing two people," I answered, with a little smug.

"Are you kidding?" she laughed, eyebrows raised.

"One of them is a guy who showed up to fix the leaky tub in my sister's apartment, and the other is a guy I met at work," I said.

"Names, please?" she said.

"Okay, ready? The plumber is 'Bobby' and the manager is 'Bob'," I say, a bit sheepishly. "Okay, now *that's* funny!" she says.

"I know. But hey, when I decided to try to keep things simple, uncomplicated, I really meant it," I said, laughing.

"I guess it *is* easier to keep track of two boyfriends if they have the same name," she agrees. "You know, it's kind of hard for me to believe it. I'm the one who was always holding up the wall at dances, unless I was dancing with *you*," I say, smiling. "I have no personal frame of reference whatsoever for what's happening now."

"What do you mean?" she asked. "Well, you know, it was kind of fun at first, having two guys vying for me, but I really have figured out some things lately that are making me want to pick one already, you know?" I said. "Like what?" Lo asked.

"Like, I know now that I do want to have a baby, which I wasn't so sure about before. Plus, I do want to get married someday, and now it's getting so that it's going to be later rather than sooner." I told her about my deadline for getting married by the age of twenty-seven.

"Well, you still have plenty of time," she said. "You're only twenty-five, and you have two fishes hooked. Pick one to cut loose."

I thought about this. "I don't know which one to choose! I kept hoping that one of them would sort of, I don't know, fade out, you know? That the 'three month rule' would kick in," I said.

"What 'three month rule'?" she asked.

"You know," I explained. "Anyone can keep up a pretense for three months, right? They can be kind, loving, honest, gentle teetotalers for only so long, then their true colors start to show, and you find out that they are really cruel, sneaky, wife-beating alcoholics." She laughed. "Go ahead and laugh, but you know I'm right!" I said. She nodded.

"I hear ya. I'm not arguing with you. I just never thought of it that way," she said.

"So anyway, I thought it would be an easy choice, that after three months one or both of them would have turned out to be the clear loser, but that didn't happen. It's been about nine months now and they're both still pretty great, so I don't know where to go from here."

"Well, there's always coin flipping," she began. "Okay, you know I'm only kidding! Well, I'm only half kidding. If they're both so awesome, then maybe you *should* just flip a coin, or just take yourself right out of the equation and have them do a 'rock paper scissors'," she said, smiling broadly.

"Cute. Why didn't I think of that?" I said sarcastically. "Well, just wait a little longer, see what happens," she advised. "If you don't know what to do, wouldn't it be best to just wait? Don't do anything right now? This timeline that you have really is not very realistic. You know that you really do have plenty of time to get married, right?" she said.

"I do and I don't," I replied. "Okay, well, have you slept with either one of them yet?" she asked.

"No, but that's another problem. I want to, but I feel like I have to pick one first, that it wouldn't be right to go that far with either of them if it wasn't building toward something, you know what I mean?"

"Is either of them pressuring you to do it?" she asked.

"Well, duh! They're men! Okay, so not so much in words, but Bob is certainly letting me know that he's ready whenever I am, and Bobby has laid in a month's supply of prophylactics and is just waiting for my go."

"Well, I'll say it again: don't do anything. Wait and see what happens. I'm glad you're not sleeping with either of them; that would just complicate it more, plus that's the quickest way to lose a guy, I think," she said.

"Now you sound just like my mother!" I protested. "With all of her 'Why buy the cow?' crap."

"Well, I can't help it! You asked me what I thought, and in this case, that's what I think is the best thing for you to do," she said.

"*What* is?" I asked, realizing that I must have missed something.

"Wait."

"Now come on; we'll be late for the show," she said. We got up, left some money for the check, and headed for the Boston Garden. It was hard to find a parking space, but that's the great thing about a Volkswagen Beetle: they're small, plus Lo was a champion car-parker, and she soon had us wedged into a spot that I wouldn't have attempted to get into in a million years. "And that's why *you* are always the designated driver!" I said. She smiled.

"Come on; hurry up," she replied. There was a line to get inside, which we quickly joined. The place was completely packed.

"Good thing we came early; this place is crazy!" she said. It was so crowded that I grabbed her arm so that we wouldn't get separated. After all, she still had the tickets.

We found our seats. We were right up front. The show was amazing, and I was singing along to his songs at the top of my lungs, along with everyone else. When it was over, I was overwhelmed by how great the show was, then I remembered that it wasn't over yet. "How do we get backstage?" I asked, and Lorraine said, "Follow me!" I did, and we made our way through the throng of people to the side of the stage.

"Where are the passes?" I asked her.

"Actually, we don't have any. We're just sneaking back here," she said.

"Oh, man!" I said. I had never been a rule breaker, that's for sure, and was panicked at the thought of getting caught.

"Relax! Probably none of these other people have a pass either!" Lo said, and I looked around at the people hanging back around the perimeter like us, and realized that she was probably right. I took a breath. Billy Joel did come back to greet us, signed a few autographs, and was gone. It was worth it to see him up close, plus it was always great to see Lo. Talking about everything made me feel better, even if no decisions had actually been made.

What I didn't know until the next day was that Bob had tickets to Billy Joel too, and had been planning to take me. I found this out because he called to tell me that he saw me there, and to ask if I'd had a good time. "What do you mean, 'you saw me there'?" I asked him. He said he had seen me when I was in line to get in before the show started. "Even though you couldn't go, I went anyway," he said. I felt bad, but I wouldn't have changed my decision to see Lorraine even if I had known that he was going to invite me too. "Well, I'll see you on our next weekend anyway, and I'll make it up to you," I promised, lowering my voice.

"Well, actually, something came up and I was also calling to say we'd have skip our next weekend too. Sorry about that," he said.

"That's okay, I'll give you a rain check for the next time we're together." I figured that I owed him that much. Before I could say anything else, he said,"Great! Talk to you soon. Gotta go. Bye." and hung up.

That was weird, I thought, but what could I do? Nothing. So I tried not to think too much more about it. I got busy with work, and let my mind ruminate on the choice that I was trying to make. Wouldn't it be great if I could figure this out before I saw him again? "Be careful what you wish for," I thought. It was going to end up being a month before that happened. Well, on the bright side, I can see Bobby this weekend instead, and maybe that will help tip the scales.

For once, I ignored my every other weekend rule and called Bobby the next day from work. "Want to do something together again this weekend?" I asked.

"Sure," he said, seeming like he was expecting me to call. This annoyed me, since I didn't like to be predictable, but hey, what was I going to do? I had to get some things straight. I hadn't seen Bob in a while, but since things were escalating with Bobby, this may be the kind of natural attrition I'd been hoping for. If so, it was time to have a serious talk with Bobby, and suddenly I was feeling a sense of urgency about making that happen. Before I made any definite decisions, though, I needed more information.

I had some real questions about how Bobby was running his life.

Chapter 34: Bobby's secret

For one thing, we'd been together for about nine months now, and he was still living in his mother's basement, supposedly to save his money. Now I was starting to wonder what he was saving it *for*. I mean, he still had the same old, beat up truck. He still wore pretty much the same clothes he'd been wearing since we met: worn jeans, white crew neck T shirts, and as it got colder, he layered the long sleeved flannels over that. That was about the extent of his wardrobe.

Besides working as a plumber, he also worked construction in the summers. These were two fairly lucrative professions, as far as I knew. He must easily be out-earning me, yet I had my own apartment. I had recently bought my new car. I had several business suits, and once you add on the requisite shoes and the blouses, these were a pretty big expense. I went out with my friend for dinner sometimes, as well as to an occasional concert. I had some money saved, but I was starting to wonder exactly what he was really doing with his, if he was saving it at all.

I started to wonder where all the money might really be going, especially since I had a past predilection for choosing men like my father. Did he have a secret gambling problem? Some other addiction, like alcohol? I mean, he said he'd quit smoking and I saw no evidence to contradict this, but if he could succumb to one vice, didn't it stand to reason that there could be others? I decided to get some answers next time we met, so I had pushed the envelope and called him, and was relieved when he accepted. Dinner would be a perfect opportunity to sit and sort out what was really going on.

As usual, we were going to a casual restaurant that we both liked, sort of a pub. We sat on the bar side, along a wall that was lined with booths. I preferred to sit in a booth in a restaurant, so I was glad to see one available. It was much easier to talk seriously with the air of privacy a booth afforded.

"Hey, what's up with you tonight?" Bobby asked as soon as we were seated. "You didn't talk much on the way over here," he said. Well, that certainly wasn't like me, true enough.

"Not too much," I said. "Just thinking about things," I said.

"What things?" he asked.

"You know, how things are going with us," I said.

"Oh," he said, "I think things are going great. Don't you?"

"Well, yes, but lately I've been wondering about a few things…" I trailed off, and waited to see what he would do with this.

"What things?" he asked, providing me with my opening.

"Let's order first, okay?" I said, hoping this would buy me a bit of time to organize my thoughts. I'd been wondering for a while, sure, but in a random sort of way. I didn't want to screw this conversation up, so I wanted to take my time with this.

I recalled a talk that we'd had a few months back, when we had discussed having kids someday. I was for it, but he was dead set against it, and I wasn't able to figure out why. That conversation had ended unsatisfactorily and I didn't want this one to go that way as well.

After the waitress came and we'd ordered, I took a deep breath and began.

"We were close to really going all the way last time we were together," I began, jumping right in with some bravado, but then I couldn't sustain it, and I felt the blush creeping up from my neck, engulfing my face. Nothing to do but plunge ahead though.

"I know," he said, "it was great."

"Well, I've been wondering about something, and I guess I just want to stop wondering and just ask you," I began.

"So. Well, you know how you've been living at home to save up your money? It's been a long time now, right?" I asked. "Yeah; a few years, I think," he replied. "So, in all that time, you haven't had to pay any rent, and your truck is paid for, right?" He nodded. "So, here's the thing. I've been wondering what you are saving up your money for." I finished.

"Oh, nothing in particular…" he began, then trailed off. I looked at him squarely.

"Come on, Bobby. Tell me what's going on," I said. I could see that he was hiding something by how his body language changed after I asked the question. "I know you quit smoking, but is it something else like that? Drugs? Gambling?" I asked. He shook his head. "No! No way!" he replied vehemently. I tried again.

"Just tell me the truth. I'd rather *know* than wonder and worry about it," I said.

I could see him getting ready to tell me something. I could see that it was something big. I was starting to doubt the wisdom of this line of questioning. Wasn't my goal to Keep it Simple? Keep things uncomplicated? It was, but now that intimacy had to be factored into the equation, that changed things for me. I couldn't just continue on with him like nothing mattered. Things were beginning to matter a lot. I decided that it was time to know the answer now, whatever it was.

"I have a kid," he said, and exhaled a long breath.

"What?" I said. "I have a kid, a daughter." Well, that was a shock. I had never considered that he was paying child support, for Chrissakes!

"How did *that* happen?" I asked, more because I couldn't think of what else to say. "Duh! I got a girl pregnant," he said.

"No shit," I said, sort of mad now. "Who?" I asked.

"Misty Robertson," he said. I vaguely remembered hearing about her; she had disappeared from the radar senior year without explanation, although whenever that happened, not much explanation was required.

"I wanted her to get an abortion. She didn't want to. That was pretty much the last thing we talked about. Every other conversation was through lawyers and the courts," he said.

"So, like, how much money are we talking about here?" I asked. I didn't feel that this question was out of line. After all, if we were going to have a future together, I didn't want to be our sole support. I wanted an equal partner. Viewed in this light, I considered it a fair question. He didn't agree, and didn't disclose the amount.

"It has nothing to do with us," he ventured.

I had nothing to say really. It was crystal clear that I could not have a future with Bobby. No way. I wasn't going to support him so that he could support his other family. Whether he admitted to an emotional attachment to them or not, I didn't see how *they* would not have an emotional attachment to *him*. Done. I wanted no part of a mess like that. I wanted *un*complicated, and this situation was about as dramatic a polar opposite of uncomplicated as there could possibly be.

My face has always given away what I'm thinking and feeling, and today was no exception. "I'm sorry," I said, but it was obvious that I didn't need to; he had already seen what was coming. "I can't do this anymore. I think we should stop seeing each other." He nodded.

"I guess I'll see you around," he said, getting up from the booth. He left the restaurant. I was sad, but relieved. I signaled the waitress to pack up the food to go. Then I paid the check and went home.

Things had worked themselves out. Not in the way I'd predicted, or necessarily even in the way I'd hoped, but the decision had been made. I was sad to be losing Bobby, but happy to be gaining Bob. With no other man in the picture now, I was ready to commit to him. He'd been intimating that we could be more serious if only I would give him the go ahead, and now I could do so with a clear conscience. It had been a while since we'd seen each other, since I'd gone to the concert with Lo and was sorting things out with Bobby.

"Hey, I miss you! What are we doing this weekend?" I asked when Bob called next. I was assuming that he was calling to make plans for our next date.

I was wrong.

"Well…" he began, then trailed off. I didn't like the sound of that.

"Well? Well what?" I asked, not sure if I wanted to hear the answer. After all, the *last* big question that I'd asked a man came with a loaded answer that blew our relationship up in my face.

"Well, things have changed since we talked last," he said. I started to feel a sense of foreboding rising up from my gut, too late. "Patty and I are back together," he finished.

Oh my God. Patty? Patty was his ex-finance. *Used* to be his ex-fiance. "What do you mean, 'back together'?" I asked.

"Like, totally back together," he said excitedly. "She moved back in last weekend. I'm sorry; I was going to call you. It was a total surprise, I swear," he said.

"You know what, Bob? Save it. All you did was live up to your reputation, right? It's a huge relief, actually, to find out now. 'Bye, Bob," I said, and for once, I hung up first.

Chapter 35: Good riddance to bad Bobs

After my personal life imploded, my professional life followed

suit in rapid succession. I was invited to a meeting with my

former district manager and the current division manager. The

meeting was to be held at a store I'd never been to, for some

reason, but hey, whatever. They were the bosses; they got to say,

'Jump!' and I got to ask, 'How high?'" I thought the meeting was going to be a performance review of some kind. I certainly wasn't worried at all. I knew that I was doing good work; I had been told as much enough times since I accepted the Training Supervisor promotion. It was supposed to be a low-stress ending to my week, although if I had considered the timing of the meeting, I might have read a little more into it in advance. It was the last hour of the last day of my work week, a traditional time for letting people go.

They arrived before I did, and the two of them were already deep in conversation when I walked up to the table. "So, Bebe, how are you?" Chuck asked, smiling, standing to heartily shake my hand. Jim stood as well, smiled a tight little smile, nodded and extended his hand as well. What was all this formality? I wondered. I saw them all the time; they were acting like they barely knew me. I was beginning to feel the first stirrings of foreboding. Where was *this* going?

"Have a seat," Chuck offered, and I slid uneasily into the booth opposite them. I thought it was odd that they were both sitting together on one side of the booth, leaving me to face them both alone. It felt like two against one, and I didn't like it one bit. What the hell was going on?

"I guess you're wondering why we asked you to meet us here today," Chuck began. I nodded. I was no longer returning his smile. He was up to something, and it felt like it was no good. "Well, we have a proposition for you. As I'm sure you know, the company has been undergoing some changes since we were bought by the new corporation," he said. Of course I knew. People were losing their jobs every day! But these were upper level managers, people on his level, not anyone at my level. That's what I thought, at least. Until now.

"Yes," I said, warily. "Well. There is a reorganization of the Training Department underway, and what is going to happen next is that one of Training Supervisor positions is being eliminated and the remaining four will split up the extra territory," he said.

"Okay," I said. "Who?" I asked, still holding out a ray of hope. I didn't care if I had to take on a larger territory. So what?

"Well, to make it fair, it was decided that the least senior TS in the division would be the position that is eliminated. So that's you," he finished.

I sat there dumbly. Me? Me? *Me*? How could this happen? I mean, really?! *Was* this really happening? Now? I did everything right. I followed every direction I was given over the seven years that I had been working with this company. I took every dirty job that no one else wanted and did it with style. I had no words that I could express in responses to this declaration that wouldn't get me into a bigger fix than I was already in, so I said nothing. I was numb.

Then I remembered what Chuck said at the beginning of the meeting. "What's the proposition?" I asked, finally. For just one moment, I thought, could they be asking me to sleep with them? As unlikely as it seemed that they would be putting the moves on me together this late in the game, who really knew? I mean, after what had just happened with the Bobs, nothing would surprise me now. I did realize how ludicrous this line of thinking was after a moment. Wasn't it?

"Well, that's the good part. You will be offered a severance package, of course, but we have another offer for you," Chuck said. I sat, waiting, not sure that I wanted to hear what was coming next. I still sat. I guess they were waiting for me to say something encouraging, but for once, I was mute. I did not nod. I did not smile. I waited.

"Instead of the severance package, which of course means you'd have to leave the company, you also have the option of going back into management," he said. There it was. Those three dreaded word. Back. Into. Management. The words that every former manager hoped never to hear in their lifetime. My heart sank, as I realized the inevitability of those words. The only variable now was where they were going to send me.

"You mean, go back to the Reading store?" I asked hopefully. I didn't see how that would be possible, since I knew the manager that had replaced me was still there and was in no hurry to leave the cushy set up I'd left for him. "No, not Reading," Chuck said, then Jim cut in.

"This store," he said.

"This store," I repeated dumbly.

"Yes. We want you to be the manager of this store," he said.

"Why? What about Bob?" I asked. Yes, yet another Bob was the current manager of the store we were sitting in. "Did he quit?" I asked. God, I was so naïve.

"Well, no…we have something else in mind for Bob," Chuck said.

Great. It finally dawned on me what was going on: they were using me as leverage to push the current manager out. Now, I certainly had an affinity for Bobs, and although I wasn't dating *this* one, I knew him well enough. Well enough to know that he was married with a kid in college, which meant lots of bills to pay. I thought that what they wanted to do was wrong, and I certainly didn't want to be a part of it. "Hey, he's out either way," Jim said. "This is a million dollar store; he isn't turning enough of a profit. You were returning twenty five percent and higher at the stores you formerly managed. We need that from you here," he said. Finally, some truth.

"I'm not interested. Thanks, though," I said. "I might be interested in managing the smaller volume store," I said. This was a little store that had recently opened up unexpectedly for the usual reason: the manager had a nervous breakdown. He locked himself in the bathroom of the shop and wouldn't come out. I'm not sure how they actually *did* get him out, but I knew the store now needed a manager.

"No, we don't want you for that store," Jim began.

"Look," Chuck cut in, "we want you to take *this* store. It's your only option. Otherwise, take the severance," he said, cards finally on the table.

"Look," he said, changing tacks, "we know you can return a good return to corporate at the lower volume stores, but we want to see if you can do it in a million dollar store. Look at it this way: it's really a promotion," he added.

"I know that I *can* do it; I just don't *want* to do it," I said. This was true. I had no desire to do it. None. None whatsoever. I had nothing to prove.

"Take the weekend to think it over. I'll expect your decision on Monday," Chuck said, and he slid across the seat and got up to leave. "Thanks for coming," he said to me. "I'll be in touch," he said to Jim, and he left.

I was still sitting in the booth, in shock. Not only did I have no idea that this was coming today, but I had no idea what to do. My life as I knew it was coming to an end. This was the only type of work I'd ever done. It also paid well, and I didn't know what else I was going to do that would generate the same income, or even come close.

"Come on, take it. It's just what you need," Jim said. Huh, I thought. It was just what *they* needed; they didn't give a damn about what *I* needed. I was at least smart enough now to realize that it was all about the bottom line, all about the money. People didn't matter. Profits mattered. If I wasn't going to show them the money, then they were going to show me the door. This was my rude awakening.

"What about Bob? Will it be good for him too?" I asked, trying to keep the sarcasm out of my voice, and only marginally succeeding.

"Bebe, Bob's out either way, so you have nothing to feel guilty about. There's no way they're keeping him at this store past August," he said. It was May. Wow, they weren't giving him much of a heads up.

I stood up. I told him I'd talk to him on Monday. "Fine, I'll wait to hear from you," he said. "I hope you make the right decision," he added. I turned and left.

That was a joke. Make the right decision? Like I had a choice! It was go to the million dollar store or leave the company, and he knew that I didn't want to do that. They knew it was practically my first job and that I'd worked my way up through the ranks to get to where I was. They were gambling that I wouldn't want to leave and start over somewhere else. Plus the health insurance, the retirement plan…oh my God. How did this happen?

I took the weekend to think about it, but of course I really didn't have any choice. I was completely pissed off. I knew that I had to take over the million dollar store. It was clear that they thought I had to prove something to them.

"I'll take the store," I told Jim flatly on the phone Monday morning, "but I'm only going to do it for one year."

"One year? What do you mean?" he said. "It won't take you that long to turn that store around," he said, laughing, "more like three months, if I know you!" he said.

"No, I mean I will go there for one year, and then I'm leaving the company," I said. For once, *he* was speechless. I'd known Jim for seven years by now, ever since my first job as a waitress, and I spoke freely. "I don't appreciate being used to force another manager out," I said. He started to protest, to give me those patronizing remarks that he he'd been feeding me right along, but I interrupted him. "We both know that there's no way you'd make him leave that store without a manager ready to go in and replace him," I said. "I'm just saying that I'll do it, but then I'm leaving."

"Fine," he said. "I'll let Chuck know. You will be taking the store over officially on July first, but you'll be reporting to work here June first and have the month overlap with Bob to smooth the transition," he said.

"Great," I thought. What could be worse than having to work for a month with the man whose job you were taking against his will? This just got worse and worse.

"You can start cleaning out your desk at the corporate office any time," he added. "Well, I'll be in touch," he said. "It so happens that I'll be your new district manager. They reconfigured the districts as part of the Reduction in Force. This store is mine now, too," he said, smiling, like I was supposed to be happy about this. Well, maybe it's true what they say about the devil you know.

I was about as low as I could be that first day reporting to work at Bob's soon-to-be-former store, but he was great to me. "Hey, I could see the writing on the wall," he said. "It's kind of a relief, actually," he added.

"You knew that they were going to do this?" I asked. "You're not mad about it?" I was incredulous.

"Hey, I'm going to a lower volume store. Sure, it's less money, but it's less work too. No hard feelings," he said, smiling. Things went much better for me after that, since I no longer felt like a villain. I began to feel a little less morose. Maybe things would somehow turn out okay after all.

Chapter 36: Hellooooo, Jason

The month flew by, and Bob left to go to his new, lesser store. I talked with him a few weeks after that, and he said the new store really was a much better fit for him. I wasn't so sure, since he'd been at what was now *my* new store for four years. Wouldn't he have left sooner if he felt that it was so ill-fitting? "My wife thinks I'm way less stressed out," he said.

"Great. That's great, really, Bob," I said. I still felt like he was just telling me what he thought I wanted to hear, but hey, what could either of us do at this point except make the best of it?

I was now a woman with a lot of time on my hands in my personal life, and I had a lot of thinking to do. I was essentially alone now, after so many lovely months with the two Bobs. I missed them both, but was trying hard to look forward, not back. For one thing, I knew that I should be glad that I found out that Bobby was supporting another family, and would be for at least the next fourteen years. I should be glad that I found out before things went any further than they had already.

I also knew that I should be damned glad that Bob decided to let his ex-fiance move back in *before* things went any further with him. I was not happy that both relationships fizzled at the same time. I applied everything that I'd learned from my less-than-successful past relationships as I navigated my way through the male maze in my late teens to mid-twenties. After my way failed -and failed, and failed again- I followed my mother's advice, giving not an ounce away. Okay, maybe I did give a *few* ounces away, but not the whole cow! What good did that do me? None! Here I was: right back to square one. I had officially crossed the border from mid to late twenties, and I was without a husband, without a fiance, without a boyfriend, even. How could this have happened *again*?

And then one day, everything changed. I was in the service aisle, working on getting another pot of coffee going so that when I finished my first pot, I would have a refill ready. I was talking to one of the long-time waitresses. You know, the kind that have been there forever and know more about the store and the staff than the manager ever could? A manager's greatest enemy or greatest asset, depending on how you worked it. I was hoping to place her squarely in the asset category, and therefore I was chatting her up, one of my least favorite things to do, when I happened to look up.

And into my life he came. A beautiful man. The most beautiful man I'd ever seen. One thing I had forgotten: with each new job came a new man, and for better or for worse, a new opportunity. I watched the red Jeep Wrangler pull into the parking lot and head directly for a space along the back of the lot, as if it had his name on it, as if he owned it. He slipped into the spot and sprang from the driver's side door with so much energy that it seemed as if he were ejected.

I watched him, transfixed. I was still nodding and smiling at whatever it was that my waitress Mary was saying to me, but I wasn't registering a single word. She caught on to this fairly quickly, and followed my gaze from the parking lot to the front door. He was just coming through it when I interrupted whatever it was that she was saying, and asked, "Who's *that*?"

"That's my son," she replied, hands on hips.

"You stay away from him," she added.

"He's your son?" I asked.

"Yes, that's my son, Jason. And you heard me," she said.

"Huh? Oh. Why should I stay away from him?" I asked. "I'm not seeing anyone," I replied, confused.

"Because he *is*. He has a girlfriend," she replied. Oh, of course. Of *course* he had a girlfriend. I mean, *look* at him. How could he not?

"Only one?" I asked, smiling slightly.

She didn't have time to reply, because he was directly approaching us. Now that he was closer, I could see him more clearly, and better appreciate his attributes. He was wearing sports gear of some sort. I'm not a girl who's into sports, really, but I deduced that he was a hockey player of some sort. He had curly black hair, strong planes to his face, and up close I could see his long lashed, deep brown eyes. The phrase "bedroom eyes" elbowed its way into my mind. I shoved it right back out. He was tall; six feet at least. He was sucking on a lollipop of some kind. This was unexpectedly endearing, and the warning bells began pealing.

"Hi, Mom," he said, as he leaned in, giving her a hug and a kiss on her cheek.

Oh, man! *Now* I was in trouble. I recalled a magazine article that I'd read (who knew when) about how you could tell a lot about how a man would be in a relationship by watching how he treated his mother, that if the first male-female relationship that he formed was strong and successful then there was a good sportin' chance that he could form others. I spoke up. "Hi! I'm Bebe, the new manager," I said, probably too brightly, extending my hand. He looked at me for a moment, long enough for me to wonder if he was going to respond at all.

"Hi," he said finally, shook my hand, and then turned back to his mother.

"So, how'd it go?" she asked him. "We won, of course. *I* was playing," he said, and then he did it; he smiled. My knees almost went right out from under me. What was going on here? My God! I'd never reacted this physically to a man that I'd just met. Well, other than Kevin, and *that* sure didn't turn out well. I was completely flustered. I didn't think that it was that obvious, but I had the feeling that somehow he *knew* the effect that he was having on me. It pissed me off, actually.

I was so caught up by the sight of him, not to mention my response to him, that I missed the conversation that ensued between him and his mother, and next thing I knew, he was calling, "Gotta go," over his shoulder as he left. ""Bye!" Mary and I both said together.

"So, why did he stop by?" I asked, puzzled. I figured that he was here to get something to eat. It was a restaurant, after all. "He comes in just to say 'Hi' to me sometimes," she shrugged. "You mean, that's the only reason? He didn't ask you for money or anything?" I asked, wondering.

"No, he didn't ask me for money! What are you talking about?" she said, indignant. "Is it so hard to believe that he just wanted to say 'Hi' to his mother?" she asked. Well, yeah, it kind of was, but I could see that saying this would be a mistake, so I shook my head.

"Oh no, not if the mother is *you*!" I said, hoping to win points. She was on to me though. "I said forget it; he has a girlfriend," she reminded me. "She works here too," she added this time.

"What?" I said.

"Christa; she works here too," she repeated. I hadn't worked there very long at that point and I was still evaluating the staff. There were a lot of part time waitresses that I didn't really know yet. I sifted through my memory for a Christa.

Nothing.

"When does she work?" I asked.

"Well, she is usually opens on the weekends," Mary told me. That probably explained it; I hadn't been working the early morning shifts much in the few weeks since I'd taken over the store, since it was the most well-staffed part of the schedule. I was still stuck coming in for the late afternoon and evening shifts on the weekend to compensate for the weaker crew at those times. "Well. I'll have to keep my eye out for her," I said, and drifted off to start my mission.

I had to find out more about this guy who had knocked my socks so thoroughly off in the span of about five seconds while saying only one word directly to me. I was used to connecting with men through the tried and true channels. Blind date? Check. Responding to lame lines from strangers during roadside pick-ups? Check. Being a consolation prize for a guy when her sister turned out not to be interested? Check. Acting as a verbal sparring partner? Big check. I'd never made a connection by watching a guy talk to his *mother*.

What is it they say about change? Oh, right. It's GOOD.

The idea of a different path became more appealing the more I thought about it. I didn't want to go down the same roads I'd been down before. They'd taken me exactly nowhere. I was already twenty-six years old with no prospects; I didn't want to be twenty-seven years old with no prospects. I needed to make some changes in my approach with men, clearly. If this was my chance, I was taking it.

I was someone who wore her heart on her sleeve. Usually everyone knew how I felt about a guy, including the guy himself, sometimes before even I did. Now that I was really thinking about it, I guess it wasn't any big stretch to figure out that Jason probably knew that I was standing there, just two feet away from him, losing my mind. It was probably written all over my face. I was going to have to work on shoring up my poker face.

Anyway, back to the mission. Knowledge was power for me. I had to find out who Christa was, and start showing up when she was working to see what I might be up against if I decided to mount a pursuit. At this point, I was just fact finding. It was good timing because I was writing the schedule for the following week that afternoon. I moved some things around. The evening shift was just going to have to do without my presence for once so that I could be there at 5:30am to open with the possible competition.

There was one stroke of luck: I was talking with my assistant manager about staffing, and we were brainstorming about how to beef up the staff for the off season when all of the college students went back to school. "Well, there's Jason," she said.

"Jason?" I asked, my heart speeding up a bit. "Who's that?" I asked in what I hoped was a nonchalant voice, coupled with what I hoped was my best poker face (I'd been practicing).

"You don't know Jason? Mary's son?" she asked. "He worked here for years," she continued, without waiting for an answer, "and he was still working some odd shifts for Bob here and there when he was really stuck," she said.

"What does he know how to do?" I asked. "Everything," she said.

"Okay," I said casually, "do you know how to get in touch with him?"

"Sure," she said. "We're friends," she added, as she recited his number. I scrambled for my pen and wrote it down.

I called him that evening from the store. I felt giddy, my stomach full of butterflies, like I was calling him for a date, instead of calling him for work. At least I had an advantage by being on the phone with him instead of being right in front of him.

Chapter 37: Jason, Jason, Jason

I saw Mary the day after I'd talked with Jason. "Hey, I met your son yesterday," I began, "and I fell in love with him!" I finished.

"Oh no, not another one!" she rolled her eyes. Yep, another one, but I'm going to be his *last* one.

Because Jason and I began to see each other frequently after that phone call. He took some convincing, but after I enticed him with my feminine wiles, he decided to come out of retirement to work for me. By way of thanks, I pretty much let him dictate his own schedule. Here were the terms: "I get to do whatever I want and work whenever I want.

Sounded good to me. "Done," I said. "When can you start?" Whenever he had time and wanted to work, I put him on. I also put *myself* on. Hey, I was no fool. I wasn't passing up any opportunities to be with him, and if I had to pay him to arrange encounters, so be it.

The grill was his preferred position to work and so that was where I put him. It was a no brainer, really. He was like poetry in motion in the kitchen. From the vantage point of the future looking back, watching Jason work that grill was like watching Tom Cruise mix drinks in *Cocktail*.

At first, I tried to be in the kitchen with him, scheduling myself to work the sandwich board, copilot to his pilot. This was a short-lived, mostly unsuccessful experiment. For one thing, he liked to work the grill with his best friend Joe, who was almost as competent (read: skilled, fast, accurate) as Jason was. For another thing, although I flattered myself that I was as good as Joe, Jason didn't share this opinion and had no qualms about telling me so.

Every. Single. Minute.

Something that I learned quickly: If you don't really want to know what Jason thinks (as in: Do these pants make my butt look fat?) don't ask Jason.

A valuable experience did come out of working the kitchen with him. One day I was giving him crap about his extra-large cup of soda that he kept by his side while he was working, which he made bottomless by running for refills whenever it was empty. Oh, and not paying for them. He was busy working while

I was reading him the riot act about this when suddenly he threw the fryolator basket that he had just finished emptying out against the back wall of the kitchen. Believe me, this is one of the loudest sounds that there is on this earth, especially in a small, partially enclosed space. It seemed to reverberate endlessly. A moment of silence ensued. Then he started talking.

I really don't remember what he said, but I don't think the actual words matter much. It was more the tone that gave the words weight. Plus, his discontent was rolling off him in waves. It was a force to be reckoned with. A dark force. I was flooded with emotions. I felt bad, certainly, and confused. I was mad that he'd thumbed his nose at my authority by acting that way. I was his *boss*, after all. I don't think anyone else actually knew what happened. So, as far as a tree falling in the forest with no witnesses goes, did it really happen?

I retreated. He, to his credit and to my relief, continued working. I certainly would have been up the creek had he not stayed. I couldn't do alone what *he* could do alone on a busy lunch hour grill. I avoided the kitchen for the rest of the day. We were scheduled to leave at the same time, which I had arranged purposely and had been eagerly anticipating all week, but now I was just wondering how to get the hell out of there without bumping into him. When our shifts ended, I stayed in my office with the door shut like a coward until fifteen extra minutes had passed, then I got my things and left. Jason never hung around even one minute after his shift ended, so I figured my fourteen minute buffer would be more than adequate.

I got to the parking lot and saw that, to my surprise, his Jeep was still there, and to my distress, he was still in it. Of course, he'd parked right next to my car, so there was no avoiding heading over there, and no way to pretend I hadn't seen him. I tried to breathe. Okay, repeat after me: Things happen for a reason. Things happen for a reason. Things happen for a reason. I liked things in threes. There is something comforting about it. Plus, three is my lucky number. I went to my car's passenger side, deposited my things on the front seat, and then closed the door.

I saw from the corner of my eye that he was sitting there with his head down. I sighed again. Without pausing to think any further, I walked around to the passenger side and opened the door. He looked up at me. "Want to talk?" I asked.

"Okay," he said tightly.

"Can I get in?" I asked, and he nodded. I got in and closed the door.

Brave.

He wasn't talking, so I'd have to be the one to start. "So, what the heck happened in there today?" I asked. He took a deep breath.

"When I'm in the kitchen, I have to be able to work the way I want to work," he began. "I can't have you standing there telling me to do." I was listening, but was not sure how to respond. After all, I was his boss in there. Wasn't I? So I just nodded. I noticed that he was looking straight ahead, not at me, and his hands were clenched in his lap. Wow, he was still pretty mad, I thought. I had gotten over *my* anger by now. At this point, I was mostly just worried. I was surprised to realize that what was worrying me was that I was afraid that I didn't have a chance with him anymore, but I was also a little worried that he wasn't going to work for me anymore either.

I remembered a study from college about how men do better talking about their feelings if there was no eye contact being made, something about direct eye contact being felt as confrontational to their subconscious mind. I was grateful for the forced parallel positioning that sitting in the front seat of the Jeep required. Maybe he wouldn't have talked to me at all if we were face to face. "What else?" I asked.

He said, "I mean, Bebe, you have to let me be the *man*." I nodded again. I didn't even know what that *meant*, but I cared enough about him at that point to realize that I was fully willing to do whatever he asked of me, both at work and in our private lives.

It's funny how when you know, you *know*, right?

I hadn't had any real men over the years that could compare to Jason. My own father was essentially out of commission for most of the parts of my life that I could remember, and I loathed my one living grandfather for the short time I'd known him. I'd spent most of my growing up years focusing on how women were equal to men, doing the jobs of men, replacing men. I concluded that I had to be able to do anything a man could do. Of course, the reverse was true in theory as well, but I'd never been attracted to a man who wanted to cook, bake, or knit, you know? For all of my striving to be equal, I still secretly wanted to be the woman, to know that I could depend on a man sometimes, even if I never actually did. Of course I was fully capable of brushing the snow off of my car before driving home after work, but it sure was nice to have my boyfriend take care of it for me.

Was that what he was talking about? Is that what did letting him be the man meant? If I did let him be the man, then would that mean I had to be the woman? Uh oh.

I decided I was willing to risk it. The discussion that had been half academic up until that point was kicked up a few notches. If letting him be the man would mean that I would be on my own with the housework, then I was not buying into that.

Wait, why the hell was I thinking about how we were going to set up house together when we were still just getting to know each other? That was so not like me. What's funny is that it's exactly what happened, and we did get all of this sorted out over time. And so the day that I was afraid would never happen for me *did* happen after all, and it really was the happiest day of my life.

When we decided to do one brave thing.

We got married.

I was twenty-seven.

How we defined our roles evolved as the years went by. As we got older, after we got married, after we finished our educations. When I was working and he was not, when he was working and I was not, the definitions of wife and husband changed. When I was pregnant and had complications and was on bedrest, the definitions changed again. When we became the parents of a son. When he decided to change careers and went back to school. When I decided to change careers and went back to school. When we were paying off school loans and car loans and medical bills. When his grandmother died. When first my mother and then my father died. When my grandmother died. When we became the parents of a daughter. When we decided to move to another state. When we were buying and selling four homes in four years, negotiating and refinancing mortgages. When we were buying and trading a dozen cars. The definition of "being the man" and "being the woman" ebbed and flowed, became fluid, crystallized, and then dissolved again, always morphing into something new.

Throughout the years there were many diapers, earaches, sniffles, and sleepless nights with little ones. There were first kittens, and then cats, turtles and fish, and then finally, chickens. There were hundreds of hockey games, little league baseball and soccer games and track meets, ice skating lessons, cheerleading practices and football games, yoga classes and gym visits. There were dozens of vacations and walks on the beach, hundreds of date nights and movies watched, thousands of books read. Throughout the years, throughout it all, there was this:

One true love.

The truth is that in the end, it doesn't matter what you do or do not give away, because in the end, you get it all back.

And then some.

30643432R00294